T0118944

GOLD, FRANKINCENSE AND MYRRH

By Slobodan Novak

Translated by Celia Hawkesworth

ÆB Autumn Hill Books
Iowa City, Iowa

ÆB

http://www.autumnhillbooks.org

Autumn Hill Books
P.O. Box 22
Iowa City, Iowa 52244

Printed in the United States of America

Publication of this work was made possible by the generous support of the Iowa Arts Council and the Ministry of Culture of the Republic of Croatia.

Autumn Hill Books ISBN - 13:978-0-9754444-6-7
Autumn Hill Books ISBN - 10:0-9754444-6–8
Library of Congress Control Number: 2007932336

CONTENTS

CHAPTER I

Through the window I have sent out into the night that whole heavy stench seeping through the cracks round the thin double door of the bedroom and gathering in a suffocating cloud of foul sepulchral odor. From the next room I can still hear the thick porcelain wash-basin ringing with the deepest notes of percussion instruments, and in that ancient chime I make out the squeezing and squirting of the sponge with which my wife's unhappy hands are washing Madonna's abdomen. I shudder in the damp south wind and do not yet dare breathe with even half my lungs. Even the tea is poisoned: I just steam my face and eyes in the rum evaporating from the warm cup. From the bedroom Madonna croaks:

"*Me romperà* the cups, *quel* wretch in there! He'll smash everything!"

The thin door shakes like cardboard as it opens.

"Hold that nose!" Cara smiles at me.

Cara smiles, oh yes, yes, she smiles, and smiles... When she carries the pot out like that, her smile is no more than a dim circle round her lips, it spreads concentrically over her chin and nose and shades her eyes. My wife, her eyes blind, dead, bears the heavy earthenware pot before her like an urn to the courtyard wall. There she climbs onto a stone, onto the pinkish marble stump of an ancient column, and tips the vessel over towards the sea. The ashes of our Madonna are borne away by the holy rivers.

The Ganges will wash away the generations, and this Madonna will continue to send her remains every eighteen days over the wall into the shallow Adriatic. She is indestructible, dying lengthily as she watches my wife and me age by her side.

The Doctor crosses himself before her and says: "Well, Signorina Madonna! How long shall we go on like this, dear lady?" She replies that he should be patient a few more days "until I recover! *Pazienzza!*" The Doctor then goes on crossing himself, in our room, angrily. Under his breath. For him she is a Great Riddle of Nature. Humane reasons prevent one, of course, there's no question of that but how humane they are is another matter . . . although it would be just and merciful for us, who are still relatively young, to devote ourselves to our children. In God's name . . . so, her hearing's good and her eyesight! And, really, every eighteen days . . . like clockwork! There's, quite simply, nothing like it in the medical literature. Nothing. And how old is she? Why, she's old, really old . . . almost incalculably! And we aren't even relations. . . . Incredible, impossible, completely unrelated! He taps his pockets, crosses himself at the door, and in the courtyard; he probably crosses himself again, round the corner, for his own sake. That's how it is every time. He is the first to greet me in the morning at the fish market, compassionately; he asks me nicely, rhetorically, just to tell him how in God's name it's possible. And why on earth should I tell him anything! I'm not surprised at the dead continuing to live and keep us in their service, submissive. I'm surprised by the living, at how they come by such strength in their frailty and helplessness, I'm surprised at myself and wonder how we can go on like this. And that is not a rhetorical question, my dear Doctor, it's a question beyond hope that I keep asking myself, and nothing is impossible for her, nor for us, we are all kith and kin, tied by blood to the dead, in faecal kinship with the dying, with the blueadriatic, with this polluted oxygen we are breathing … But we'll buy these few fish that have been fattened beneath Madonna's courtyard wall, Doctor, and all go about our own business in brotherly and kindred peace. We shall be united by grey mullet. Enjoy your meal!

My own business is worse than the Doctor's, but I've almost learned to enjoy my food.

"You make a start," I say to Cara, "start frying the mullet so I can't hear the old woman ranting."

She has washed out the pot and turned it upside down on the terrace to drain.

"Start frying those mullet," I say, "they're clean."

My wife goes on washing her hands for a long, long time, poor thing, I'll have to fetch water tomorrow.

"Child!" calls Madonna.

"What is it, Madonna?" I ask from the doorway. "What the devil is it now? Tell me!"

It is dark in her room. She moans as she breathes from the depths of the room. She's hardly there. She's crumpled up in the hollow of the bed, as in a rocking cradle. But she fills the empty, acoustic room with her wheezing, and it seems as though she has squeezed all this murk and gloom out of her body like a cuttlefish.

"Child! Are you deaf, eh?"

Cara pushes me away from the door.

"We did everything beautifully just now, did our business and washed; so what is it now?" asks my wife, stepping into the darkness of Madonna's room. She doesn't find it difficult to enter this mausoleum; she spends days and nights here, poor creature.

"If you aren't quiet, I'll sleep right through the night and I shan't come at all, all right?"

"She would too, she would, *si.* If there were no Hell. Criminals! But then I'll cry at the top of my voice, my dear, and shout. *Tutta la notte.* I will, you know!"

"What's wrong?" asks blackmailed Cara. "What's wrong now?"

"I can't hear the Hail Mary being said, that's what's wrong. A Christian soul needs ... "

And what can I do, I quickly start mumbling anything that comes into my head, withdrawing into our kitchen-living room, and Cara has come with me, she has started rolling the fish in flour and praying under her breath: "Give them eternal rest and eternal light for our souls you'll have to bring some water there's none left and I must wash before the journey souls in Purgatory and then you can rest as long as you like rest in peace. Amen ... "

The nuns have been ringing the evening Angelus from their little bell-tower for nearly a thousand years now without ceasing. Since the eleventh century mesdamesetmessieurs. A model of architectural achievement. More precisely, St. Andrew's, as you see ...

I took the zinc bucket as one takes a child by the hand and carried it through the back yard into the garden, I rang it, ringing out a response to the thousand year-old ditty of St Andrew's by the Southern Sea, drumming my knee on the bucket. The bell hopped two or three more times on one leg, shocked by my shameless zincogram and then fell silent as though it had dropped into the sea, not leaving even so much as a romantic hum in the air over the warm evening furrows.

There is none of that at St. Andrew's. Its bells are tin. Once they've done their clanging, it's all over, and you can't any longer tell where it ended.

And one day no one will be able to tell exactly where my one and only life ended either. Here — so many years ago, when I took up my watch over the dying Madonna— or in freedom, if I survive the captivity.

I had not yet left the back yard — on the edge of the verandah behind me I made out the clatter of my wife's overshoes. I thought I heard "for the priest". I stopped, and then I almost ran to her. Out of the darkness she held out the rag ring for my head. I had forgotten it when I set off with my bucket. But still I asked:

"What.... has anything happened?"

"Lord no, don't be daft!" sighed my wife.

"Piero! Little Piero!" came a call from the other room. Madonna was now calling my wife by the name of her brother, who, they tell me, died while still in his cradle.

Cara called back crossly and then whispered to me:

"We can always change our minds. I'll stay. But please don't act the fool!"

The bucket suddenly seemed full of wet clothes; it had grown heavy in a gust of the south wind and was pulling me through the garden. I'm not clever enough to know how to act the fool. The south wind was blowing. There were eighteen days ahead of me in this huge house. Solitude. The vestibule of the grave. Life with a corpse.

The fresh air was stifling me, with its sticky damp and the smell of decay from the gardens. And there are no warm furrows here or any of that romance, of either dusk or dawn. The little bit of earth that has collected in the gardens among these rocks is not even earth. The houses, walls, streets, courtyards— everything is rock on rock, and the gardens are dunghills and rubbish heaps and graves, rotted bones, skin, where something clammy is fermenting, left behind by the passing generations, like sediment in a quarry. Where else would the black humus in these great stone bowls of walled courtyards have come from? Anything that could not rot in this compost heap is still scattered through the gardens, lurking in the wings: cement heads with buns, capitals, tiles, glass, earthenware vases and chips of majolica. In the viscous, greasy, amorphous gravy of decay which is earth for us, where magnolias, pittosporum, laurel and evergreens are planted.

I knocked at a neighboring ground-floor window, holding the rag ring like a halo over the balding top of my head. Then I raised the halo, as though removing a mighty tiara, and, as though paying my respects to Christ's grave, I greeted the terrible face of my neighbor on the other side of the pane. What I bowed to was in fact the image of fear, disfigured by natural ugliness and unnatural boniness, blueness and whiskeredness.

The most attractive thing about her is her name, which seems neither attractive nor hers. Our friend is called Hermione. Not Erinye. Hermione. And for some years now, ever since we began neglecting our well, several times a week she has been frightened all over again, because I am eccentric and wicked and her nerves are bad in any case, bad fro fromher mother swomb!

"I said didn't I that this was sanpietro come forforfor water, motherofGod! With a ha-lo!"

"And my wife has invited you to come over this evening for a while."

"Alright, for goodness'sake, the poor woman's go go going away ... oh, but you gave me a start!! I know, I know she has to go. I'll go with you. Why shouldshe shouldshe worry, just let her go!"

We drew the water from the well, poured it into my bucket and some of it over the bucket; the wind ruffled the water and sprayed it over the top of the well, which Hermione does not like, for the old folk always taught us that water that comes out of a cistern is no longer healthy if it fallsba fallsba ckagain inside, *indrento*.

She took one of the bucket's handles, and I the other, and I did not need the ring, so I waved it about to keep my balance, because it is heavy. It is stuffed with stitched up remnants of old-fashioned homespun waistcoats, bits of felt slippers, hats, wool and silk in whip-shaped shreds, ribbons from old ladies' gowns, moth-eaten plush collars and the sediment of centuries-old lye, and this heavy, tightly filled pie wafts from my hand an acrid smell of slops and boiled vegetables, which, when combined with the sweaty fumes emitted in waves by my breathless neighbor, lost its individuality and merged into one single bitter taste of amaranthus and these courtyards, this south wind and this destiny.

When we reached Madonna's garden, Hermione put the bucket down in the dark dangerously suddenly, just in front of my toes, and said solemnly:

"She's going to die, you know! Didn't I ss sayso before? Well, she will, the old lady will die soon now while you're on your own. I swear. Before Christmas, before. Any anyday now."

I lit a cigarette so as to turn away from her face, and silently blew the smoke off to the side. If she had spoken the truth, maybe I would have lit a candle to St. Andrew instead of a cigarette. But then, again…

"She's a devotee of the Co … Community of Worshippers of the Mo … st Precious Blood of Christ. She is. Perhaps you know that, but you don't know that they all died before Christmas, all of those … them. If not exactly on the Eve, then a day before or after. This one and that one, and all. I know them all, on my honor (I am untouched!), not all the women, I didn't say that, but those dev … otee … dammit, you follow? Not one of the worshipful sis sisterssur survived Christmas Eve! *paroladonor!*"

"Oh come now, Hermione! At least seventy, each one of them."

"No, no, lovey, they haven't, not that that last … most important one. That's what I'm saying. No, really. They didn't when I sayso! Now you know."

We couldn't reach an agreement. I bent to pick up the bucket, she bent down quickly as well and we set off like two dumb fools through the dark garden into the courtyard, lashed by the south wind. No one should ever dare think that he might not one night find himself in this windswept universe humping the same stupid load with a person he does not understand, who has wandered off somewhere onto the other side of reason and settled there in some dry bloodless little bed forever.

"We won't say anything to Cara, remember, will we. Hold your tongue like this … as though you didn't have one. Why, it's as clear as clear! Because poor Cara will be al … armed, because then she'd stay. And that would be some Chris … tmas and Newyear, honesttogod!"

We soon reached the terrace, put the bucket down and plunged into a cloud of smoke from the frying oil. My wife was blinking over the spitting pan the way she blinks over the crater of the chamber pot, and Hermione hurried into Madonna's room to savor another's inferiority. I stretched out on my couch and heard the same conversation I have heard goodness knows how often. First, the identification process takes a while, although Hermione spends as much time in our house as in her own. But Madonna often meets Cara and myself all over again, so it's only to be expected with Hermione. And when she has finally established that she is neither this nor that late relative but little Hermione, her late father … *bel campione!* … and that late hussy's daughter, then Madonna concludes that she does not know her, for she has not seen her since she was in nappies.

"You are … that is … young. Little. It's alright for you, Godknows," Hermione laughed jerkily: "why, Hermione isn't in nappies any more, goodheavens! She'll soon be restin … restin-peace, too! How … how old are you?"

"A hundred," says Madonna firmly and proudly. "A hundred *inpunto.*"

"Ah now, it can'tbe … can'tbe … beso much, signora Madonna!"

"How much then, exactly?" asks Madonna inquisitively and provocatively. "In your opinion."

"Well, roughly, oh how should I know. Lotslotsless. Plenty."

There was a short silence. Suddenly Madonna screamed:

"*Aiuto*, my little one!"

"Oh just leave her," said Cara, "she frets the whole day whenever there's a south wind."

But Madonna was roaring hysterically by now:

"Give me back my Kampor you thieves! Criminals and *farabutti!* This is my house, all of it's mine, from top to bottom!"

Cara was draining the last mullet on a fork. She flung the whole thing onto a plate and went in.

"*Dunque?*"

"My guardian angel, drive this witch and Beelzebub out of my house!"

With elaborate gestures, Cara drove Hermione out of the room.

"Shoo, *maledetta* Communist witch! Shoo! There, sit down, while the fish is hot, have some with us. I'll close your door, Madonna, so the smoke doesn't hurt your eyes."

"Close the gates of Hell, the committees have taken everything away from me! Kampor, the woods, the Sheepfold, Pidoka, the Kopun vineyards, the Castle, everything I owned, Barbat and Supetarska, Kalifront … all those villages and relics … and now they send witches to steal my years! *Ladri! Assassini!* Which I came by honestly … accumulated. *Cento anni precisi!* I am, I am! A hundred! *Esatto!*"

Her tears reminded her of her losses, and their memory provoked more tears. That is all she's still living for: to mourn her possessions, which she exaggerates hugely. And that is all she still remembers from the time of her more lucid old age: that confiscation of twenty years ago, which completely unsettled her. Since then her spirit just staggers through the wrongly disconnected regions of her younger days, among so many dead and in the timeless gloom of the non-existent.

We ate slowly, and my wife prepared a fish for Madonna, arranging flakes of pure flesh along the edge of the plate. Crunching little bits of fried skin and licking the bones clean as she went, she told Hermione to be sure and keep an eye on me and Madonna. Hermione just repeated from time to time:

"Forgoodnesssake, I know, I know! He doesn't need comp … company and letsay … let's say friend-ship from me. Just look in and lend a hand."

She always talks rapidly, breaking up her words crossly and chewing her thin whiskers as she stretches her skin and lips into grimaces of inexpressible contempt and disgust, and her eyebrows leap and collide above her nose as though they were artificial, stuck onto the face of a melancholy clown, while beneath them two little bulbs spark in turn, as though each eye belonged to a separate head.

Then she went, saying goodbye to my wife:

"You don't have to tell me morethanonce, *farrò quello … quelloche potrò!* Don't you worry about anything. 'Bye!"

For a long time after we were left alone, we could hear Madonna crushing her soggy little supper greedily and eagerly with her gums. Cara prepared the tub and heated the water for her bath, and I put on my pensioner's cape and stepped out into the somber Lane of the December Sacrifices. I'm not saying that is actually what the street is called, but it is December and my real sacrifices are just beginning. And anyway, it doesn't matter what these streets are called. Everyone calls them by the name of people they know who live in them in any case, or the arcade, or the tavern, or the well. They all display new stone plates with presumptuously huge historical names fit only for the devil. They all bluster with heroisms or boast of army divisions, and even the most bare-handed and blustering division would have to file through them endlessly one by one, from daylight to daylight, on dry rations, suffocating from each other's foot-cloths in the narrow passage. The ancient, bashful past of these little streets is disfigured here by the arrogant history of the new world, so that old Kekina's courtyard is actually called Thomas Woodrow Wilson Square, and not Kekina's Manse or The Green as it has been from time immemorial. Each of these signs takes up half the street, for porches are Squares here; little broken flights of steps are Streets. And it would all warm a local heart if Madonna would only be done with her stools once and for all.

It would all be familiar and treasured. We would live up

there with our Son and Daughter, with their exams, notes and little problems, and in summer we would find a room and an electric ring in some acquaintance's house, and everything would be, as I say, familiar and treasured as in prehistoric times. Even that stupid Woodrow. Or Hermione could cook for us. Or it could it all be, heaven knows, quite different. God could walk on the Earth as he did with Enoch and the Mother of God could cook oriental food for us and I would eat *baklava*. It could be as it never was and never will be. I would not have to go out wandering like an idiot in the dark and the south wind, while my wife washes herself with soda in a trough so as not to take any traces of Madonna up to the children in town, and I would not have to be glad that I am here, airing my lungs from the hundred-year-old stench of a rotten stomach. I would play cards on the kitchen table in Zagreb instead. Or children's roulette, mahjongg, dominoes, or whatever. Perhaps I would survive a serious tram accident, report objectively from the scene. Walk along leafy Zrinjevac Square and criticize, fart softly, write reader's letters. Be a member of parliament! Elect and be elected!

But no. I am a civil peacetime war cripple. The old woman up there — she is a cripple of confiscation, nationalization and collectivization ... — an historical cripple! While my poor wife and children, drunk on freedom and electrification, amply enjoy the fruits of Madonna's and my great sacrifices. *Deo gratias!*

If they ever succeeded in forcing me to be what I would never agree to being forced to be, I would have all the brochures, large scale and nautical maps of this dear Island reproduced ... somehow ... in negative. Where the Island is, there would be a lagoon, maybe even a brackish lake, and the sea would be drawn like dry land, pasture. Everyone would have to abide blindly by the decreed order. To live, finally, in a new way! No longer to interpret the world, but change it fundamentally. Scientifically. Or at least cartographically. Then whoever survived would have to make it to the cliff under which Velebit mountain washes its corns in the Barren Island Channel, get there as best he could, and then hitch-hike along the coast road to the next garrison ... and get on with it!

For the time being it's better if I just wander in lightlessness. At this time of year there aren't any visitors, it's not the season, there's no "tourist traffic," so there's no light on these heroes and divisions, only stone steps in the gloom and acrobatics, you have to choose where to put your hoof. And be chosen.

"Good evening!" I say. "Drawing something again?"

"Just copying these few more plots for some land-registry summaries tomorrow."

"Of course ... of course...." I quiver like a moth in the light. "You alone have the fate of us all in that bottle of ink."

"Of what?"

"Er, of us all. Us all."

"Aha, not Saul? No, us all, you say." And he goes on drawing, ruling lines, inhaling smoke from his cigarette, then says again: "Us all, eh?"

"That's right ... I was thinking about something.... You know!"

"Yes, yes, one does think," my one ... friend here replies with understanding, or –what should I call him—we play cards from time to time. A stupid game that I never find entertaining. "People do think when there's a south wind. Indeed. Not that it helps."

It doesn't help in a north wind either, I think to myself. It does not help even when it helps. In the silence the little steel feather of his drawing pen does not so much as squeak, but it still carves out boundaries and dry stone walls and chops through little roots in the sandy, salty red soil: this is yours . . . that is his, this is how it is, that is how it will remain. The steel tip glides along, greased with sweat and blood. Complain unto the Lord, oh ye ploughmen!

And into the room comes my one . . . or how shall I put it . . . his lady. She usually watches while we play cards. And makes us coffee. She asks compassionately:

"So, please tell me: how is the poor old lady?"

"Thank you. Oh just the same. Aha. In fact, she's a little better today."

"Oh that's good!" says his lady.

Hehey, couldn't be better. And I see there's no chance of that game of cards. What do I care! The man just keeps on inking and sketching those plots. . . .

"Pardon?" she asks out of the blue (perhaps I've already begun thinking aloud). "I said 'that's good'!"

"Of course," I said. "I've even been able to pop out for a bit . . . Makes a difference straight away."

"Excuse me, I'll just go and put some coffee on!" says this one and only wife. Although other wives say the same thing.

"Oh no," I say, "thank you! I must be off."

"This wretched thing's urgent, damn it. But if you waited a little . . ." says my one and only.

"Besides, my wife's leaving on the midnight boat, so. . . ."

It was as though I'd lit a fire-cracker. Leaving! And how will I manage with Miss Madonna? Of course, the children, Christmas, New Year, holidays. Once a year at least! They're quite grown up, it's true. But always so far away. It's not easy, but then what can we do. We all have our cross. Still, it's the most sensible thing we could have done. Radical. Only, how will I manage?

Besides! Besides, my wife is leaving! Besides what? There is nothing apart from the fact that she is going. Not even a cross. Nothing so significant has happened for a long time. And it won't again soon either. There is no salt lake, only these plots and the land-registry, we affirm ourselves on the old ground. And there are no cards either, not today, or for the next eighteen days. Nor good black coffee. Nothing. Farewell!

Freedom Square has huddled completely under the umbrella of its one solitary holm-oak. It was planted forty years ago, while its symbolic adoptive sister Freedom was being born in torment, stunted and then regenerated, but the oak spread beautifully and, lice-ridden as it is, arched over its space. Beneath the tree the square is dry when it rains, there is no sun or sky over it, and in fact there is no more square either really. Only the tree of Freedom scattering acorns into its too narrow concrete bowl. But no little pigs come here. Others come, people with no need of acorns, who find no freedom ... they come because of the sea breaking against the town's foundations below the square, as below a captain's bridge. They feel stronger here. They come to dream of sailing or of death, like me now, while out there lighthouses wink rapidly like a devilish brood, illuminating nothing. They light up for their own sakes. At the end of the land or the edge of the sea? Somewhere in the heart of the endless dark that has no contours. As in a dream.

CHAPTER 2

And so, at midnight, the boat sailed off, off sailed Cara — and I shall no longer say "poor thing." She stood in the yellow light of the deck as though in the town square, dressed for an outing, upright under her hat, serious beside the beautiful suitcase, as though she was already waiting under the chestnut trees for a tram. In the engine room, a ram-like tram bell clattered and the boat slipped imperceptibly away from the shore — a black river poured in between its side and the quay, and then overflowed. They switched off some lights, and everything seemed to stand still; only the distances grew. The boat revolved like a moveable operetta stage with coquettish white waiters stepping autonomously over it. They sailed off into a south wind with no waves to speak of; disappeared with their red and green lights behind the pines. And — that was that.

Now it is absolutely clear that this poor shore has been left with just a few of us scattered and alone on its moist rock, that it is not moving, not revolving, that it stands useless, except for those rare boats that may never come again. I have to leave this empty auditorium. Alone. Back. Gone too are those Swedish girls who bathed by the Big Rock last summer and came urgently one by one into my room at night. Uninvited. At my mere harmless thought. And I did nothing . . . After all, I didn't insist ... Maybe I tried a little in various languages ... *Entrez! Restez! Tombez!* ... Please, what can I do for you, I ask. I act the fool, I stroke my hair ... that sort of thing. They always smile like Lucias; each time they just come in, but they don't know French or *rester,* let alone *tomber* or the like. Everyone learns English these days, but they don't respond to any language. They smile, and I see that they speak all languages. That's how it used to be once upon a time. All in all, one way or the other ... they're not bad! Although people might say, for instance, a man with two grown-up children, or else, his poor wife, and ... it's all true. Ah well, the demands of the flesh, Cara is Madonna's slave and every evening she's weary, weary.... And to give her her due, it has been hard on her. But now, for eighteen days, I won't even remember to give a thought to my body in conversation with those naked Lucias. It may be laughable, but it needn't be: one man will be wanting his sleep. A nursemaid. A nursery nurse.

While I was still a long way off, I thought I heard my foster child crying. I hurried up the quiet little street, brushed aside the oleanders on the courtyard wall and listened. The house was silent, as though she had.... I was about to say "died." As though the house had died, of course! Because I don't intend to start thinking about tragedies in the first five minutes. Although, let's be honest at least with ourselves, at least at midnight with our head in the oleanders — not every death should be mourned. We mourn some people so much in their lifetime that they die ready-mourned and we have no more posthumous sorrow left in us. By dying they have done nothing bad that we should mourn all over again, nor any good that we should be grateful. And if something nice comes to us from their death, again it is no thanks to them. What is — is. If it is. Oleanders always make one's head spin.

Cara had, as always, made up my bed in the kitchen next to Madonna's room. When I went in, Madonna had, of course, noticed that hideous creaking of all century-old doors, but in her death rattle she simply mumbled: "thieving thieves!"—well, not a death rattle, but whatever they say when nothing serious is going on.... And I ought to oil the door tomorrow. It would be good to oil everything straight away, the oven door, if nothing else. That's the easiest. It's true that it would smell of burnt oil. But I certainly ought to do things around the house ceaselessly, every day, all eighteen days, or rather, tomorrow first thing make a comprehensive plan.

I lay down, half-dressed and did not respond, for fear of waking Madonna completely ... and, besides....

Outside, enormous fig leaves are leaning heavily against the windows like a shoal of little stingrays, scraping their sandy skins on the faded crumbling stone under the window ledge and cheeping as they rasp against the glass, while somewhere down by the Municipal Loggia the town clock is striking an uneven *ritardando* of some forty or so chimes, which could have meant midnight, but doubtless actually means that time here had fallen apart after the great plague of long ago and broken into bits of any old size, which mean nothing (not even the wrong time), and that the extinct clock strikes only when the boat leaves, any old way and just so much, the way a seagull cries or an owl hoots. The south wind rocks the clock chimes in the air, sometimes carrying them far off, so the little tower itself seems to be shaking them into random windows, bending over roofs to give everyone a chance to hear a bit. Out on the open sea the express boat is rocking too and in it is my Cara with her suitcase.

She is going to be deluged up there with senseless questions from her mother, who "couldn't ever, try as she might" gather from me exactly why we were "sacrificing" ourselves for that woman at the seaside or at death's door or wherever. Cara would not be able to talk to our Son and Daughter, but, tired as she was, she'd have to explain that it wasn't for the sake of any inheritance, because Madonna didn't have anything any more, but a sentimental commitment to a lonely, abandoned person who had presumably done a lot for me in my childhood (she could say put me through school or whatever would sound even more convincing) and who had besides promised unequivocally she would soon be standing before the Lord, but had now forgotten her promise, and was taking her time in moving on, slowly forgetting all her good deeds and even the name by which she should present herself at the heavenly gates.

I must have dozed off just as the express boat with Cara in it was emerging through the Middle Passage into the Main Channel. Far too early, therefore, to start to sympathize and far too early to start being jealous. In front of her was nothing but the dark cube of the Kvarner Gulf, through which the little golden steamer was plunging, boring its way through the thick south wind. Damp, sticky cold. Her hands washed with soda. The smell of sour cheese, or beer, in the boat's grimy lounge. The rumble of the engines below the deck and the murmur of the sea under the portholes like the rush of a waterfall. And here — the rasping of rough leaves on the window-sill, their mouse's squeak on the thin glass, a cold bed. Stillness. Sleep. Waiting. Whether we are transposing ourselves half-consciously from one point of the dark globe to another, or sailing in our thoughts half-asleep on a musty couch as on the wings of a fever. Waiting for a life that could come with a death that doesn't come. Stillness that opens up sores on the soul's back. Waiting and stillness, and sleep stolen as on a night watch.

I woke up when Madonna's throat grew arid: as the parched might once have put it. She was moaning on the other side of the open door, slapping her dry palate with her tongue and sucking the cactus of the bitter air:

"Her-bs ... her-bs!"

I tried to hide, but in vain, for she moaned tenaciously and steadily with no prospect of ever stopping. She must have set some vital pendulum in motion with her respiratory goat-skin, stimulating the rhythm of her heart and sustaining herself. And if she stopped suddenly, it would mean she had expired or was drinking.

"Her-bs ... her-bs!"

That was how she called for her herb tea at night: she found the word more resonant and suitable for calling and waking people. During the day she would simply demand briefly: *El te*. She may also have been brighter at night, just because I was myself so sleepy.

I flicked the switch in her room and something like a faint light lit up in the branches of the chandelier under the ceiling. Then I switched on the electric ring where her pan of tea stood. The light silenced her moaning so that I turned, startled, towards her bed, thinking that God had beaten me to it and instead of pungent herbs granted her eternal bliss. Out of a little cloud of grey curls two glass eyes stared fixedly at me. Madonna occupied only the upper half of the bed, lying as was the fashion at the end of the last century to lie in one's mother's womb, hunched up, with her knees and hands under her chin and a little petulantly pursed toothless face. It suddenly seemed to me she had lain motionless like that ever since she fell into the world. The midwife had forgotten to slap her and the new born-baby just opened its eyes but never woke up. Seeing nothing and comprehending nothing of the world through its glazed eyes, it had slowly grown and aged on the same sheet from which its mother had long since arisen and gone to her grave, and where anxious generations had then succeeded one another, with chamber pots and herb tea in their hands. The only thing that had happened to this fetus, apart from a few whiskers and sparse bit of beard, was a nebulous but inalienable awareness of an inheritance and possessions bequeathed her by her forebears as they each went one by one out of this great room. Or if not awareness, then an instinctive power. Or an illness. We looked at each other for a moment in the half-dark of this incubator like two forgotten people immured alive *where there is no hope, where fortune is evil.* But we lacked even the contact that might have been possible between us. Sitting on Cara's empty bed, I heard behind my head the unreal hum of the current in the fat spirals of the electric ring, the only sound in the room and the whole empty night around us, around the house, in the ocean of solitude around these houses, these rocks and sea, so that exile and despondency under the faint glimmer of the dim night bulb appeared as a living cell, the only remaining diving bell of life after a cataclysm. But still I looked at her as though we were both dead. Then the pan of tea came to life and started jingling and Madonna shifted her two grey beads in their dark sockets. They glinted like mother-of-pearl as they moved, like cats' eyes.

Before she drank, she glanced at me again out of her grave and sobbed without tears, in the voice of St. Andrew:

"Her-bs . . . her-bs!"

She slurped the liquid, grinding her gums as though kneading clay, her little beard trembling. She looked at my hand when I reached for the empty cup and asked sternly:

"And all the others?" and she would not let the cup handle out of her clenched forefinger.

"They died, Madonna. They've died out," I said quickly, as I did not feel like any nonsense.

But she would not let go of the cup. Her forefinger had become terribly entangled in the porcelain handle, as though it had wrapped itself round it twice and grown into it, and it gave no sign of life. Her hands lay on her chest, like two empty discarded gloves, distorted and twisted, but ossified in that grotesque disorder, petrified in a random movement, and dead. The cup's little handle was lost in that tangle of lifeless roots. I wondered whether we wouldn't perhaps have to bury Madonna with that cup under whose now greenish glint were the drawing of a wondrous building resembling an antique jewel box and the blue curlicues of the inscription: Hotel Esplanade Zagreb. I just took the spoon out of the cup and said impatiently:

"Come on, Madonna, come on. It's nightime, for goodness sake. I want to sleep!"

I was afraid to yank the cup away more forcefully, because the old woman might have slipped from her high pillows and then I would have had to lift her up again, put my arms around her, thrust my hands under her thick armpits, breathe in the somber fumes and raise once more into its half-seated position the whole pitiful spasm of life that was so senselessly hunched up and enduring. I simply gave it a careful twitch, inviting her to surrender. All right, Madonna, come on, come on. But she did not take pity on me, she would not give in, she panted like a dog in the heat, which meant that she was laughing with all her strength and then she managed to say, through her panting:

"He-he, why that means I'm stronger than you. How is that?"

I let go of the immovable cup, took just the spoon over to

the table and turned off the light. She stopped panting and began to call for Cara.

"Cara's not here," I said, turning the light on again. "She's not here. Give me the cup, and we'll see where she's got to."

"Cara's not here? Well, well! Ho, ho," she meditated in surprise. "She must have gone to the graveyard?"

"Yes," I said, finally removing the cup. "Do you need anything else?"

"Or to first mass?"

"Uh huh."

"Insomma, tell her, if she ever comes back, just how everything is and what's what. Let her know, the poor thing. What's she to you anyway?"

"She's my wife."

"What?"

"My wife. *Moglie."*

"I thought ... it seemed to me, that she was an *infermiera."*

"To you, yes, to you she's a nurse. To me she's my wife. Okay?"

"How many you have, *porco!* Listen, listen, first of all, alright, tell her that they called me up and sent me to the army, alright, and that I ... that I'm not here. And you go and hide...."

"All right, all right. We'll certainly fool her. Goodnight!"

"That'll teach her, the minx!"

"Grazie, grazie. Altretanto."

I sprawled back onto my couch and heard Madonna continuing along the path of her associations. Just when everything was quiet again, she asked from the darkness:

"How are mama and papa?"

"Fine, thanks," I said, shaking with laughter. Then she herself started panting, laughing as well as though she understood everything, as though her consciousness had been restored for a moment and she had remembered that they had been dead for a long time and her question was foolish. Or as though she were mocking me in a strange, mad way. But then she really started to reason, and as usual my blood ran cold. She puffed as she said:

"Haha, if you hide, *sempio,* how will you be able to fool her? If you hide, how will you then tell her 'I'm-not-here'? I'll have to be the one … the one who hides. It's silly of you to say 'We'll fool her'! How?"

I propped myself up on my elbows and began to listen, but all I could hear now was endless gasping laughter, barely broken from time to time by those already spoken words, twisted into all conceivable convolutions, and it was clear that her little half-extinguished flame of wit had burned itself out, that her spirit was delighting in a ray of light which had chanced to wander past and reach it, breaking unexpectedly and joyfully through unknown cracks in her consciousness.

I got up and went out onto the terrace facing the sea. And lo and behold, a young north wind was already swirling in the exhausted southerly. Madonna had begun to snore, clattering like a gas meter.

CHAPTER 3

Early in the morning that wretched door creaked again and brought me back from a deep sleep. Hermione was already standing beside my bed, thin, long. For winter clothes she had only a grey woollen shawl thrown over both her shoulders and fastened on her chest. She was laughing soundlessly, but with her teeth bared, as though something had really disgusted her, she squeezed her eyes tight shut and sniffed:

"Whyfor g-good nesssake, What a sight, wellwell, well! *Bella roba!* Let him get up, then. *Checheche coraggio!* Why the wom an knows no shame or modesty, for godssake, here she comes straight to the man's bed. And he could be naked, godhelpus, who knows! Eh, not that I mind a bare bum! Go to the Devil with all your men's smut. I have grown old un unsullied!"

I removed the crust from my right eye with my thumb and forefinger and cocked my ear in the direction of Madonna's door, leaning up on my elbow in bed. Hermione followed my glance and peered into Madonna's room. Then she stepped inside on tiptoe and returned with the tea pan.

"What might the time be?" I asked.

"It'll be God knows. I didn't hear St. Andrew's. What whatsit matter. She's asleep. Asleep. If she's not dead. She could be dead. Her eyes are open. You never you neverknow. You go on sleeping, what do you care. It's cold. I'll make some tea....' Her legs are so long, she stepped in one stride out into the hall, and I heard her swish the water round in the pan and empty it in the garden. On the town tower some maimed hour struck, barely audible in the distance, as though the clock itself were weary of its barren task. You could not count the chimes, but for a moment Hermione fell silent, she was probably listening to them, and then said from out there: "Whywho who the devil would try to count, you have to wait for godssake, you have to wait and wait and there's no end to it! And what's the point! A bird st ... st ... stands on that hand and straight away it's ten minutes later, ten minutes earlier ... if three pigeons fall off it ... ohmygoodnesme ... that's three times ten." She put the pan full of water on the stove under the window and began to light the fire. I could smell the match and the thin wisp of smoke in the fresh morning air. I reached for a cigarette and asked Hermione:

"What are you going to buy, how much shall I give you?"

"Give me fivehunfivehunfivehun ... a thousand. A thousand dinars. And I'll give you the change. Some milk for the old woman. Then do you want fish or some of that black mutton? What's a dinar today! And some potatoes, you have to have some. As for eggs, eggs, that's toomuch, that's a luxury! We won't have any. Daylight robbery! I was for this commucommunism, but when I see whereitsallgoing.... Give me five hundred and we'll see."

Madonna suddenly called Cara in a gurgling voice.

"You're still alive, Miss Madonna?" Hermione sounded genuinely surprised, standing in the doorway to Madonna's room and huddling in her shawl in the sepulchral chill.

"Is that you, Hermione?" Madonna asked soberly. "But I'm calling Cara, Cara."

"Cara sent me, makes no difference. What would you like?"

"And Cara?"

"What shall I say?" Hermione turned to me, "Cara?"

"You be off, Hermione," I said, "I'll get up."

"Cara's gone dancing. Early in the morning. Um pa pa," Hermione called into Madonna's room, and, presumably imitating a train, she set off, hopping, towards the door. She went on calling from outside: "There's a storm blowing out here like on the opensea!"

Madonna was patient today. She fell silent wondering where Cara could be. I can read her every thought. Apart from those transcendent ones. A few years ago we explained my absence by saying that Cara's mother had died. Madonna was bound to have forgotten, but still this time we had decided to bury her father, just for a change. So now Cara had been left quite alone. I dressed and went in to Madonna to carry out that stupid duty too. I knew she would go on asking for Cara every day, but it would be easier for me simply to repeat a formula, even if it meant constantly burying my father-in-law, than to keep dreaming up silly answers which might anger Madonna, or which would not satisfy her. I put out my cigarette, rubbed my eyes as though I were washing, because we had to save water, and because it was too cold for major hygienic exhibitions.

"I want to make water," said Madonna.

I took the pot out of the bedside cupboard and pushed it under the covers, but I don't feel like mentioning all that I had to fiddle with in there and what a complex business it is to bring even the most trivial things in this world into some sort of order. Waiting for Madonna to make contact with her supposed motor centers and mobilize her small nervous system and warped sensations to summon up the thin shudder that activates the narrow pipes, loosens the loops and opens the little canals, I briefly announced in an emotional tone the sudden death of my esteemed father-in-law.

To gain some time, at the worst moment, Madonna gave me a sharp command to close the cupboard.

"Can't you smell the stink! Shut the door quick, immediately!"

I had to rummage with my foot round the door, which was all I could do since my hands were still under the covers, and my whole attention focused on the deceased; and now I know that nobody really knows his potential recklessness, especially not spiritual acrobats: everything remained whole and dry, and the door banged shut! Madonna immediately functioned at these gloomy tidings. For nothing sets her system going as effectively as talking about death. Not a storm, nor an anti-cyclone, nor high atmospheric pressure, none of these raised the remains of her consciousness to such clarity. The vessel in my hand reverberated with muffled ringing and Madonna sighed:

"Peace be with him, *angelo mio!*"

Later, when Hermione returned, she said vaguely:

"My son's father-in-law has died. My daughter's father. We got a telegram."

Of course. I hadn't thought about how we had received the news. But we could show Madonna any old piece of paper.

"You don't say, Miss Madonna!" mocked Hermione. "Who's died? Who was who to whom? Why then that'll be your husband!"

"Husband?" asked Madonna. *"Selvatica,* not a word of regret, she just makes jokes! Husband?! Idiot! When have I had a husband? Ne-ver. And what for?"

I turned to Hermione with extravagant gestures like one sailor to another in the distance with little flags.

"Ah!" she got the message. "Ah, well, him today, you tomorrow: oneaftertheother, we'll all go. Blessed d... blessed-death!" She grinned at me, "why you're an old devil yourself!"

"It'll be you tomorrow, and not me, you fool!" snapped Madonna.

I was actually speaking to both of these demented women, because they both had to understand me. From one I was looking for support so that the other would spare me from reproach:

"Cara had to go, she had to go in this cold, what could I do, you were asleep, weren't you, there was nothing for it, he was her father. There's snow and floods and volcanoes and hardship up there in town, Quite dreadful, but a father is a father . . . let's just hope it all goes smoothly."

"Si, si , si, e, come no! I was sleeping, sleeping. Day and night. *Brutto bugiardone! Ti lo senti?* May it all go smoothly, ah! Fools, both of you. Well, really. A man's died up there . . . and all he . . . just hopes it all goes smoothly! Did you hear that? *O, corpo di Bacco!"*

"And what grief that is, I ask you!" Hermione took up the theme, "grief for a father, not to mention the shock! She'll have to stay, poor thing, up there at least . . . I can't say . . . she'll have to stay . . . who the devil knows. . . ."

I did not dare let her finish. I asked Madonna anxiously:

"What do you think, Madonna, how long will it take? And when could she be back?"

"To get him buried and everything?" Hermione joined in again.

I must confess that this stubborn insistence of Hermione's on grief, death and burial was beginning to make me a little uncomfortable. Especially the "get him buried." As though he were carrion. But she thought it a wonderful discovery; this banal lie — a brilliant invention. She was delighted by this game of misleading a naughty child. She overrated her role, but she was more intoxicated by the honor I did her intelligence by asking for her collusion and help.

The old woman was scowling as she inspected her little hands. And then I suddenly realized where I had gone wrong. I should not have claimed she was asleep. She will not admit it. She never sleeps. Sleep is a pleasure, laziness, rest, evil, sin, for it is a sign of health, a sign that nothing hurts, that you do not need anything, that you can be alone, or something like that. She rejected death, but she would exaggerate her illness if that was possible, because she thought that nobody believed how ill she was, and because she sought care and attention insatiably like a spoilt child. She scowled at her fist, trying to separate her index and little fingers. When she thought she could just make out their tips, she glanced at Hermione, glanced at me, jerked her hand slightly in an unseemly gesture, saying:

"There! That!"

It was an expression of impotent fury and malice. And I felt and I knew that there would be no question of contemplation or philosophizing for some time. She would demand impeccable service from me, harass me night and day, reject any kind of explanation, criticize her food, her care and everything I did.

I withdrew into the kitchen with Hermione, conscious that at the very outset I had forfeited what miserable chances I had had, and that I had brought on myself the worst possible treatment Cara had ever experienced. Hermione's face showed what her instinct had dimly gathered: horror at the fear of the unspeakable malice that threatened from that deathbed. As though the force of Death itself had declared cruel vengeance on liars and chatterboxes.

She showed me some meat wrapped in paper on the table,

a string bag of vegetables and the change. Without a word she poked the fire in the stove, put on her shawl and left.

From the room could be heard calls for help and then weeping that was indistinguishable from her laughter. Just a dog-like panting interrupted by little coughs. I went out into the garden to look at that wondrous white rose by the wall that blooms in December. And to escape Madonna's fury.

That was the beginning of my conclave; my service to Madonna and my isolation with her began on a note of hostility. The rose is in full bloom. The densely crowded petals shine white, burnt at the edges by the north wind, without any sparks of dew on this sharp, dry morning. Far to the east, over the mountain crests, heavy tubers of low cloud and snowy rags in the rifts. And beyond it all, in the mist of the mainland — people are living! Surrounded by high walls of white stone, hung with little dried campanula bells, I can see only the cold, pure sky above me with the tip of St. Andrew's sailing across it, and the distant outlines of Mount Velebit, the furthest and highest wall beyond which volcanoes of fog are puffing. I stand like a nun in a convent garden, and instead of feeding white hens with feathered legs, I am tending a quite bizarre creature; instead of stroking a white rose, or dreaming of Lucias.

My holy neighbor, you can see from up there that I'm lying. Go ahead and strike me down if you've any reason to think I'd send her to the devil! I ramble on and prattle things I don't mean, for you know yourself that I'm not going to pray, but I have to do something! I would care for her just as tenderly as I touch this white rose, if there were any point. If I knew what for. If you told me for how long. Let's say that within the area that a tram covers in half an hour, a multitude of my friends are pottering around and bumping into each other. They are together. They are there. It may be that if I sifted through them all, there wouldn't be a single real friend left. But people would still be pottering about, I would always meet someone. Or at least I would travel in a tram for half an hour, hoping. I would be within that area. Somewhere around — for all of them. I'm not saying it's important whether one's here or there. Just moving about isn't more important than life. It's not in itself anything more than vegetating. But then it would be good somehow to find out what life is! Is happiness life, or could life itself be happiness? Or is it vegetating, both here and there. I'm a nun here in the bottom of a stone bowl with a little humus and vegetation, under the dried Istrian bell-flowers on the wall, under your bells, and under the bell of the pure arc of heaven. They are there in an ocean of fog, less together than it seems from here. But I tinkle and jingle somehow drily here. There I would reverberate dully in the damp and smoke and winter gloom. I would hate, or perhaps I wouldn't, but I would have the opportunity. From there I'd even be able to say what this Madonna was. What the devil is going on here. I would make use of two or three medical expressions, it's such and such, I'd say in passing: I have to stay there a little longer, until her organism quite packs it in, actually innumerable organs have already given up, but the vital ones haven't yet, the heart is resisting, and so it's just a matter of days, and then, and so on, it would all be clear. I would set off here again as though for the weekend.

Perhaps the cleaners would not even have swept my tram ticket from the pedestrian island, and I would already be back from this sandy island to that pedestrian one with the story of Madonna's death, of how we had to force her straight while she was still warm, how we pushed down her knees and elbows and simply snapped her and stretched her out so that she could be fitted into the coffin, how everything had clicked and more or less fallen apart inside the sack of her thin skin, how she had flattened out and covered the bottom of the coffin, like a crumpled newspaper or an empty goatskin. From there I'd know how to see myself here, say what I had been and why and what principles I had acted by; what good I had done, who I had helped and how much harm I had done myself.

Cara has a long white soul like a nightdress and whiter than the whitest rose. Today she will forget all the bad things in an instant. Sitting in the kitchen, she will drum her fingers on the table and say to her mother, father, Son and Daughter, herself and perhaps me in her thoughts: "It's only a matter of days and we can get through it; but how is life with you?"

CHAPTER 4

What can they say about how life is with them and what is life anyway when one is living? It's a city, up there, municipal services, advantages. You glance to the left, glance to the right, you're a chance passer-by, you turn up — you disappear. You do have to stop for a moment when you see a red light, but not always even that. You choose streets according to your personal inclination and your whole life you never know all the most important boulevards in both directions. In the army no one believes you are just from Zagreb, they always want to know more precisely. The radio station does not broadcast from somewhere in the ether, but from round the corner; professionals, head offices, this or that person's history, popular musicians, it all rubs shoulders with you on the pavements, in entrance halls, in ice-cream shops. But that is not the point either. Who loves the Island more than I do! Life is not all rubbing shoulders, let alone head offices and pop musicians. If only I did not have to sit here, my head on one side like a mangy dog in a nettle patch, listening in case Madonna starts droning. If I were not a watchman, if I were exempted, like someone disabled, like a pensioner, seeing that is actually what I am ... Oh brother! An invalid nursing an invalid! An invalid of the past tended by an invalid of the future, as it were! I do not mean to say there is anything wrong with me, thank the Lord, I'm not missing an arm or a leg or an intestine or anything else perishable. But I have not been, let's say, pensioned off just like that either, because of my tousled hair — some comrades must have found something about me, some other impediment or roguery, that some committee found damaging or that did not suit them, so they did not much care for it, obviously!

And if I didn't have to cook, if I weren't constantly washing up ... dealing with dirty dishes, rather than cultural history! If I could take *Gods, Graves and Scholars* under my arm and spend a couple of hours in the morning, a couple of hours in the afternoon, wandering through the park, reading a little, making a few notes on who dug up what when. Or it need not even be that. We have this garden. You can read there, you can even do a little digging there, you can find sand there too. You don't have to be a scholar, nor does everything have to be conclusive and epoch-making. Why?! Your respiratory canals can simply set consciously to work on these iodine vapors and this forest oxygen, you can breathe, breathe in; watch boats and fishermen in the harbor, visit all the moorings and anchorages one by one; one foot in front of the other; paddle barefoot through the dewy grass of the football field for the sake of the magnetism. Who cares if anyone says that lunatic's taken off his shoes. Who cares about anything. Who cares. And I would even be quite happy as things are if only that scatter-brained Hermione had not frightened Madonna. If she could take over from me for two or three hours a day. At least I could go to the market myself and perhaps save the occasional piddling dinar ... all right, I know ... but even that is not absolutely pointless. And, it goes without saying, on my way I'd look at the sky above my head, see a little of the changing tides ... people would actually see me suffering my samaritanism. And I wouldn't rush anywhere, I'd have a bit of a rest. There, that's all. More than that, I can honestly say, I don't need at the moment. Why should I pamper myself? I'm done for in any case.

But not all this again. Not having to be a nonentity again for a mummy ... for a medical specimen. In methylated spirit. With her calling me before it even occurs to her to want something, then chasing me out of the room like a filthy cat. With me squatting outside her door like a puppy and pricking up my ears to catch her grunting. In these two days since she has not been able to stand the sight of Hermione, or the sound of her voice, she has run me off my feet. I'm lying here exhausted, reflecting on how one ought to live, while she keeps flinging out official statements from in there without let-up, just so that I don't imagine that everything is rosy and I'm back in favor. Outside it's a sunny afternoon, in the sheltered spot below the park women have undone their blouses and are feeding their young in the sun; my pensioner colleagues with their hands crossed on their backsides watch it all uninterestedly or return an interested glance, but towards the pensioner class. Outside, the mild winter sun is yellow, everything alive has crawled out into the open, there is nothing evil, nothing to be afraid of, small time politics — there's fish, there's no fish, someone's got a raise, someone's got rheumatism, perhaps someone even feels sorry for Madonna, no one feels sorry for me and I stop my ears, stop my ears here in the half-dark, but it does not help. I try in my thoughts to wrap myself in a white coat, I try to imagine Madonna as some kind of intricate electronic control board, as some kind of super robot, and myself serving it ... Oh, my, how he too has fallen, the man in the white coat, but so much more purposeful than me! He serves machines. While I serve an old wreck, and at the slightest creak of an old sprung bedstead all my cybernetics are reduced to the blue enamel handle of a chamber pot decorated with medallions of rust. And if my hands were as frightened as my eyes are afraid and my nostrils wrinkle, the job would never be done.

"They are not people!" shouts Madonna from in there, "they're Saracens!"

Steady on now! And why Saracens in particular? Robbers, by all means, fools! Wasn't this island besieged by dangerous Norman ships as well, and had it not been for our St. Christopher, who deflected the cannon balls from the town walls with his head and sent them flying back at their stupid galleons, we would have no Fiera here, nor would you kiss the silver chest with the ceremonial skull in it, on St. Christopher's Day. Only we've fallen for that Crusaders' skulduggery from time immemorial, because from the pulpit Saracens sound like Satans and sycophants, while the Normans — polite, docile — South Italian Normaaani, wouldn't you say! Ah yes, you have to adore your island and have its turbulent history at your fingertips, and not simply rattle off what the curates rattle off at the Nine-day Devotion. You should know who the real enemies of the people are and who it was enslaved the Croatian rulers *in mysterious circumstances* — and all those fine things, of course, of course! But what am I doing straining my nerves here, because of an old scratched tape-recording! All it does is spasmodically reproduce the remains of words it recorded unconsciously under the pulpit and in the confessional of St. Andrews! What am I getting so worked up about! Let her shout, let her say Saracens, so what! Until she calls: come here, damn you! Until she says clearly what she wants — I'm resting. Perhaps I'll even doze a little. And meanwhile let her grind away, it sends me to sleep. And all that history . . . I really couldn't care less!

"And worse than Saracens, worse! Worse than all guerrillas!"

Madonna was mumbling somewhat more quietly now, as though she was not sure whether anyone could hear. Perhaps she had begun to question her own reasons. Perhaps she was listening to her own words and trying to make out what they meant. Or she had not found the right expressions and was losing confidence. In fact, I think she simply does not know why she is angry any more and by being angry out loud she is trying to dream something up as she goes along. That is why her voice is flagging, and that is why she suddenly says softly to herself: "Poor old fool that I am! Really!"

These are my only moments of rest, when Madonna sets off into those remote regions and when she talks to herself. No one would believe it, but it really is a rest. I lie on my couch in the kitchen, and look at my fingers. One is truncated, the whole top joint is missing, instead of a nail there is a hard, round, horny cap. On the other hand there is a double nail on the index finger, one rigid joint, numerous scars. I could tell a lot of sad little stories about these fingers of mine, and, without exaggerating, they would be strange and somewhat horrifying, because there is always a little multitude of cruelty, human filth, evil and stupidity gathered round such insignificant and peripheral, yes, one should say peripheral mutilations. Wrong-doing even. Crimes, indeed. But forget it. I have not been left here in the forecourt of death to reflect on people and crimes. Nor, a stone's throw from a hideous disintegration, to discourse on the insignificant scars every crazy wolf-cub gets as soon as he has scrambled out of his lair. I belong to a nation that has hands like this, chewed off fingers, contorted tendons, stumps, man's most precise tools — variously mutilated. And I belong to the generation that excels in this. For if we were to line up and examine all the peoples of Europe, if they put out their hands, well, what did I tell you! The majority of the maimed ones will say: countryman! And most will try to tell you it was for the fatherland. But it is not true. It is a mark of belonging to a particular civilization and ... so there's no point ... Forget it. I am on duty beside a medical wonder that does not belong to any ethnic group. For if she and I are countrymen, then God is our only ruler and the galaxy our fatherland, if there are such things. Galaxies, I mean. I am hanging about beside the abyss of a grave, at the end of the Earth's horizon, by the shore of that enigmatic river that surrounds the world, I am sitting on the brink of the world, like a sleep-walker on the edge of a night roof and reflecting on my Balkan scars instead of wondering why it is I have to wait for my own anonymous death here in this deaf mortuary and not even outside there by the cemetery wall since I cannot be anywhere in any blessed civilization. Instead of being a hoplite, or an oiled gladiator in airy, sunny meadows somewhere or in the open spaces and meadows of the soul, I am condemned to listen to innumerable bubbles of gas from a rotting hulk of flesh, popping out under the sheets in the next room as from a barrage balloon, and to find the rhythm of my afternoon recreation in those snorting anal pulsations. But if I look away from my hands, if I lay them down by my sides or put them together on my stomach, suddenly I too am nothing but a corpse preparing to tread the heavenly paths and I see myself as her room-mate — Madonna there, me here, the two of us abandoned like lepers are waiting only for death. And if I look with a vestige of consciousness into myself I feel as though I had suddenly found among my old papers a photograph of myself from the time when I shall be ninety or so, and in firm handwriting, on the photograph, something like a psychogram of myself at this moment, this moment that has been going on since the beginning of time and that is becoming everything. That is what this respite of mine amounts to. And it seems bliss to me, after all my kitchen and nursing cares, bliss between two of Madonna's summonses. And if I could, if I didn't have to cook for Madonna, I would float lethargically on this couch to the finish and presumably die of hunger, but I would never again flicker an eyelash.

Perhaps frightened by my own thoughts, I got up and went to Madonna — for the first time without being called. When she caught sight of me, she began to spell out some of her blurred verses. If anyone imagines they could understand what she says at all it is only because I know how to decipher and convey it. Her lips are two fins, sadly stuck together, sticky and slimy as a dead fish's, with a hard, swollen tongue twitching in between them, scarcely parting them for a moment, poking out now in one place now in another to achieve a vague lisping. With fear in her eyes, she spoke as clearly as she could:

Anima serena
Conta mi la tua pena
E sta lontan di me!

But in case anyone imagines one could see the sudden fear in her eyes as easily as I know how to interpret it, it should be reiterated that the little windows into her soul had long since been frozen over by the breath of death which had nested behind them, and that for a long time now they had been framed in rings of uniform fear at the prospect of that invisible guest as though in surprise.

"If you are a spirit from Purgatory, cross yourself and stop!"

Instead of "stopping" I moved towards her bed with a little pan of cold chamomile tea. Perhaps I would quite simply have killed her if I really had crossed myself and stopped in the middle of the room like a ghost.

"I've stopped, halted!" I said, approaching her pillow. I knew no sign of the cross could save me from this hell. "I've stopped," I said, "now come on, let's have that mouth open!"

I folded a little piece of gauze into a tube and raised her upper lip with two fingers. Then she thrust out her hardened tongue the way a deep-sea comber thrusts out its swimming bladder when it's caught, and, using the tube soaked in chamomile like a paint-brush, I began to moisten that rough, cracked and crusty muscle that was still swelling to say something. I dipped the tube back into the pan, and she slapped her moistened tongue contentedly against the velvety roof of her mouth; then I ran the wet tube once again over the furrowed burnt phallus protruding from the cavity of her mouth, and she broke into a secret soft cat-like purring. So we went on tirelessly until twilight, by which time my hands had begun to shake and spill drops of chamomile over the great bed and I threw the gauze into the pan like a barber tossing his brush into the lather and went to put the beet leaves on to cook. It was only then that shots rang out behind me from that newly greased weapon:

"*Cretino,* to do me a little favor did you have to slink in like a thief or a ghost! *Vigliacchi* and Saracens! Beelzebubs and torturers of Christian souls is what they are and not holy souls from purgatory, neither here nor there, but devils disguised, *doyoucapisci* … ergh … disguised … ergh…."

I thought for a moment that Madonna was choking, that she was foaming at the mouth in her agitation. I dashed back into the room, turned on the light and sprang to the bedside. She started shouting:

"He's going to murder me, help! Save me, I've been murdered!"

"Calm down, my dear Madonna, for God's sake, this is the beet knife, for the beet, from the kitchen … I'm preparing the beet leaves, do you feel ill? There, look, to hell with the knife, I've thrown it away, there, I've thrown it away, *lo go buttà* ... I'll give you a little tea, just let it warm up, I'm heating it now, sweet-sweet-sweet tea...."

"Make me some lemonade, devil take you! Lemonade with lemons," said Madonna, quite calm by now. She knew that lemons were expensive.

I might have expected it, she had not acted the bit about having her throat cut for nothing. I picked the knife up from the floor and went into the kitchen as into a slaughter house. I squeezed a lemon with one movement and supernatural strength. A little saccharine disk for her pancreas. Then I rattled the spoon, announcing my arrival, as an acolyte announces the Last Rites, so that no one should think spirits were stalking the world again. She drank as though she were eating: chewing every mouthful while it was still in the saucer, as in a nosebag.

"My will is that I be burned at the stake, like my, how should I say, *il mio antenato, avo lontano*...."

"Ancestor, your ancestor...."

"My Markantun. That is my last testament."

"All right, what must be, must be."

"Not must, but MUST!"

"Your will be done. We've got beet leaves with hard-boiled egg, Madonna. Would you like coffee or just plain milk?"

She was scornfully silent for a long time. I turned and went out but she was roused by the clatter of the spoon from the kitchen, because I sometimes put the cutlery down clinking and clattering like all the furies, particularly when I am as pissed off as I am today, and as I have been for three days now, because of her reign of terror and official declarations. She summoned me resolutely, as people do when they do not intend to give in.

"Get them to bring it so that I can sign!"

"There's nothing to sign, Madonna You've signed everything already and the lawyer's got it. You can't do it every day."

"I've made it all out to you, fool that I am! And have they written down all the rest, my last testament too? And that my ashes be cast into the ... into the Tevere? They have, eh? All right then. Go on, go on, cook the beet, you ninny."

Madonna hummed softly until evening "From the rising of the sun unto the going down of the same," the words of the psalm to a sad aria from *Il Trovatore*. And one might have assumed that she had come to terms with this world again, and even with me. As she arranges her last things in her mind for the hundredth time, she will soon begin to look around this vale of tears once more without impatience, perhaps even beginning to wish that the black train that travels West should never arrive.

CHAPTER 5

Madonna was angry with me for three days. She was offended, but no longer knew why. She did not remember the reason, she only remembered her anger, and today she forgot even that, when she heard it was Christmas Eve. She did not hear it from me, which was bad, but she heard, which was so good that she quickly forgot my lapse.

This morning old Tunina came with a pine branch and a skinny little cockerel under his arm. He said good morning to me in the garden and asked whether the mistress had risen. When I led him into the house, he simply nodded his Zeus-like head and chanted:

"Then the poor lady still hasn't recovered since last year, or the year before, or the year before the year before...."

I told Tunina it was old age and she would not recover from that, although it was foolish to say so to him, as he is older than any living thing on the Island.

At the door he bowed without putting down the branch or the cockerel. With his free hand he raised his little tomato-red riding-hood cap and sang out in a sweet voice:

"Praisegod, *signora parona,* and the Lord grant you good health and the greatest happiness in all the good cheer and festivity of this holy feast day...."

"Who are you," asked Madonna inhospitably "with that creature?"

"Your serf, Tunina, your devoted and humble servant, *signora parona*. Old Tunina."

"Tunina? Bravo, Tunina, bravo! You've come to ask me for something or other again, I know. I'm not giving you anything. Go to the manager, if he gives you something, if he does, well and good, let him do so! But I shan't give you anything and I don't acknowledge anything! You've cheated me enough."

"God grant peace, my *parona,* to the sad manager!" said Tunina solemnly, as though it were just a little mistake and the manager had still been giving things away to all and sundry only yesterday. "The Procurator, my good people, has been why, how long.... There, the young gentleman's one of them, he knows! They killed him right there, lying in his bed like that, in the name of the people, may God and St. Lucia forgive them! Ah, yes."

I could not get involved in conversations with centenarians, I just observed, out of the corner of my eye, that Madonna had fallen into a vengeful rage at such a business loss, while Tunina was explaining that there was no question any more, regrettably, of resurrecting the procurator. I went to get brandy and biscuits from the kitchen and heard Tunina explaining:

"That's not why Tunina has come, my *signora*. He barely comes into town now at Christmas, for the sake of the fact that it is a sacred custom and God's ordinance that every peasant should offer his respects to the mistress and do what he can according to his means, here with God's blessing this cockerel, all I can do, but from my heart. A little pine branch to decorate the house and smell sweet. And thanks be to God. For all your beneficences."

I brought the biscuits and a bottle of brandy on a stool. Tunina smelled of the stormy morning and the forest, his skin quivered on his cheeks and his nose and cheekbones were red and blue.

"Povero diavolo," said Madonna. "Tunina must think it's already Christmas Eve. *Ma che da rider…!* What's the use of his having good legs, when he forgets what's in front of his nose and mixes up all the days in the year! But take that creature all the same, take it. They owe me so much, it should be Christmas Eve every morning."

"But we said it was Christmas Eve, or have you forgotten?" I lied brazenly, expecting the worst. "Hermione said it this morning, he's right, Tunina's right."

She started thinking, and I began hurriedly to make myself busy, carrying the biscuits and brandy to the dresser, encouraging Tunina to sit down. I took the pine branch and laid it on the dresser too, and then grabbed the cock. Its legs were tied, it flapped its dusty wings helplessly, and then calmed down in my hands like a pigeon. Although it did have more feathers than a pigeon.

"Show me!" called Madonna, "let me see!"

I pressed the cockerel to my chest with one hand and handed Tunina a glass with the other, and then went up to Madonna's bed. She probably thought she could stretch out her hand and touch the cockerel from down there. I myself thought for a moment that a miracle was going to occur, but it didn't. I stood by her pillow, and she barely glanced at my hands out of the corner of her eye, without moving her head.

Tunina wished us good health and bent forward, then sniffing noisily and clearing his throat he began dipping biscuits in his brandy.

"She isn't heavy," muttered Madonna, as though to herself.

"He's fine," I lied again. It weighed less than the feathers alone could have done.

"I can see," said Madonna resignedly.

With Ancient Greek frankness, Tunina said calmly: "Can't be done, what with the women and the kiddies, *signora parona!* Thank God for small mercies. The good old laws aren't respected no more, and that's it, my good people! Communism. Everyone does what's best for himself. You've got to steal to take your master something. But there's no debts, mind, if I'm to speak the honest truth. No, there aren't. That I can say. There's no debt."

"Give him one little cake and two hard biscuits. We must keep some for the others."

Where would we get cakes? And for what others?

"We haven't any of those," I turned more towards Tunina than her, "we haven't baked for ages, you know that, Tunina. Here, a little brandy. There's more, help yourself. It's stormy and it's a long way home."

And no one else would come. Tunina knew that too. Once there had been a hundred of them. On Christmas Eve the peasants would fill the garden with turkeys, capons, chickens. They filled bronze bowls with eggs. For a long time now, Tunina had been the only one left. And it wasn't that they had all died. Communism, my good people! Nowadays on holy days and on all other days poultry flies unplucked into new refrigerators instead of into our old courtyards. And that's it, that historical justice. But there aren't any warm bread cakes either. No one bakes them. Nor do they dry biscuits either. Everyone has his own refrigerator. Progress, my good people....

I took the little cockerel into the empty garden. First I clipped its wings with scissors and then cut the string round its legs and let it have a bit of a walk.

Although I had long ago forgotten everything, this brought back a little whiff of earlier Christmas Eves. I used to clip feathers like this only at my Uncle's house, where livestock would arrive at Christmas, perhaps in even greater quantities than here, because there every donation was received with gracious approval, and not indifferently as here. Tunina used to come there without fail. He was as old as he is now. Piles of soft cakes and dry biscuits and bottles of grape brandy were spread on tables. Curled up on a camp bed, in new long socks I waited for Mada to weigh the capon in her hands, before I took it, armed with scissors, into the courtyard for execution, while Tunina stood by my Uncle's desk, wrapping cakes in a handkerchief and coughing from the brandy. He did not mention communism then, but he said "my good people" and answered my Uncle, wiping the drops from his beard: "I won't be allowed to vote, *signor Procurator,* for the reason that, they say, I'm in advanced old age, that's what they tell me, the devil only knows. In advanced over-ripeness, ... and it's not legal." My Uncle was expounding on something, saying it didn't matter what he thought or what they said over there but did he know who he ought to vote for, WHO to vote for my good man, and nothing else the peasants told him mattered, it was all stuff and nonsense, as long as a man knew what was what and wished to have a clear conscience in politics. Whoever's my master, I'm his servant! My good man! And as for you, Tunina, don't be a peasant ass like all the others, forget them and all their stories, we know how it goes and where it's all heading. We know it all, for God's sake, we're not idiots. And we're not Mamelukes and all the rest. But tell your master something else, Tunina. Say, truly, from your heart: I'm not old, because there's no limit! But they want me to vote for the so-called peasant rebellion and peasant party, isn't that it, and

I can't do it because of my honor and my obedience to the government, and so on, to Signora Markantoni, Mr. Jeftić and the Lord God, *insomma,* you tell me that, and I shall take off my hat to you, look, like this, old friend, you see, and God grant you good sense, happy Christmas and goodbye! But don't come twisting things and telling stories in front of me! All right, eh? Child, give Tunina two more fresh cakes, Mada, will you, let him know it's Christmas as well, that's the way! You see, you understand me, the Procurator wasn't born yesterday, uh-huh.... God be with you! Now go in peace." And then Tunina had nothing left to wrap the new cakes in, and he was confused, and his grey beard twitched and Mada slipped him some more brandy, even though she's a Starčević supporter, for my Uncle approved with a sign of his thumb, and I ran headlong down the steps with the capon as though it were a double-headed eagle.

There's no courtyard filled with poultry any more, one could say nostalgically. The cheerful little opposition cockerel was now hopping about in the garden pecking at lumps of earth. I picked up the feathers and took them onto the verandah in case Cara could use them, and poured a ladle of water over my hands.

Tunina was sitting quietly in Madonna's room right beside the door, as though he had decided to give his old legs a good rest from his long journey before doing a round of the town. It is impossible to believe he had on his feet those same canvas peasant shoes that he wore on that distant Christmas Eve I remember. And that same sleeveless jersey, which serves him as a coat and a jacket and a vest on his bare skin. Stiff as a knight's chain mail. Black and greasy as though it were not knitted of roughly spun wool, but stuck together from a combination of sheep's and goats' droppings, and that was how it held, glued together, tanned by storms and old age. It is impossible to believe that all these years of mine, a whole lifetime, are the same in the life of this old man as the lifetime of a jersey and a pair of canvas shoes. From my new long Christmas Eve socks to my disabled serviceman's pension. And it is impossible to believe that the world could have changed at all through its wars and misfortunes, through all the blood and upheavals, if all these storms and leeches have not destroyed one peasant's jersey. From the old man's viewpoint, his clothes and shoes are not particularly old. They date from the moment when a hand known to him had spun, knitted or sewed them for him, as he watched, and now they had grown worn, now when it was time, and is that not simply natural aging! Possibly from the perspective of the millennium, nothing has occurred even during this time ringing with the sound of tanks, ideologies and revolutions. Perhaps the world is only slowly aging and wearing out in the most natural way, changing its clothes, and we see dramas in the microcosm of our day-long life, in order to justify our weariness and our departure, and in order to create a false notion of our own importance. Are not our truths as insignificant for this world as Tunina's jersey and shoes are for him: garments that have replaced old ones, which will be replaced by new ones? Tunina's jersey and shoes were essential to him. Was the pinprick we made in the globe essential to the world?

I stuck the pine branch in a jug on the dresser. Madonna said:

"Hang my rosary on the pine tree and find a candle to put under it."

Tunina was still soaking biscuits in his brandy. Stretching out his hand in which he spun his red cap with its worn tassel, he pointed towards the bed and spoke as old men do, turned in on themselves; to no one directly, but to the days of yesteryear, which we were unable to hear:

"What possessions they had, ah-ha! And what wasn't theirs, my God! Three quarters of the Island, the best, the most fertile land, and the strongest peasants. Everyone used them and got things from them and needed them: you want zinc, you want sulphur, you want fertilizer and seed, they'd measure out a third or a quarter of their maize, grapes, wool, cheese, oil. Now there's no one anywhere near, eh? And the forests! The lime-kilns. No one. Not even for God's birthday, the way you used to come, my good people, in those olden days to the master and acknowledge what was right and honest. To see the sick master lying like Jesus in the manger, unable even to hiccup, so sick and ill!"

"Thank God at least one robber sees the injustice and robbery." It seemed that Madonna had suddenly realized that this was not one of the old-style Christmas Eves. That she was celebrating in poverty, and that there would be no procession of peasants with gifts today. But she closed her eyes and said: "Now, my old Tunina, go home in peace, and let me pray. And don't let those others come into the room, let them leave Cara whatever they bring out there, for this is all nothing but a disturbance, a stench of brandy and riches."

I invited Tunina to move into the kitchen, because Madonna was going to sleep. She was going to pray ... to pray, pray! He got up without a word, his shoes rasping on the worn floor, then from the door, holding his glass full of yellow crumbs as though drinking his own health, he said in a half-whisper.

"Ah, my *parona,* may I see you again next year and Godbewithyounow!" Then he came into the kitchen, bearing his glass in front of him and driving on his rickety body his huge, god-like head, wreathed in a halo of long papery grey hairs. "The poor, sad thing doesn't know what she's saying!"

I sat him down by the window near the stove, poured him some more to drink and said that she was no longer a human being — which was not true, but near enough — and I was just on the point of mentioning her age, but I remembered again that it was stupid to speak of it to him, as he was older than any living thing. I told him he was older than everything in existence and that was how I had always known him.

"I haven't kept track of my age, what can I say, young master, such were the times and the world then, what can you do. I saw you not long ago when you were, forgive me, still a child. And these last years, I see you as a man, there you are. In a word. But it won't be a hundred, I would say, but then, it might be more, no one knows. There's nothing older than me alive, apart from some plants maybe. A pine or an olive tree."

I began to toast Tunina expansively, for I too had been sipping something or other since early morning. His little runny eyes sparkled as though they were still being stung by a piercing wind. His two or three withered eyelashes stuck out, glued together, protecting nothing; they had moved away from his eyes, and fluttered somewhere almost in the middle of his wrinkled lids; the whites were washed by cloudy, stagnant water.

"You've been salting olives, I see," he said, pointing to the earthenware pot on the terrace by the window.

"Well no, Tunina, that's, er, for Madonna, when she needs, you know…."

"Eh?!"

His toothless mouth with its sticky lips did not open in surprise, but his eyes examined the pot in the shade of the wall, and, staring out of the window, he said in an almost tearful voice:

"It's a shame, young master my lad, to use a pot like that for shit, my good people! You can't find a pot like that even at the grandest houses, not any more. Imagine! How well they'd keep in it, how long they'd last! Hey-ho! If only they'd grown well this year. But they didn't. Maggots, maggots."

I toasted him again, smiling, and we drank. Tunina's eyes only watered all the more, as though that thin brandy which had been sparkling in his glass was now seeping out from under his lids and spreading over his eyes. He kept repeating "maggots, maggots" and then said quietly and thoughtfully:

"Well, if I had one like that, you'd have a fine crop. You would. And there'd be plenty. I know what I'm saying."

I went on laughing, what could I do.

"I've got a copper bucket," Tunina would not be put off. "A new bucket is even better for the use of people and gentlefolk."

"That wouldn't do, Tunina, the pot is her … comfort…."

"The sea would clean everything properly. Of course it would do. It would, my master. The sea cleans ulcers. And of course it would clean that … comfort!"

"But it's not mine, I tell you! That pot."

"Everything that's hers is yours, God and everyone recognize that. But I'm not forcing anything, Heaven forbid! I'm just saying how it is. She's still got things!"

"What shall I say. She hasn't really. That pot there. Some crockery…."

"And the house … of course…."

"Only as long as she's alive. So they don't have to pack her off somewhere. Then it's all over."

"Eh? And what about your charity, your nursing when she was sick over all these years, I suppose God will repay that, is that right?"

"If He's got any small change," I replied, shrugging my

shoulders, and turned on the radio. "That's what killed her, my Tunina. Confiscation."

"Ah yes! It will too, I know. But, then, say all of it was somehow suddenly given back to her, the joy'd kill her. You can't go back no more either. What is - is. It's best the way it is. If someone took the land from my family, there'd certainly be maggots and fierce fire over that as well. Changing is worst. No, it's best the way it is. Each thing becomes good when the people it shook up die out and when you forget the beginning. And the poor old padrona doesn't want to die ... that's all there is to it."

Never, not even from the spiritual fathers, had I heard so much cynical experience condensed into a few brandied sentences. Tunina sipped his drink as he spoke, and I started seeing little black devils flying out of my glass, like the ones that poke out of St. Nicholas the Traveller's hood, with hard little red horns and hairy behinds. One was beating his breast, some little Zulukafer, a little mythological demon with goat's hoofs, some knobbly little ram from who knows where, from Asia Minor, or, if you like, a little Illyrian, pardon the expression, was curling his tail, like a New Year sucking pig and beating his little hoof on his shaggy breast "I am," he said, "an Internationalist." "What is he?" I wondered, shoving my nose into my aromatic glass. What could he be, my good people? An Internationalist! Well, and what shall I say now to the big long-nosed haughty French devil, shouting out of the radio: *"Oui, nous aussi, nous sommes les Internationalistes!"* When I don't find that half so funny? I can only tell him I don't believe it. But I don't find it funny. But the rest is suddenly funny, however, all those little devils, just because I do believe them, honestly, just because it's easy to believe them. Who wouldn't want to stand beside the big long nosed one! If only he's being serious. If only all these revolutions aren't a fancy-dress ball of collective egoism. Oh, what an ugly poison you get when you mix Tunina with brandy, a war cripple with Christmas Eve, a dream about the capital with island emptiness and long term celibacy! Were I the mythical Aeneas, my goddess mother would now protect me with a little cloud, and my reckless wanderings would remain invisible to the evil guards and patrols on this slippery shore. But I'm nobody's mythological pet or pin-up cared for by well and ill-disposed gods alike, but a ridiculous vagabond who must decide everything for himself, since his ancestor God, because he was far too busy or because he was a bad organizer, or because there was only one of Him, or in order to be able to amble untroubled through the hunting-grounds and meadows of the cirrostratus, I don't know why, but in any case He lumbered me with free-will and left me to toss about according to the impulses of the self-managing convolutions of my brain as though on the waves of the Mediterranean towards Ithaca. That was the god I had inherited, and how stupid it would be to have invented Him myself! And so, whatever the cause, this ridiculous vagabond decides everything for himself, and does everything against his own wishes, because he thinks in a way he would not want to and because wishes and will don't go together; will follows thought and thought flies in out of the darkness, out of a glass, out of a radio, out of the naive-experienced suggestions of any old poisonous centenarian, or simply out of the divine anus of St. Ethics, as the Inevitable and Whatelsecanyoudo.

The radio was almost blaring by now, and Tunina was probably saying the same thing again, or was it for the first time: "Everything becomes good when those it shook up die out and when you forget the beginning." But that may all have been, it had all whirled through my head in a flash, the length of one single last sentence of Tunina's for that must be why the radio was blaring like this, I had turned the volume control too far to begin with, Madonna would surely be yelping with horror by now if it went on any longer. I quickly hushed the noise box, and in the swaying air, which was condensing following the pain in my eardrums, I heard an angelic greeting and a tiny perverse bell from the throat of a little maiden who was already standing in the kitchen doorway. She said in a descant, like Gilda from the sack, in an almost inaudible voice, but with hissing Old Slavonic sibilants, that she had brought the laundry wassshed and ironed for Sssignora Madonna and me and Madam, and that the nunsss sssent many greetings and where should she put the wassshing. She could feel that Tunina and I were glowing white-hot under the burners of the brandy gas, and she lowered her eyes, fluttering her lids at the same time as though she were looking for protective spectacles and she rocked those clean nappiesss of hers left and right in her arms, not knowing what to do with them in her confusion. I said dear God, what dear little funny shoes she had, black, with buttons, like St. Gulliver, who had pumps with buckles, like St Andrew's maidens, lacquered actually, but even nicer, but, never mind, it doesn't matter, he had white knee-socks like hers as well under his soutane, if she had knees at all that is, let's see, let's have a look, because he didn't wear the kind of concoction the maidens from our convent did, and he was mad about traveling, so she probably wouldn't stay forever with the poor Claressss either! I'm only asking, why are you so shy, my child, I was only joking ... Tunina, admit that God knew what he was doing!

"Things shouldn't be changed," he replied. Perhaps he had not said that earlier when he was talking about confiscation or whatever it was. Perhaps he said all this for the first time only now about the little maiden, but it had all got somehow jumbled up in the brandy. He wasn't even looking at the girl, although it would have been worth his while, but talking to the ground under him. "It's best the way it is. If you suddenly told her: here is the whole wide world, it's yours ... the joy would kill her. Everything becomes good when you forget the beginning...."

"Actually, we're Benedictines, sir. We're not Claresss."

"Admit it," I shouted, "God knew what He was doing! Just look at her! A goldfinch! Tweet-tweet!"

"Probably. Probably He knew," and then he added bitterly and irreverently, "only she didn't know."

"It's no good changing things, eh?" I shouted as though I had caught him lying. "Not for those who are well off, my old Zeus!"

"Not for her either. We know one, she left the convent. Modest and colorless, she was. Now she paints herself red all round Rijeka and she's a great whore!"

There! There, there! He's chased away our little virgin with those coarse words!

"Let's drink, then, Tunina!"

St. Andrew rang as though he were summoning his wandering lamb urgently back to the safe, squeaky shadow of the convent's quiet corridors, and it was unutterably comic that, close as he was, a mere dozen steps away so to speak, he should use such a thunderous means of summoning people and sounding the alarm. We could even hear the ministrant's tiny bell from St. Andrew's Church, or the bell at the entrance to the convent which calls the nuns when people come begging them for slops for their pigs (one should say "swine fodder"), or when they are brought wool to knit jerseys, or when people just want to visit them, with a little hard currency donation, or for any reason.

And what I wanted to say, for some reason, what I mean is we can hear all of that, all their little ringings and tinklings, devout and secular, while he, my respected holy neighbor, let out a great clanging from the bell tower, as though he were a volunteer fireman, and all for no reason, say for the sake of our tiny little chassste goldfinch, who doesn't herself know whether she has any knees under her habit, my good people! Who doesn't know where anything is. And so on, not to be filthy. What a job for saints, eh! But imagine, my Tunina, what this saint is driving at!

"Tunina, what's on your mind?"

"I'm saying, I keep telling you over and over again, the mistress is calling you, but you do nothing. I'm wondering what's got into you, she's been ringing and ringing!"

I rushed into the bedroom, as though to an assembly point, stopped at the door, bowed and stretched out my arms:

"All my humble powers at your esteemed service, my *contesssa!"* It was stupid, you'll agree, and actually at the very same moment … maybe I'd had a bit to drink and … er … muddled things up … I was a little ashamed of my histrionics and so I quickly stepped towards the bed, speaking prosaically and profanely. "Of course, dear Madonna, I can't hear you in the garden, while I'm in the garden for instance. We ought to have a little bell you could just lightly ring, ding-ding, if I'm in the garden, or any other distant lands, like St. Andrew for instance … his bells deafen me, and then where does that get us? I don't hear you and I don't know and I can't hear you. Please. Here I am. Proceed. An old friend of mine made up a little song, which goes, how does it go:

In the chill you bring warmth for me, cool in the heat,
Fair clothing for my body, for my bitterness sweets,

You sate all my hunger, you quench all my thirst,
You soothe all my sorrow, when my heart it would burst."

As I say, I felt somewhat abashed even during that stupid declamation. That's my personal freedom and weakness, and altogether....

Madonna watches me, watches, watches. I see now. That would really be too much, if she too, if she is mocking me. Or starts to with time.... She's watching me with special understanding, but, mercifully, quite benignly. Mercifully quite reasonably and quite knowingly she says:

"You quench my thirst ... and *i ghe da bever, dunque.* And ... and all the rest of it, *ben,* good, that's all Christian and as God commands. *Ma dell'altra parte insomma,* nothing is known. I mean, no one knows who does the quenching, *caro mio,* no one knows whose thirst is quenched, and all the other things."

"Quenching? What do you mean no one knows? That is, it's the poet who is quenched, who is nourished! Of course we know that!"

"Quenches, I know. But what do you call *questi due?"*

"Due? Two? Which two? Who do you mean?"

"El tuo friend. *El suo* benefactor."

"Benefactor? I know no benefactor. No benefactor do I know."

"A, ecco! A quel altro?"

"That's that Hannibal, the poet! Not Hasdrubal, but Hannibal. Not Cannibal...."

"I know, I know, but I'm asking what his surname is?"

"Oh, I see. That's Mr. Lucić. Our countryman. Hannibal Lucić."

Madonna was more or less content. She took a respectable

little length of time to think privately about the whole affair and how it was that poetry had found its way here to us. But there was no longer anywhere she could escape or withdraw to. She had become resigned in this discussion, and she was even thoughtful enough not to bother me any more about the benefactor. And of course, if I may say so, I could not possibly know all those things! It was quite refreshing when she concluded our aesthetic duel with a quiet sigh:

"Ah well, God help him in his old age! *Bon poeta. Vero poeta.*"

It doesn't matter what had made her conclude that Hannibal was old, now it's more important to see what she wanted and why she needed me. That must always be the priority. I tried to challenge myself in a way, to see whether I could somehow guess her wish myself. Examining myself and the room. It isn't easy, to be honest. It isn't easy to guess. It isn't easy to examine oneself. Then there's that percentage of alcohol in my head. And after all, why should I exert myself. I ask: what do you want? She tries to think but she doesn't know. No, she just doesn't know. She can't even remember calling me, as I say she did. And I of course haven't a clue. Tunina said so, damn him. I can't say she called me. But again, I must say so if Tunina is so sure. She must have forgotten. But she didn't forget to launch in an exalted tone into a dazzling, old-aged oration about what a noble and godly deed it is, my son, that at least once a year I should treat her, helpless and piteous as she is, according to etiquette and her nobility and behave with her as is fitting and as once others, greater than me, and saintly persons, were all obliged and duty-bound to do. I accepted the praise and self-praise by clicking my heels together and during that lost time I tried to think of how and what our Madonna could softly tinkle ding-ding, as we had said. With my thick head I quickly concluded there was nothing she could do it with. Not her hand, nor her foot, least of all her head. Then I thought some more and finally concluded that after all there was nothing she could do it with. Unless the bell was electric, and we put a push-button on her chest. She would be able to do that, Heaven forbid, without any effort and set the whole house clanging as though with a thousand telephones, day and night, and it would seem that the main switchboard of Interpol was right here. And she is saying that health and property don't make a title, but blood in the veins and a family tree and martyred ancestors, and I, if only I'm not mocking her, am doing my humble duty, offering her what is hers by God's will, and that if I were not depraved like everyone else today, I would behave like this always and forever more, for it is balm and salve for the spirit to her. And here — imagine — she bursts into tears.

"I'm not mocking you, *Contessa,* honestly I'm not!" I exclaimed, placing my hand on my sword hilt and clinking my spurs. I almost started weeping myself, for here, beneath the family tree, the last little leaf that had dropped from it was withering away!

And while she dragged from the folds of her nightdress an endlessly long ribbon of yellowish gauze, I withdrew discreetly so that she could pour out her chronic tears in solitude into such a stage prop as this with no coat of arms embroidered in gold and no perfume, particularly no perfume, like that utterly low, dirty, *misera plebs contribuens.* But the horrendous creaking of the boards in the bare floor of our improvised kitchen betrayed my discreet flight and Madonna called out in a still tearful voice:

"Send him my greetings, *figlio mio,* send him my greetings!"

"Who, Madonna?" I asked vaguely, stopping in the middle of the kitchen.

"Your old friend. Send him my greetings."

I knew she didn't mean Tunina, because even I couldn't see him here any more and I had almost forgotten all about him.

"Did you hear me?"

"Quel poeta?" I asked, somewhat frivolously, without stirring from the spot, *"El signor* Lucić?"

"God help him in his old age. Send him my greetings."

Instead of sitting down and penning that missive straight away, I started to look around for Tunina. He was on the terrace, examining the pot, I went out into the air. The morning was still cool, and I could see that the keen north breeze had cleared Tunina's head as well. Thin rivulets glistened in the sun in the furrows round his mouth, like the apostle Peter when he heard the cock crow, but that was presumably because of the brandy and the sharp air.

"So be it," he said, when he saw me, "so goodbye then!" and he went straight to the door, along the passage and through the garden. I wanted to tell him as he left to call again as soon as he heard that Madonna had ceased to function, and I'd give him that wretched urn to take away. But I must have felt that both he and the urn were more fragile than Madonna. So I just muttered goodbye and closed the courtyard door behind him, maybe forever.

CHAPTER 6

I stood by the window of Madonna's room, watching the sky flicker and fade. Hermione, unannounced, was sauntering round the garden feeding and watering our one-and-only little cockerel, which I had forgotten all about since this morning when I adopted him. With his clipped wings, light and transparent, the little cock was hopping about in front of Hermione, keeping always the same distance away from her, and Hermione had screwed up her face and forehead, twitching her whiskers and eyebrows like one of Genghis-Khan's bloodthirsty Tatars, not with the intention of wringing its neck, but from an intense desire to win its affection. Her teeth gleamed white and in an incomprehensible whisper which I could not even hear through the window, she was sending Madonna through me various evil wishes for a long life. Knowing that I had to hide her presence from Madonna, she was making a bit of fun of me as well with crude and unambiguous gestures, calming down and moving away only when our wild little cock, shaking his comb like an Italian *bersagliere,* began to march, Roman style, towards a small pile of potato peelings.

Madonna had just finished her afternoon cocoa. I must confess that I had enriched her menu somewhat with food and drinks that in my layman's view wouldn't at least stimulate stools, so that nothing untoward would occur before its time. She was still trying to reach the bottom of her cup with her tongue, thinking that the non-existent sugar must have sunk down there, and when I took her well-licked cup away from her, she looked at me lovingly and said too loudly:

"She does everything the way she wants, but you are like my son."

Then she motioned to me with the fish-hook of her finger to bend down and said into my ear: "Did she hear, eh? Well, let her hear!"

"No," I said with relish, "she's in Zagreb."

"In the grave? Well I never! No one told me that." I didn't feel like submitting to her free associations, which she sometimes entertained herself with, playing on my naive nerves. I barely mumbled again, through my teeth "Zagreb," but she seemed to register it; in any case she went on quite calmly: "I thought she had died as well. Thank goodness you ... you dispatched her before she died. So many have died already, my whole cellar stinks of the dead, so that I can't stand the taste of my *prosciutto*. But that doesn't bother me, *de resto,* because I've got a tooth or two missing...." She thought for a moment, then pushed her crooked index finger between her sticky lips and began searching over her bare gums. "You've decorated my room with rosemary and I didn't even notice."

"That's pine, Madonna," I said loudly, in an effort to drown Hermione's clattering dishes in the passage. "Today is Christmas Eve."

"Oh! *Che sorpressa!* Then we're fasting today, are we? And there I am, thinking about *prosciutto!*... Have we fasted?"

"Oh yes," I said, "we certainly have! The house smells of dried cod, because of the fast. If we did even have cod, that is, because a fast is a fast, not just a meatless day, isn't that right! *Insomma,* we fasted, I know that for sure."

"Because if I didn't...."

"No, you haven't sinned, of course not! Absolutely not!"

"E, neanche per idea, you know!"

"Heaven forbid! I tell you we've been starving ourselves since morning, since last night ... since God knows when ... " and as I walked towards the kitchen, I tried again to stumble and tread on that creaking board. I hurried into the passage and hissed at Hermione: "What the hell are you doing crashing and banging about like this?"

She was just pouring a pitcher of water into our bucket and she answered in the same hissing whisper:

"I'm bringing you, bringinging you water! The old girl hasn't got ears like a babat. I'm bringing you water, Water's not cottonwool, what can I do, you hear it, you're bound to. I hear all kinds of things myself, and...."

"... so you keep quiet, poor thing!" I tried to push past her towards the door to the garden, to chop a bit more wood.

"Of course, that too! But I'm never lost, neverlost for an an answer. What needssay needssaying I say!"

In the bluish Christmas twilight that smelled of soot, the cotton-white roses had petrified like curiously large stars, still glowing, but turned to ash. There was also a smell of the thin acrid smoke of holm oak and scorched oil in the air. The thin pure membrane of the sky suddenly faded, but it was still brighter than anything under it, walls or earth. Only the white roses were not exinguished, but phosphoresced from the half-dark corners of the garden as though they did not get their light from the sky, but from their own calyces, and, illuminated like this from within, they were hanging in the bluish air like inflated gas balloons.

A few blows with an axe in God's good air would undoubtedly clear my head and drive away the muzziness from this morning's brandy better than standing apathetically by the window. Only it seemed inappropriate to think about Madonna with an axe in my hand. There was a damnable evil foreboding in that, or at least if not a foreboding, then a symbolism that was quite out of place, reminding one of that sinister Fyodor Mikhailovich, or if not even that, then surely that prehistoric tool, my blows and my grunts would in some way preordain, direct or at least simplify my limping, idle thoughts. I kept thinking that I must somehow pull our relationship together, if only for a short time. I kept thinking that it was somehow a relationship after all. I'm incapable of living beside so much as a plant as though it were something dead. Madonna had been tormenting me for three whole days, and now our relationship had changed. Yes, our relationship! Actually, it is Madonna who changes her moods and I have all too little influence over that. If one of the two of us is a dead thing or a passive plant, then it's me and not her. That is, I would be, if I didn't react, if I lived beside her as though I lived alone. That's why this, whatever it is between us, is a relationship! Because I didn't feel put out only because she was ill-treating me, but also because there was a ball of semi-organized matter living beside me which hated me inexplicably, as in science fiction, which wanted to humiliate me, which pulsed (even if it sounds silly to say so) with some full-blooded feelings towards me, even if they were negative. However unclear it is, one must presume it was Cara's departure that had driven her into such a state of irritation. And today here she is, rejecting Cara, and calling me, adopting me. Maybe it is just revenge and a sign that she is offended. But what will happen if I now become indispensable to her, as Cara was before? I could perhaps make things a little easier for Cara that way, because Madonna would stop shouting that I'm a layabout and a squanderer and wouldn't be insulted by my coming into the room as she has been up to now. But what if she actually came to hate Cara? If she chased her out as she has Hermione now? Dear God, there was no need to wave an axe around to know how inexpressibly likely it all was, after all! What I call a relationship is perhaps only an axe blow, the uninterrupted alternation of two simple meager possibilities: a tormented, weary life with Madonna's feeble support, and that same life without her support. But still, it is hard to say what that support depends on. And harder still to call it "support." I would be a bit happier if I could say of Madonna that she is one thing or another. She isn't defined, nor is she so exceptional that I could adapt myself to her as to some misfortune of fate. There's no goodness in her, I know, but what sort of deformed goodness could flow from a withered soul and an irresponsible consciousness? Maybe that spiritual darkness dulls her malice, but it would also deform any goodness. My difficulties with her stem from the chance fluctuations of atmospheric pressure, or from the unpredictable rising and falling of her disrupted subconscious, and the only law governing our relations lies in me. I the barometer. The weather-vane. Rusted in a different way. The graph of her moods. And for her I am good; and I am the wicked interpreter of her malice. I'm not neutral. I was never indifferent; not as a child, nor ten years ago when I decided to stay here with her. I never loved her, not even in those most bestial wet-dreams when reptiles, or wax models, or warm quagmires copulate. Let alone in daylight. But still — I'm not indifferent. One would probably say: compassion. But the petit-bourgeois have succeeded in placing that on some ethical scale of values too, so it is more a tool for the protection of animals than a human emotion. So, maybe compassion. Perhaps something like that. Something devoid of all qualities, like a retreat of discipline, false human pride that masks flight in conscious withdrawal. Something like a sense of tidiness, like cats burying their excrement. On the surface of the earth, beside every human corpse, there must be someone to watch over it and scatter it with dust. So that its soul should not roam, so that scavengers should not snatch it away from the gods. In short — so that it shouldn't stink. But when it is the soul of a living creature that is wandering, one can only wait, with a handful of dust, and while the dust slips through one's fingers during the waiting something is born in the heart. Love? Hate? Feelings? Probably nothing so straightforward. Unless a grave-digger just happens to be appointed to a corpse by chance, simply as a nameless scatterer of dust, a coverer with earth. But even if it's only that, even then the icy worm of a relationship, or something like it, can sometimes settle on the grave-digger's spade, and one simply never thinks about it. With or without it, one's responsibilities are the same. Only in that slimy worm, if he's lucky, befuddled and has time on his hands, a man may sometimes come across hard lumps and knots like those in a branch of old olive wood under a blunt axe. And then he stops, puffs and throws down his tool.

Hermione walked past me twice carrying water, and then did not reappear. I found her preparing supper, and told her she should not trouble herself today, but she did not reply. What will happen if Madonna remembers the fast again during the meal? I thought I should take Hermione in to Madonna again as soon as possible to see whether she had forgotten, and to know how it would be with Cara when she came back. Thankfully, Hermione did not have to be asked twice. When she had put the supper on to cook, she went into Madonna's room herself, sat down just by the door and took up her knitting, as though she were preparing to spend the night here.

"Oh!" I remembered, and asked Hermione quietly, "are you still thinking of that?"

She did not look up from her knitting, only clicked her needles a little faster, nervously and jerkily, firmly pressed her eyes, lids and eyebrows together all at the same time repeatedly, twisting her lips into a scornful grimace. I asked her if she was thinking of staying long because then I could slip into town for a bit. I had not stretched my legs for four days. She calmed down not knowing what to answer, and then went on with her knitting quietly and steadily as though she had never been nervous fro fromher mother swomb. Then she raised her eyes slowly and meaningfully towards Madonna's bed.

Madonna was watching her in the half-light, as an octopus does: you cannot make anything out, just sense two eyes, you feel a stare, then you gradually begin to distinguish on the rock those two eyes looking at you, like two little deep black pools and all you can see are those two eyes on the rock, not the limbs, everything has merged in camouflage colors with the rock and the seaweed.

It seemed at first that something was rasping somewhere, and then Madonna's voice could be made out:

"Light the candle under the tree. Light it. The child will soon be born."

"Oh, not yet, Madonna," I said thunderously. My voice reverberated like a clap of thunder in that silence, and I was probably only speaking a little breathlessly from wielding the axe. "It's only seven now. Midnight's a long way off."

"You hear me?" asked Madonna, as though my sonorosness had not even come near her. Terror gripped Hermione. She glanced at me in alarm, then looked back to the bed as though she could see a terrible chasm in that space, that my voice could not reach over. It did not occur to her that perhaps Madonna did not want to hear it, because she wanted her little will to be carried out, she wanted to show the unknown visitor who was the one and only master of the house, and at the same time to make out by the light of the candle the face of the visitor who was clicking knitting needles and guarding her door. Madonna was too "thrifty and house-proud" to use up a candle simply for the sake of a custom.

"I hear you," I said quickly, "I'm just looking for a candle."

But there was not a single wax candle in the house. There was a glass on a shelf in the hall with a wick that had been floating on green oil and dirty water, since God knows when. I put it onto the cupboard under the pine and lit a match. Hermione tried to stand up, realizing that Madonna would recognize her in the light and drive her out, but I hastily put my hand on her prickly knitting and stopped her. She sat down again, if you could call it that, she did not settle on the chair but stayed rigidly upright and stiff as though she were squatting and there was no chair there at all. But that could also mean that I had offended her with my mocking question, or not so much the question as the tone of my voice. Because the question was apt enough. She was here just because she was thinking of that. But it was silly to go on doubting it. She was not thinking of that, because she did not doubt her prediction. She was simply waiting for what had to take place on Christmas Eve, since it had not happened before. And it was pitiful and stupid of me to have thought of it by chance, instead of taking it for granted from the break of day. And she had come to be here and help me, to call the priest and all the rest, to wash, to dress … it was not curiosity that had brought her, as someone might have imagined. So that meant that I had still been wondering why she had come without fear or circumspection and why she had settled in and set up camp and brought her knitting. I mean if I had found that strange and peculiar, and I had wondered, and I had happened to remember, and I had been rude, and I had said what I said and asked what one should not ask and all those crude things from one fairly educated.... Fine, splendid, quite right and proper! That is what her rigid position on the chair meant, that was what her knitting said, behaving as though it were the only thing here worthy of Hermione's attention. The light under the pine flickered, sputtered and put out a tall tongue of pinkish flame, so that I had to move it away from the pine needles.

Madonna went on looking at Hermione and now two straight thin little flames from the light really were glowing like cats' eyes in her pupils. Instead of bristling and bellowing at the unwanted visitor, she looked her over with growing warmth, in a kind of trance, and started to say, word by word, in the tone of a lullaby:

"St Thomas in a golden ... in a golden bower ... Thomas in a gold ... "

And something immediately shifted in the air, everything became different, more homely, more intimate, more Christmassy, not only because of the cheerful flame of the little candle under the pine, but also because of the long-forgotten carol of our grandmothers which Madonna had dug out of some other Christmas nights on the Island in such a soft voice.

Hermione caught her breath jerkily, so that little teardrops scattered around:

"I'm Thomas ... she means, saintthomas knitting, oh my, knitting hose!"

I wanted to help Madonna remember the carol, but she

had acquired a heavenly smile that was lighting up her whole pillow, and she went on by herself:

"... in a bower sat,
weaving little nets,
ensnaring evil witches."

Hermione recovered from her laughter and surprise, and joined in:

"The witches said to him ..."

Then the three of us began to chant, in a totally muddled choral recitative, tuneless and unharmonious, but throbbing with the onrush of inner tenderness:

"St. Thomas let us go,
To our homes for Christmas!"
"When you will have counted
The fishes in the sea,
The cherries on the trees,
All the varied feathers
Of the birds in the air,
Then I shall let you go,
I'll let you all go free."

Although we all joined in, Madonna was actually singing the part of St. Thomas in a bass voice. This should of course have been Hermione's role, but she and I were in a way primarily interpreting the witches praying, witches weeping, witches in captivity. That's how forgotten words come, like a cough, a fit of crying, laughter from the belly, or they well up like a prayer and then your mouth and heart are full of them, and they are spoken tremulously, in a babbling flow, and when they dry up, when they come to an end all too soon, those words that are always niggardly, always short, the wondrous words of magic formulae of respite and relaxation, then uncontrollable laughter bursts out with the surprise and delight of the sudden discovery of sweet magic and understanding and health. Madonna was panting, Hermione laughing and laughing, and I thought almost joyfully that tonight Death was once again far from this house, and that our Pythia, beguiled by the vapors of prejudice, would see the birth of the child, and she would not see the death of the worshippers from close to, not tonight, and not before who knows how many Christmasses to come, for Madonna was now pushing her leathery tongue between her gums and again searching through her dried-up memory: *"St. Thomas sat in a golden bower . . . weaving little nets . . . ensnaring evil witches . . ."*

Hermione went on hurriedly knitting her pointless stockings. The light sputtered and the already drunken little flame swayed. Suddenly I got up from Cara's bed and told Hermione perhaps only with my eyes that I was just going to slip into town, I don't know whether she received the message, I don't know whether I said anything. I almost ran out of the house, dragging my cape (my old mac, that is) in one hand behind me like a dog, and it swept the pavement as it is otherwise swept in tragedies when a man is left alone following his tragic insights or ordinary realizations, although there were no insights or realizations of any kind for me, just a desire for solitude, and not for some kind of special romantic solitude, but escape from that loneliness there, for escape. I was not going to play cards, or to the cemetery, I was not looking for anyone, I did not head off anywhere. There was air and biting clarity and tiny stars.

Bright bare electric wires stretched across the blue of the night. In the windows there was light behind the shutters, no one in the streets, dry, resonant Christmas concrete, washed stone flags under my footsteps. I did not particularly hurry down the steps that twist down to the shore and stink of ammonia, like Madonna's bedside table. But nevertheless I came to the sea for confession.

Dear Mr. Sea!

I've had enough of you, it said, of you and your shitting from the heights!

Honest to God, the sea's right! A person in my position would pine away, if it were not for him ... God, and the sea. He wouldn't have anyone to talk to.

Oh, that's only a topsy-turvy sepulchral rite, my good sea, that ... from the heights! *"And the nearer we are to Heaven, the further from Heaven we are."* And that, in the urn, that wasn't me, remember, let's be perfectly clear!

Beneath the town on the leeward side, on rotten beams sleep the boats turned with their undersides towards the sky and the sea doesn't reach them. They've turned their registration numbers like rolled eyes to the strand, and all those "Sonyas" and "Katys" and "Adas" are lying like dead bream on the bottom of this frozen night with no shooting stars and no holy signposts. Naked, empty.

Dismemberment.

You take away a boat's oars, sail, tiller, everything; sponges, ropes, buckets, even the anchor. Dismemberment. That's demotion, demobilization, disarmament. Dismemberment. Amen.

That's when they turn it onto the side where the sun doesn't warm it. That's when they start riding its keel. When the boat, which is made to travel, becomes a tent under which someone crawls to foul the sand. So how could the sea want it! It's right, the sea's right! And we, Mr. Sea, are neither a forlorn "Katy" nor a sad "Ada". But an upturned urn, temporarily disarmed. And we count the fishes in the sea.

We count our defeats, we who have turned our sailing hulls over.

If that idiot Hermione hadn't asked where I'd been, Madonna wouldn't even have noticed that I wasn't there. Or she would have thought I was in the garden or the kitchen or doing something somewhere nearby. Where had I been all that time? Oh fool of God … I was, I don't know, by the sea, down there below the walls. I wasn't there all that long … I was so long … all right, I was at Tariba's, *better here than there* and, to be honest, I got a bit stoned. But first and last I was by the sea, well, we got talking, and then I slipped in for a glass, that's all, I didn't count, what's it matter, a glass here, a glass there, only I don't know how long I was here, how long there, but I was by the sea twice. That's for sure. It was closing time at Tariba's and that was that, it wasn't *in this season of the year* unlimited! But he … but he … you don't go to him for midnight mass, but you know … so, there are regulations, police, today like any other day, time gentlemen please! So I withdrew myself unto the sea and a great multitude went forth … went forth in all directions, but I went to the sea. However. I went back there to say another word or two about our situation … but forget it … I didn't see him either to begin with, so that by the skin of my teeth … in the dark….

"Where was I? I was here, of course! What do you mean, where?" I say to that stupid Hermione, winking with my left eye, then my right, but what's the use!

"I don't care, forgod'ssake, what do I care," she mumbles,

pointing to Madonna, "but she called you, signora Madonna shecalledyou. You weren't here, I gave gaveher her her dinner, she asked for aspi aspiririn. I gave her some, I found it. Aspirin. But she called you, and called you, and how was I to know where the hell . . . "

"Aspirin?!" I say, staring at her. "Aspirin?"

"She had a pain, hada had apain!"

"Well done, Hermione, well done, well done," I whisper and hiss: "let me shake your hand!"

"Why?. . . It's Christmas . . . we already . . ."

Madonna was angry that I wasn't taking any notice of her but amusing myself with St. Thomas, and she growled from the corner had I at last sorted something out and what good was it if I'd been in the forest, and didn't know how to tell them what was what. I was at the Town Hall, I said, naturally, where else! And I told them all what was what, of course, and I could tell her, I really felt somehow, that this time something would come of it. They promised, just the way I'm talking to you now. They were afraid I'd start shouting the place down, especially the ones in the central committee, they just stood and stared like this, and then they tried to calm me down and begged me and promised. So that . . . it bodes well, bodes well! I filed a petition . . . which adds some hope to my optimism. That is . . . I'll take it to the Top!

"To the King!" roared Madonna, *"come si chiama quel mascalzon de Turco?"*

"Ssssh!" interrupted Hermione, "there's no Kara any Karageorge any more. Now there's a repuplic!"

"Of course there's a king, you fool! There must be a king!"

"No, signora Madonna, now there's an execra excru executivecommittee, believe me! A repuplic. Everyone does what he wants!"

"God in Heaven!" exclaimed Madonna, delighted at the splendid prospect. "No more beating about the bush! He'll give the committees what's coming to them! *Sursum corda!*"

"Coda, coda, of course" said Hermione calmly, "weighted scales. Specu-lation and rising prices and turnablindeye and dongiveadamn!"

It's not a question of not giving a damn I explained to Hermione, but Madonna will get what's hers, because justice will prevail in this transitional period and so on, and you, my dear, had better have an aspirin for EVACUATION yourself, and I'll congratulate you once again and then you'll be able to meddle in judicial affairs and in progressive politics and the intricacies of property law relations.

I'm not going to start betting with you ... I'm only saying: Madonna will get what's coming to her.... That's what I said, and it was clear that I was having great difficulty coping with the ethyl vapors in my head. She was a bit startled, she realized that she had tossed a purgative and not a sedative down Madonna's throat, and she realized perhaps what a delight it would be for me if Madonna started to call for the urn before the appointed time. She knew what a crime that was, and that all her favors and assistance could not outweigh this one immeasurable mishap she had arranged for me. I could already see in her eyes the self-abnegating decision to tackle Madonna's labors on her own, if they came on, and so redeem her mistake before Cara and myself, but behind that apparent masochism peered the blind, still unshaken belief that all worshippers withdrew before the hour of Christ's birth, according to the laws of the heavens, and that she would redeem herself tonight by washing the corpse even before the bell for midnight mass. I, on the other hand, was sustained by the great hope that Madonna's stable machinery — because all the subsidiary organs and all the secondary functions had ceased — would successfully withstand this insignificant Aesculapian attack, and that the remaining two or three organs, in all the simplicity characteristic of lesser breeds, would stick to their persistent time scales naturally and constantly, like polyps, jellyfish, like worms, like geysers and volcanoes, and as the Moon in the sky keeps to its changes, and as in starry space … what goes on there God only knows, but I can believe and I know that purgatives do not attack the heart or lungs, and luckily I have watered any other surviving organs copiously over the last few days with my layman's cocoa, and with God's help may no ill befall!

Madonna wanted to hear more details of how things stood at the Town Hall with her estate, she demanded persistently that I should declaim to her all that I had flung in the face of those committees of theirs and, since I had embarked on that exploit, I started describing the people I had seen at Tariba's, and as though I were holding a glass of tart red wine in my hand, I went up to her bed as though it were a bar, raised my little finger in the air and said:

"This comrade here has all three laws of property relations on his side with the amendments and annotations and regulations, here, see, and all the rest, and so on, under paragraph such and such, in this and that section, I listed it all, I knew all the dates of the relevant submissions when an item was filed, I listed it all, clearly, and then I said the following. They gawped at me, like blockheads. I did not wish to humble myself, I said, I had not come, I was not begging for all those le-ga-lly guaranteed rights for my protegée, those which flow and follow! Now, however, the afore-mentioned — because, my Madonna, you can't talk to them like ordinary people! — the aforementioned is making a claim under this heading…."

"I would have said to them, I would: Signora Contessa Markantoni! And not that *sopraddetta* . . . aforementioned . . ."

"That's no good. They know who they're dealing with. With their adversary!"

"I wouldn't be ashamed, *invece,* let them hear!"

"But I said that, I said that before, at the beginning, I said: the Case of Contessa Madonna Markantoni, her application for the return to perpetual possession and all the other things that follow, and then I listed in my deposition, before living witnesses, the Land Registrar, etc., etc. Kalifront, Dundo, Pidoka . . ."

"Per Dio!" she shrieked, "you probably forgot *el mio Kastel!"*

"Ma che forgot! What are you thinking of! And Kanat! The Kopun vineyards! You think my mind . . . my mind's a sieve! Forgot indeed! And Kampor!"

"Why, is Kampor ours as well? *Per Dio,* how much there is!" she asked in a desire to take on still more. "And that wood was ours, and we had lime-kilns . . . And there's probably a lot I've forgotten. . . ."

"Everything," I said, triumphantly, "everything, we won't make them a gift of anything!"

"Bello mio!"

"Nothing!"

"Everything?"

"Everything!"

"Bello mio. And how did it *insomma, andato a finir?* What did the plunderers say?"

"They said they didn't know the exact date, that I should come again, in the near . . . it was closing time, regulations, police, time gentlemen please, but Tariba himself, who replaced ex-King Farouk, took the matter into his own hands, and I believe. . . ."

I did not even hear the knocking. Hermione led into the room my one and only associates here, with the destiny of our population in their pockets. Madame had a black fox round her neck, and the fox smelled as though there was going to be a fall of mothball snow at any minute. They had brought in a sad little compassionate smile on their faces, and after I had exclaimed enthusiastically, and after I had expressed my amazement why look who's here, look who's here, and while I was still clicking my tongue, they, partly in unison and partly each separately, so that I did not know which of them to look politely in the eye, they hastily explained, rubbing their dry night hands, that they had just popped in, as they were on their way, to church, they had just popped in to see, they were actually going to midnight mass, more because of the custom, not any kind of clericalism ... just to see how I was coping, if I was alive, if I needed any help, to wish us a Happy Christmas before anyone else, but they would not stay, because it must be a nuisance for Signora Madonna. And you could see on their faces how scented they found the air here.

"Signora Madonna," said Madame, in an appropriate voice, but almost cooing, as though talking to a child, "well, how are we, how are we, my poor Signora, are we better, a little better, of course, you're better. It will soon pass, you'll see, just a little patience," then she turned to us, the living, to Hermione, her husband and me, and, as though the outcome of Madonna's illness were fateful for the nation, she showed us an anxious, suffering, made-up and unmade-up lower lip which meant ah, I don't like the look of it, I don't like it at all, and she whispered conspiratorially: "She looks bad!" and involved herself with Hermione in death-bed diagnoses.

"This is the comrade from the Land Registry," I introduced

my guest to Madonna distantly. "He will sketch all that they have taken from you. Sketch. Sketch."

"My respects, madam. In the Property Files," he said, bowing his head with great tact and delicacy, because my words sounded ironic to him and he did not know how much Madonna understood.

But Madonna did not answer, she was accustomed to having people paying their respects to her, even in property files, and having them greet her and not returning the greeting, and she would probably have driven them out of the house immediately, if I had not introduced them properly; and when it penetrated her consciousness that these were people in authority, she pressed an imaginary handkerchief to her eyes, as though hiding her burning tears discreetly and with dignity, and said sadly:

"We have written to Pius XI, the Holy Father, *La Santa Sede* will redress all injustices and crimes done to us believers. For the Russian Tsar himself trembled before the Holy See!"

The Registry administrator bowed in approval, then set about staring attentively at his right glove, as though it was a bunch of geraniums.

I saw them out into the street, among the festive crowd who were squeezing in the half-darkness into the narrow lane on their way to church. My guest opened his mouth to suggest that maybe I could after all slip away some evening for a game of cards, but it probably occurred to him that I might invite him here, to me, and he hastily embarked on some municipal remarks, concluding that he felt too, à propos, perhaps it was a superficial impression, that Signora Madonna was sometimes even mentally absent, or he could be mistaken because who on earth knew which Pope it was now — as though he were afraid that our island state had fallen out with the Vatican Council.

I excused myself, saying it was pretty chilly, and I'd have to go in, they accepted this enthusiastically, and we wanted to wish each other something along the lines of "have a good time" but it did not seem appropriate to refer either to that holy midnight service, and Heaven knows not to my duties, as "a good time," and so they stumbled backwards in their confusion into the passing faithful, and I leapt back through the garden towards the house, reeling from the deafening peal spilling over the town from the great bell tower.

I found Hermione trying to conjure up the Christmas spirit by waving her arms about. She had struck a match and was looking around for something to light with it, she waved the little flame round the feeble flame of the oil light, then she noticed the rosary on the pine branch and took it hastily to Madonna, explaining that those were the Christmas bells ringing merrily on high, that Christ was born on the midnight hour. But Madonna looked blankly at her, took the rosary limply like a shoe-lace, then dropped it helplessly onto the floor, closed her eyes and began breathing heavily and rapidly. I watched for a few moments. The situation was becoming increasingly dramatic. Hermione picked the rosary up from the floor and stayed stooping in the air without a breath, her mouth open, with only her denture hissing softly as though it were about to slip off her gum. I sat down on Cara's bed. The bells outside stopped ringing, and the death-rattle could be heard more clearly, and Hermione could be heard pushing her denture back into place with her tongue. I said to myself: gentlemen, this is the end!

"It's my fault," whispered Hermione, with a horrified expression. "I told her that the Papio, I said, fool that I am, thatthe that the Papapio . . . that wretched . . ."

"Calm down, sit down, you see how it is," I said in the soft voice of a confessor, more with looks and gestures than words.

She crumpled her shaggy lips with her hand and trembled, her eyes wide open as though she were expecting a clap of thunder. She went into the passage and drank some water in loud gulps, moaning into the copper scoop like a cow. When she came back, wiping the drops of water from her chest and chin, she called from the doorway:

"The Eleventh! The Eleventh, that wretch, I said he'd died. Popius, Popopius!" she beat her forehead with her fist. "And the Twelfth, and God knows who else. What was I thinking of!"

So that's it! In other words, Madonna was crying, not dying. That's why Hermione was doing her Christmas dance and explaining the bells to her! I stretched out on the bed and told Hermione to blow out the candle and switch off the light as Madonna was bound to fall asleep now. She said goodnight eagerly and to call her if it should come to heaven forbid ... She never went to midnight mass in any case, her people were unbelievers and commun communists, and her brother and that other brother, goodness, they had beards to here, like Chetniks, and they would have been, I don't know, top people in the local council, always and everywhere, had they not died of diarrhoea, of dili dili gence or whatwasit dysentery in Bosnia and Herzegovina, and the other one as well over there in Slovenia, godonlyknows, from canons and petards. Everyone in the family, as long as anyone could remember, had always been in favor of this mess. She had been a little pioneer even then, and the red cross and in processions and all the rest, a comrade and at rallies, oh yes, the greatest! Andhow ... and we all clapped and off to the polls, my dear! Only, devil take them, such robbery at the market, and mackerel at six hundred dinars, that made her cross! As for all the rest — goodnight! She had already set off, but came back to remind me of the supper waiting for me on the kitchen table.

Her maiden tread could still be heard in the garden, then the creak of the garden gate, the mumble of the hurrying faithful between the stone façades and their thudding on the paved street, and Madonna had already slowed down to fourteen inhalations a minute. She was whistling sharply, as though she were blowing at a blade of grass, my tired blood rang in my ears, and from the parish church, which we traditionally called the Cathedral, the muffled drone of the organ puffed from time to time, and the shrill singing of euphoric sopranos from white throats sunk in ticklish dark fox-fur: prayayay for-or u-us. A hum as from a distant Sunday stadium.

"Little One!" Madonna suddenly came back to life.

I kept quiet to hear what she was dreaming about, but she was not dreaming.

"Light the lamp, Little One!"

"Oh, Madonna *santissima!* There's no oil in the glass, what do you want it for? Come on now, go to sleep!"

"Light it for the dead, light it *per il Padre Santo,* bring some oil and light it!"

I had to get off the bed, add some oil and light the little soul in the glass.

"Come closer, *bello mio,* sit beside me."

"There. What is it now, Madonna?" I sat down on the edge of her bed, yawning and scratching around my ears and under my arms. A smell of death and some kind of tangy cheese wafted up from her so that I felt a terrible, bitter thirst, although I had not eaten, although I could not even contemplate that cold little supper on the table and the hard Christmas fritters that Hermione had made for custom's sake. I was overwhelmed by thirst from Tariba's tannin brew as though I had drunk my cup of gall and vinegar and my executioner were now thrusting an acrid sponge under my nose as under the Crucified One.

"Madonna, my dear, what is it, do you want something to drink?"

"A little later, later, *bello mio*. First you tell me, tell me slowly and calmly, now that spy has gone, from the beginning, how you came to the council, what they told you, what you listed to them . . . Everything. How they were flummoxed!"

CHAPTER 7

An evil thought has been conceived in me and I could curse poor old Tunina for it. I can already feel it swelling under my peritoneum, somewhere in my belly, it's going to make me hiccup, my head is beginning to spin, I feel the evil thought shifting and kicking like a living embryo, pressing on my spleen, and I shall give birth to it, shaggy as a little demon, and nurse it at the breast of my despair and my unhappy fate. And then I shall live in damnation with my odious secret under my shirt, or all four of the policemen on the Island will simply put me into their blue motor boat, switch the engine onto half-power, throw out their fishing line and take me over to the Prison Island, to the kitchen-tile workshop. Something is going to happen, my friends, I feel it in my bones, and let it, damn it, if it is ordained, let it be born since it has been conceived, and I shall not curse Tunina, God grant him long life, not even if Mr Böcklin himself were to take me to the Bay of Kotor.

One day I shall simply rush into Madonna's room, shouting: Hosanna! Eureka! I shall shout that we've got everything, that everything is ours, or rather hers, that they've given everything back. I shall shout that Madonna is rich again, just as she was before! That she's got all she had back, half the Island!

And, if what Tunina said is true — the joy will kill her!

I'll have to get well oiled at Tariba's first. I'll burst into her room, and that'll infuriate her for a start. I'll shout from the doorway, then from the middle of the room. I'll raise my arms in the air like a statue, as though the heavens had opened; I'll shout from her bedside. Perhaps I'll even hug her! Perhaps I'll hug her if I have enough to drink, perhaps I'll give her a good shake. Congratulations! I'll shout anything that comes into my mind: Kastel, the vineayrds, Dundo.... Hey, Madonna, *sursum corda, porco ladro,* we've won! Then I'll suddenly drop her, in my rapture, let her fall onto her bed.... Oh, dear heavens, I've completely lost it, that would be too much! It's hardly surprising. But she'll soon revive, I needn't worry, I bet she'll even slowly raise herself up in her crouching position, raise herself on her elbows and look at me, devouring me with her eyes, she'll ask me how it's possible, she'll ask me to tell her all about it in detail, how I went there, what I said, how they were flummoxed. I'll lie like a trooper, I'll lie, I'll spin yarns, I'm not a cheer-leader, nor a people's tribune, but I can be imaginative, God knows, if necessary, like all the party programs and proclamations put together and all the long-term liars and imposters and charlatans and poet-laureates and Clever-Dicks all over this angular globe, let's not deceive or underestimate each other! What more is there to say: they've given it all back! Do you know what all of it is? Three-quarters of the Island, for God's sake, you can't know or see it all with the eye — serfs, forests, sheep, hills, valleys! Landscape! It's all yours, get up and bow to me, let's go and inspect it all. Or no, that's not necessary, no, look, it is I who bow to you, my fine lily! In the fields, by the roads, in the meadows, in the olive groves, beside the flocks stand serfs and the sons of serfs ready to fall on their knees before you, and you, Madonna, stay just where you are, do what you like! Sleep! Spit on your vassals, order caviar, if you want, switch on all the lights, we needn't save any more! We needn't spare anyone any more, there's been enough slavery and plunder. Knock and the door shall open, seek and ye shall find, lie and ye shall be believed!

And she'll stop, she'll watch, she'll listen until my delirium passes.

It won't be hard to turn on all the lights in the house, my pension will come eventually, we'll economize. I've saved a bit, because Cara isn't here. She probably won't order caviar. She didn't eat it even when she had everything. She'll look at me and most of all she'll want herb tea with two or three biscuits. Then she'll sigh contentedly and have a little weep: thanks be to the most priceless blood for this gift and that I have lived to see my rights! She'll roll up her eyes, piss on the darned yellow rag under her, roll herself up into a hard ball and give up her little ghost, for great is His mercy.

This evil thought was conceived on Christ's Christmas Day on an empty stomach, some time after six in the morning. And as soon as it appeared I consciously thrust it with all the strength of my will into my dark subconscious, where it slumbered in reserve, unworthy and base. Maybe I'll need it.

Hermione felt defeated that morning. Because the old woman had not obeyed her — she was alive, and still seemed to hear. And on top of that there was I, idiot, ordering salami and mandarins, as though I was flinging all those delicacies and dinars into the sea, over the wall there, into the sea, onetwo, heave-ho, herewego, into the sea! Idiot! And I'm so contrite, and submissive, good God, you would have thought I was about to inherit the imperial treasure of Doge Orseole! Like Hell, it'll be a house of straw, a pumpkin coach and a crooked sixpence for me! That's what I'll inherit and that'll be my thanks, a crooked sixpence! She's even regretting giving us water from the well, Mamelukes that we are!

"I know she is ac ... a Christian soul, as well, alright, although I don't recognize God and don't care a fig for him. But, good gracious, there must be something, there must be some thing or other up there, at least a Holymother to curse ... or my crazy old mother, seeing as we live so miserably and meagrely and our soulsinGod — Goddoesn't want them, there must be, mussbbe musbe some sacramental thing! And we do have souls, I know that. We all have souls, *perdio,* because not to have one of those either is all we need!" — Hermione became quite confused in her helpless anger, she too had evidently had all she could take. For a moment I though she would secretly sort Madonna out for me, delight her, shock her, or anger her in some way, or overload her system with some food. But that would be too much to expect from our good, kind Hermione. She's just jittery, she isn't wicked, she isn't wicked, what can you do. That's how she's been fromherm ... other's womb.

Madonna and I celebrated the afternoon by ourselves in silence and holiday solitude. The holy sisters sent us a little plate of cakes and a small bottle of maraschino, like ear-drops. But the little virgin was less frightened. Carrying the plate in front of her like a gold Communion platter, she raised her eyes even as far as my mocking chin, and spoke quite coquettishly, with an excited female hormone between her vocal chords which made her little voice sound husky. She spoke straight to my chest, because I went up to her, trying to frighten her in some way. She said what it had been ordained for her to say, but she did not step back so much as half a step, she did not look for protective spectacles and she did not hurry or squint. On her head she had a reddish crown of hair in the most perfect Slavonic single plait that was ever carved in marble, and little yellow wisps round her forehead and ears; and the wisps jiggled as she made her speech but the thick loaf of her plait lay motionless on her head like a heavy serpent on the tree of knowledge. I accepted the Christmas greeting and took the plate, I almost gave her a little tickle under the chin, but at that moment a muffled booming was heard from Madonna's room, from under her covers, and it drove away all my male dominance of this twittering child. And then again and again a boom, loud and unmistakable, driving out all doubt! Could that be Hermione's aspirin, divine Jupiter, God of Thunder! After the beginning of our Christmas festivities had been announced in this way, the little virgin blushed with embarrassment and slipped away through the garden, tripping along like a sweet Japanese girl with trimmed heels. Madonna was reciting again:

Santa Barbara, San Simon,
Liberene de sto ton,
De sto ton, de sta saetta,
Santa Barbara benedetta!

"Did they say why they came?" she asked sardonically, when I went in to her with the sacrificial gifts in my hand. "Did they say how much they're giving?"

"Yes," I said, "it's sold. They say the house is a ruin, so I sold it for a song."

Rubbing her crooked elbows, she began looking about for something to kill me with. But I knew how much such a stupid joke could cost me and I said hastily:

"It was the little girl from the convent. Here," I said, laying out the small floury cakes. "They sent Christmas greetings. And this is maraschino for you."

She looked at me suspiciously, she was thinking about

something. Did she still believe that the cannon fire had driven away the buyers and saved the house, or had she ridden straight off into the pampas grass of her inner landscapes? It was not clear which area of history she was now in. She looked at me, then at herself, examined the coordinates round her real bed, and then returned her gaze to the tangled garden of her ghosts, trying with all her mental powers to determine whether I was there, where the ghosts were, or here, where there was nothing, and which space I was moving in, speaking my words for her.

She tried to make out where the words were coming from, as though this room were a tomb in which you would not expect to hear a human voice and where the only thing that was truly real was the outer aspect, which was inaccessible to us. But the incomprehensible primeval vanity which had unexpectedly switched on her system of defenses and fear of ridicule, froze her face, hid her doubt, and all at once there were just two stern, angry eyes looking at me with a ruler's superiority; they spoke like the familiar poses of the enthroned: "We are not trying to penetrate your unknown insignificance, but we graciously maintain that you are trash; we do not permit the superfluity of your vassal's speech to penetrate to our consciousness, we have decided to consider you a hypocrite; can you not see that we do not see you? Can you not see that we do not hear you? Can you not see — you do not exist. If you see anything, you see Us; We are the only proof that you are alive, if we so wish!" That is what her eyes said, her mask from a majestic portrait.

To an extent I know it was not quite like that. And perhaps on the contrary I was the only proof of her existence. Because, did she really exist anywhere else, other than through me? I admit her existence every day: I move her, feed her, hear her, see her. I am the only one who understands. It is through my actions that her wishes are confirmed, her words realized. I straighten out her twisted thoughts and so give them life and sense. I am host to a parasite, but this infusoria, tick and coelenterata will in time infiltrate its slimy larva into my soul, this phytoparasite will strangle my sinews and arteries with its unbreakable tendons, and this tapeworm will make my most vital juices dry up — and, sucked out by this fungus, I shall disintegrate. And it will be true: I shall be trash. I shall exist only as long as she wants to drink my blood.

I sat down by her pillow, crumbled one of the little dry convent cakes into a spoon and, feeding her the sweetmeat, I dripped into her ear a drop of my poison.

"This house may never be sold or given away. By law. If it could, it'd be worth selling it even at a bargain price. Then you could use the money to munch away on all your favorite things, every day!"

Surprisingly, she did not react badly. With relish in her eyes, she sucked the sweet dust from the spoon like a hungry child, and perhaps she was only trying to remember whether she had received those generous promises yesterday in a dream or before a heavenly jury.

"*Sempio*. You think I didn't go to the council this morning!"

That is all she said. Tentatively and guardedly. She was testing her own doubts in my eyes.

Our little Christmas feast was spread between us on a low stool: the sugar rings and the little bottle of maraschino. Through the window a ray of afternoon sun, woven from rusted gold, had lodged in the floor in front of my foot and spread over the uneven surface of the scrubbed floor, gleaming and burning on the splintered threads of the scratched pine and casting a shadow over the greasy whorls and knots in the worn wood. This light decorated the room with wisps of half-darkness which made Madonna's face and the white lace trimming on the sheet glow. And in that stillness my crumbling of the crisp little cakes boomed like the clatter of a stone-crusher, and Madonna's sucking of the pellets resounded like a smack with a battledore.

Like a monk's cell. The prior has sunk into a pit of metal springs, and the prior has long pants with laces, and I am giving him Communion *corpus domini nostri,* and I can hear leaden drops rattling in the cloister into the bottom of the well and somewhere far away in the sultriness dry cones are cracking in the tops of the pines. If there is any vestige of eastern darkness in my soul, if there is a need for the regeneration and cleansing and rinsing of all earthly shells, then once, before my reincarnation, I must surely have been a solitary monk, and now I am suddenly being visited by surreal memories and fragmented visions. And always that indistinct cloister of long-ago which causes all my inexplicable associations to resound and which makes even my insides square and all my horizons angular. Those acoustics of a quiet space, which alone are completely substantial in a way that no actual volume has ever been real. And this day seems to me unbelievable, it is incomprehensible that this should be a jingling, singing, noisy, dancing, toast-drinking, festive day, full of snapping fire-crackers and shiny, fragile little balls. Yesterday seems unbelievable too, it is incomprehensible that I should ever have waded headlong through the whirlwind of war, grenades, shouting. Unfathomable. The screech of a tram turning, processions, and all those important parties. That this is Christmas afternoon, that the world is inhabited, that in the air above this roof huge clamorous bells hang under the dome of St. Andrew's, their bronze jaws only temporarily still in this replete afternoon. It is incredible. We have sunk into this peace as into the calix of a man-eating plant, Madonna lies silent, as though deflowered.

In dumb ecstasy, she is following the sweet gruel as it drips down her gullet, while I brush the unpleasant sugar dust from the tips of my fingers, sitting in the sheaf of light that has now climbed onto me as onto the Lord's Chosen One, I can feel my big, cold, friar's tonsure on the crown of my head and I crouch completely in my ascetic's body as in a rough habit, and it is as though I really were now irrevocably nowhere, apart from here on a stone beside a dead well in the centre of a lost cloister.

In the silence I crumbled the cakes with a crackle and snap. Madonna merely indicated with a sigh her minimal return. The crescent-shaped cake percolated through my fingers into the moist spoon, and when my greedy little ward parted her lips, I tried to offer her the spoon again, but she shook her head and I withdrew and asked:

"How about a little drop of maraschino now, eh?"

"Wait," she said, "I want to tell you something."

"Go ahead," I replied, knowing that it would again be ... how she went to the council, and how they were flummoxed. "Go on, tell me, tell me ... "

"What? Tell me, you say. But you don't know what I want to tell you! I just want to say, you know, that now I do remember you. Yes, you. I remember you. When you were little. I never could remember you, who you were, whose child you were. And now it has come to me. I remember when you were small and that it's you and who you are and everything has come back to me. Like a holy inspiration, it's you but it isn't you. Look at the light round your head. *Il cerchio dei santi! Insomma,* it's you and no one else. My child, you were an angel, do you remember when you were dressed as an angel, *bello mio, mi ricordo come se fosse ieri!* But, tell me, ah, you don't remember, *poveretto*. And I ... do you understand, no one ever tells me anything, and so I, poor thing that I am, I don't know,

I thought you were my lawyer, my lawyer, and not my angel, that it was you never occurred to me!"

Madonna talked and talked as she had not done for a long time, and her speech almost began to resemble a barely intelligible prayer, it was tiring to follow it, like incoherent rambling in half-sleep. Although it was true and real, surprisingly accurate. It broke like a spring out of the darkness and gurgled, barely falling over her lips, but it emerged pure and in fact unreal in its clarity. Distant days shimmered in this room, untouched by time, and the past can never have been so directly present as now, through this medium, through this immovable time-ship through which memories were coming so clearly to life, wiping out all the intervals between the years.

At our door stood Uncle's sister Icita, on the very eve of the Three Kings, and it was such an event! Not because it was Epiphany, but that she had come at all, she who never came to our house, because of Aunt. She said straight away to Uncle, from the door:

"I've come to see my brother. Brother, the only reason I've come is on business for the congregation and the Tertiaries, and our president Contessa Madonna Markantoni, who you are the first to respect and serve, so listen to me like a Christian and don't trot out those slogans as you usually do."

Uncle betrayed some unease, brushing imaginary crumbs from his desk with both hands rapidly and uninterruptedly, moving his hands over the desk, pointing to all those papers waiting for him, he gave a little cough, shifted his feet under the table and looked at those files of his like a culprit. He hurried her crossly and timidly, looking furtively towards Aunt, who had moved quickly and demonstratively away from the door into the middle of the room, where the old Mattress Maker was filling and sewing up our old blue mattresses on the big table. Aunt started to pick up the small tufts of wool from the bent nails of the notched comb, as though every little sheep's hair was suddenly valuable, just in order to turn away from Icita and give Uncle a chance to say his piece as was expected of him. Her fingers started to tremble, and seeing or sensing that, Uncle repeated with offensive abruptness:

"Well, tell us, *finalmente,* what you have to say and go in peace as soon as possible."

He would never have spoken to his elder sister like that anywhere outside his house, but she was big and important here as well, for this was the house of their fathers.

"Thank you, brother! Thank you, dear brother! But there is someone! There is someone who sees all of this!" she began her vitriolic dirge. "You only do me a deed of mercy if you abuse me and humiliate me and insult me. I shan't say you ever 'raised your hand against me' because it hasn't come to that yet, but there has to be a first time. Never mind. It's all for redemption and penitence. But yourself. You are harming yourself, *ma cosi sia,* they've so ruined you teaching you to behave like this. I shall have to redouble and increase all the abundant and humble prayers I offer to commend also your soul, dear brother, and it would be better if we directed all those prayers for the souls of our dear departed!" Icita raised her huge rough hand towards the picture of their shared father and mother, which hung, terribly enlarged, on the big wall.

The Mattress Maker, an old witch, bent and gnarled as a skinny cat, glanced automatically towards the picture on which the little white beard and black eyebrows of Uncle's and Icita's father and their mother's grey head stood out, exactly like the head sleepily praying now in our doorway. Sticking her huge crooked needle into the mattress, as though she were on duty in Hell, she said in a gruff bass to Aunt:

"What a lot of words, gracious me! My goodness! What a lot of words, in the name of toiling Saint Christopher! What a lot, from a sister to a brother, oh my! My late spouse never said 'get out' to me. I remember him under my breath, to myself, I don't interrupt. I say: 'My lovey' and I give a little sigh, and there you are, that's all. And he knows, he hears, and I carry on sewing. And these people would do better to do some work, and not go round sermonising, if you get my meaning."

Aunt said nothing, and who knows if she could make out anything of that bass voice other than an indistinct murmuring. She had heard all that about the late "lovey" and "get out" all too often, and now she was preoccupied with how long Icita would stay on her doorstep.

"You see and hear all of this," Icita was saying to her old father in the picture, "and you know how I am received and met at the door of our house, which I avoid and steer clear of until a holy mission and the holy errand on which I am engaged drives me here. Thank the Lord!"

"Come on now, that's enough litany and exaltation, for goodness' sake, I'm not in the mood, I've got things to do; if you've something to say, out with it, if not, *va te . . . far . . .* !" exclaimed Uncle, starting to fiddle with the papers on his desk.

"All right," said Icita with a sigh, "I've come to say that your little boy is this year's angel for blessing the water. Wash him and clean him, nails, ears, knees, and let him empty himself inside as well, don't give him any supper tonight, or coffee in the morning. He must have an empty stomach, as though for Holy Communion. He is still in a state of sin until the spring, and this will be like your first purification and trial before His face, my child, so you should be like a communicant. You know the holy customs, brother, if you haven't forgotten them, and there's no need to give you a lot of instructions!"

Aunt immediately flared:

"My child is clean! And who says, who says it must be my child that has to do it, those old . . . !"

"Sssh, come now, that's enough, be quiet! It's God's will, and it's a great honor," Uncle said meekly, afraid that Aunt's resistance might turn into blasphemy.

"He was chosen by the Assembly of the Maidens of Mary," Icita began to reply, enunciating exaggeratedly, but she did not deign to glance at Aunt, she went on looking straight ahead, at her brother's feet, with a somewhat contemptuous reproach for his submissiveness. "All old, virtuous women, servants of God, with no children of their own, who have no children, and whom the parish and tradition give the authority to choose."

"Servants of God!" Aunt swore, and it sounded like "Serpents of God." "So why don't they make angels of their own, if they need them? You leave my child alone!"

"Per l'amor di dio!" Uncle was scandalized, knowing that *Contessa* Madonna herself was at the head of those serpents. "Be reasonable, woman, you realize you're insulting the *Signora Contessa!* But you don't know it, or you wouldn't, I know. Be reasonable!"

"Any other mother, or, in truth, adoptive mother, would be pleased and delighted. The sweetest and prettiest little male child, nearing his confirmation, from the more prominent families in town is chosen without malice or envy, for his qualities," Icita went on in the same tone. "We vacillated, like a weighing machine, because there is more than one good family in town, my dear brother, and more than one well-groomed child of noble appearance, but *Contessa Madonna,* and, to be honest, I too, singled out your little boy, *testardo,* because, as your sister, I wanted to increase your standing and do your house good. And I know that the child is neither yours nor homegrown, nor, as I said, the only one.... To my misfortune I stood up for you, *cuore ingrato,* only to be insulted. Thanks, brother. Why, God forgive me, you didn't even make that angel, one could say, if you want the truth, did you!"

Aunt was silent, barely managing to hold her tongue, as she bent painfully over the carding comb, while the Mattress Maker sighed painfully, moistening the string with her lips and thrusting fiercely with her needle, as though she were piercing the devil's hoof. Uncle then hastily promised that I would be ready and worthy in the morning, and carefully edged Icita out of the house, evidently full of simultaneous gratitude and anger, despair and fear. But Aunt was silent as the grave all that afternoon. Uncle sat down at his desk again and in his emotion spent some time wiping his misted glasses, and then he put them on and went on reading his book. He just happened to be reading that book. He was reading it because it had somehow come to be on his desk, otherwise he never read. It was an old boring book with Latin words, crosses and the history of the far-off ancient town of Grič, which I did not understand, but someone had leant it to me, so I had to keep it and leaf through it a bit. My book so occupied him that he soon forgot the threatening silence filling the room behind him, and, untroubled by the Mattress Maker's occasional deep mutterings, he applied himself to it seriously like a student. He had probably first begun to read in order to protect himself from Aunt's looks and angry arguments, and to give himself more courage if he did after all have to reply, because at his desk like this, with his back to everyone, it was always easier to settle quarrels and resist attack. Aunt and Mada and I were used to him sitting all day long, with his back to all of us, in some world of his own, talking the whole time to himself and his papers, strewn always in the same tremendous disarray over the whole table and stuffed like rubbish into the open drawers. He was always looking for something, or calculating something in his head and would make a note only of the problem and its solution. He would say proudly:

"Exactly. I don't know and don't wish to know all those operations. Operations on paper. I have the operations here!" he would tap his forehead, "and what operations! You take a pencil, I'll do it in my head, let's see what your operation amounts to! Idiot! An operation is when they cut your stomach with a knife, and not calculation, you little fool! When a man doesn't have anything in his head he has to scribble and scratch with a pencil, like an illiterate while I do it all *einzwei!"* But he always forgot and lost his little notes and would quarrel with himself all day long: *"Maledizion de sti biglietti!* First I had it there, I had it there, then over here, *dapertutto,* and now neither dear God nor the Holy Mother of God knows, I've been looking for them in vain everywhere, try here, try over there, they just aren't here. And they might be right in front of your nose the whole time, like the other day.... But how can it be, *santo Dio,* how can they be lost, when they've got the estimates for last year's olive harvest on them, I can't do without them, everything was precisely noted down, and a list, and everything numbered, which worker did what. There you are, it isn't here. It's not, no, it's not! So? So what now? Huh! And now, what's the use! Shall I kill myself or go blind! But how could that be just the one that's lost ...!" And then, all over again. That was how his long sittings passed, and we only ever saw his back, round and fleshy under his tight silky waistcoat, behind which could be heard the rustling of papers and the hissing of his toothless monologues. These were sometimes threats to a debtor, scoffing at some expert who had submitted naively low estimates in favor of a peasant villain, for they were all equally villainous, but mostly he would just be chewing over any old words which his enormous energy had to spill out in order to maintain its balance.

But this afternoon Uncle was silent, and that could not have meant that all his great energy was employed in reading, but that it was being expended on supporting the leaden atmosphere behind him, that he was preparing to meet bravely the onslaught of Aunt's fury, when it finally broke over his shoulders. A long time passed like that, while the Mattress Maker rumbled on dully and her needle thudded with each prick as though it were being thrust into a taut blister. Aunt was almost calm, she sat down on the lower board of the carding machine and began to use the other toothed board to scrape, pluck and comb the mounds of old, hard, compacted wool. The bent nails knocked against one another and caught each other as though they were being sharpened, clanging loosely in their rickety beds, while Aunt untangled and re-twisted the wool over these crocodile jaws and then went on carding, banging one board against the other. Through that rhythmic knocking Uncle plunged into his reading, absorbing himself in his book, for the rhythm of the work encouraged and isolated him. And the carding had already stopped, nothing could be heard but the punching of the Mattress Maker's needles and the grinding of Aunt's teeth as she chewed her thread, when Uncle suddenly banged his foot on the floor and hissed sharply, horrified:

"Oh my, *lo mazza!!!*" then he drew back abruptly and said dejectedly, "that's it then, they'll kill him!"

Aunt just clasped her heart, turned pale and sighed painfully. She passed her hand over her forehead and glanced at her fingers, which had become like wax. If there had not been weightier problems in the air, she would have swirled all the air in the room onto the head of the man who had startled her with this sudden brutality. As it was she merely went rigid, emphasizing by that dearly-paid silence that the insult was far more enduring and terrible than all these assaults on the nerves.

Uncle, however, was not fully aware of the effect of his panic-stricken cry, which had taken him by surprise as well to start with, and then a little later, absorbed in his reading, he cried:

"Assassino! There he is, this very minute, good for him! *Bella roba!* What did I tell you! *Guarda,* but the fool sees nothing! It's criminal! Before your very eyes! And with a knife!"

"What are you talking about," the Mattress Maker consoled him, not understanding. "It isn't written that the child will automatically die! It used to be like that in the olden days. Nowadays a lot of them survive." And then she spoiled her consolation with a loud sigh: "It isn't written, but then ... you never know."

"He isn't thinking about the child, my dear!" Aunt disabused her reproachfully, "His head's full of novels. Novels!"

This brought Uncle back to reality. He wanted somehow to show concern for me, but whenever he tried to put anything right, he always managed to ruin it utterly. Not knowing what the Mattress Maker had been saying to Aunt, and what was in fact going on behind him, he suddenly said, as though waking from a dream:

"Well, child? What is it, have you been to the toilet? And don't put any food in your mouth from now on! Think of tomorrow and saintly cleanliness, inner and outer. And be contrite." He said that without turning round, as though reading from the book, but you could see he was agitated and that he was not reading any more, but had turned his ear towards us.

"Oh Lucheni, cursed murderer!" In her moments of greatest depression, Aunt would choose indirect speech: she began to

recite not to herself, nor to Uncle, nor to the Mattress Maker, a bitter little verse against cursed Lucheni, who had thrust a needle into the Empress's heart, probably reminded of it by the upholstery needle, and not by the murders with golden needles in the historical town of Grič about which Uncle was reading and about which I was the only other person to know anything, Aunt knowing nothing. That long drawn-out tooth-gnashing of Aunt's was her special mixture of hatred, half-mockery, disapproval and sadness, which Uncle understood very well and even felt perhaps like a needle in his throat and dripping water on his motionless head, like Lucheni, and so he began, injured, to defend himself in an equally round-about manner:

"You'd do better to go on sewing those mattresses, wouldn't you, Mattress Maker, which is what I'm paying you for, and not interfere when I'm speaking! I'm talking about what's here, in the book, and not about the child! What Lucheni, you two foolish women, what Lucheni, what murderer, what offensive words! What do you mean, the child will die, indeed! You fools! I'm talking about this lucheni here, and it would be better if you did some reading yourselves, ignoramuses! In the book, in the book, doyouhearme! It shows how people murder and assassinate, that's what, how they ... I don't know. But not the child. The child indeed, for Christinheavenssake!" Uncle was even a bit angry, probably ashamed at having been caught reading. He equated the reading of novels with mortal sin and always threatened to tear up all that rubbish like this ... like this, and burn it like Sodom and Gomorrah. Now he had forgotten about that, he was just overcome with shame and somehow to regain his ground, he snapped at me: "As for you, child, you're never disobedient, so why don't you go to the toilet. Go on, when you're told to, go out there and push, push!"

"Push, push!" Aunt suddenly bared her teeth at him,

because she had had absolutely enough. And things really were getting silly. She flared: "You go and push yourself! What a tongue you've got! You can use it with us, but with your sister . . . ! And don't you insult the woman who's working for you in your house! You're the one who's ignorant!"

"Graaah," sighed the Mattress Maker, wheezing, "leave the Signor alone, go on."

"Work, work . . . that's why you're paying her, to work!" he muttered to himself.

"She knows what she's saying," said Aunt, evidently now wanting to express her fear.

But Uncle did not want to take up this conversation, he merely made light of Aunt's and the Mattress Maker's anxieties by mumbling over his book. That was when I realized that they were all hiding as much as they could from me. But a great fear had in fact overtaken them all. Including my Uncle. Only Uncle did not want to show it. Although there wasn't much point in hiding it from me, because I already knew perfectly well all those stories about the angels usually dying after they had blessed the water. Some died right beside the organ in the upper choir. Some would get home, undress and lie down dead on their beds. And some died later. It depended on the angel. And none of the grown-ups could ever claim that he had been an angel and survived. Some did, in fact, but no one took them seriously. All those angels came to an end God knows how and where, therefore. Gradually or suddenly. There were none left. Only last year's and the year before's and one or two other angels had happened to survive, and that was because I remembered them, or had seen photographs in front of the Photo Shop. Although they could still always die one of these days, for no reason. Besides, children today are not even worthy of being taken by God and being given straight away the trumpets and fanfares they had in the choir while they were crossing the water. No one took any notice of the ones who survived, and their selection was, actually, a simple mistake on the part of the congregation of the time and those Maidens, because it meant they had not chosen the right one. Always, every year, the right one had to be somewhere in town, the one God had made to be his angel, but those old women did not necessarily know. When they chose the wrong one, and the angel did not go up to the sky, then it was all hushed up and not talked about, because it is better not to mention things that annoy God and make his Chosen ones ashamed. Besides, last year they had wanted to choose the son of the Agronomist, and maybe they had got the right one then, but the father began shouting that his son was not a janissary, and that he was not letting his children be thrown, I don't know, to the Sphinx, to be devoured, and he went around explaining through the town and houses and alarming people by saying that in the old days sphinxes had swallowed all the janissaries one after another because they could not answer their riddles. This got him publicly condemned in the church, and the best of it was that his son still died afterwards. Whoever is chosen by God is not any kind of janissary, no matter what kind of godless or even Agronomist father he had. Everyone had begun to call the Agronomist "Sphinx," which was something terribly insulting, even worse than being called "dragon," but when his son died they gradually stopped, no one even said anything when he reappeared in church, first for the funeral and then for the May devotions. The priest himself pretended not to see him. And so by chance that other angel, who was chosen by force of circumstance instead of the little agronomist, was still alive today, except that his right eye watered, and the true, predestined, one had died instead of him.

“The child is truly worthy,” the Mattress Maker remarked solemnly in the evening. They were having supper, and I was sitting to one side, reading “The Guardian Angel,” and I was glad that I did not have to eat and that I was the most important person in the whole house. It seemed to me I would never have to eat again, because I was already an angel, and I was thinking about how I would become a guardian angel to someone or other, maybe even grown-ups, maybe the teacher … my goodness, and perhaps I would even admit to my charge that I was guarding him and watching over him, and perhaps I would sometimes tease him: you must not do this, you must not do that … drink your fill of the sea. But in fact that all falls through if I am chosen to be a trumpeter. The Mattress Maker stroked my hair twice and repeated: “He's worthy, he really is, look at that curly hair, gold and curly like a lamb's fleece!”

“Ah! What d'you mean worthy! He's not worthy. He's just a kid, a bundle of trouble, he's naughty enough, thank goodness, and more than enough of a tease!” said Uncle as though justifying himself before Aunt, for the first time stressing my faults as virtues. “Why the kid's wild enough, for God's sake, and all these novels he reads, how could he understand everything like a grown-up …”

“May God hear you! Why, he's even an altar boy, he sings in Old Slavonic and in Latin, in two languages, as well as anyone, like a little saint. I watch him kneeling. Following everything. Ringing the bell for rising. …”

“Oh, that'll do! Or perhaps you don't know what his father was! He was a barrel-maker, for heaven's sake. Well, then if you know! How can... go on, go on with you … how can a barrel-maker's balls produce …”

“Oh my goodness, what are you saying?!” Mada was scandalized.

"Parolazze sporche!" exclaimed Aunt, although she was not sensitive to coarse words. And that was where Uncle had her. He knew she did not have the right to protest in the name of refined expression and he abandoned his indirect discourse via the Mattress Maker and began mocking her good-naturedly and harmlessly to her face, in the hope that he could turn the quarrel and Aunt's anxiety into a joke. He began drooling in a forced way, and, stuttering at the top of his voice, through his teeth, so that I would not understand, he recited the well-known lines:

Down flew a bird from the walls,
And pecked off Gabriel's balls.

"Well, anyway," said the Mattress Maker hurriedly, embarrassed by this indelicate joke of Uncle's, which she had at first tried to drown by whistling, ostensibly because of me, "the child even did his business before the usual time, as though he were, God forgive me, inspired!"

"Oh, go on with you!" Aunt now joined in excitedly too, "you really are asking for trouble. Be quiet, you witch, don't provoke him!"

"I did it because I had a pain."

There was a peal of joyful laughter, as though I had said goodness knows what. They seemed to have been waiting just for this relief. They laughed happily as they would have laughed at someone dying if he had suddenly returned from his coma, stuck out his tongue and asked in a vigorous voice: "What are you staring at, I'm hungry!"

"Well, yes," I confirmed, "everything was tight here, and it hurt."

They burst out in a delighted guffaw again.

"I'll go again a hundred times before tomorrow if you go on frightening me!"

By now Uncle was already wiping his nose and eyes. Poor Mada rushed out of the kitchen and ran down the steps groaning: "Oh, oh, I'm going to wet myself, oh . . . !" And then, when the laughter died down, when there was a little pause in the nervous laughter of that evening, Uncle tossed the final safety link into the chain of his optimistic proof and said, nodding, in a tone of mock reproach:

"An angel, eh? *Bel campione, cara mia, ti lo senti, a?"* and began weighing me up the way a man surveys his successful crime: *"Tu es primus inter castigandos. . . ."*

Sometimes it seems to me that Madonna is the same as Icita, the same as that whole choir of maidens. Now, when none of them is left, I think that Uncle and the Mattress Maker and poor leaking Mada, and that whole sad, grinning world around me has crumbled onto the bed in this quiet room and I need only a few more moments to free myself. Just those few more moments. Those days when I really did escape from my fetters to that fiendish committee seem to have been only an illusory liberation. And it is only now, even if only for a few moments, that my liberation is perhaps really near at hand. Between the meeting of Mary's maidens and the meetings of electors in the building of the former gymnasium, maybe the whole of history had passed, but my headlong life had connected those two meetings, and for me now everything that happened then seems — real and present, while all the rest is improvisation, it should perhaps have meant more than a refugee camp, but it has remained a mad chase without refuge. I was caught up among those fugitives until yesterday, and it was enough to stop for a moment and find myself by chance beside this pillow, to forget that I had already been apparently saved, and for fear to creep once again into my spine, fear of what could be, fear at the realization of all that could be done to a child, to a person, always and in all ages, in all committees and assemblies. And who will believe that I am still shaken with horror beside this pillow and that I feel all over again like a man who does nothing but constantly leap over chasms. Who will believe this is always our shared destiny, and that it is only afterwards that our knees start knocking. Liberation is only an instant of illusion, it is always just a moment or two ahead of us. It is always just in front of us, because we are brought up in false hopes. And every moment that is behind us is nothing but terror from which we are running away. So both escape and improvisation become our refuge, for, as long as we can still look around us, we believe that we are saved. As soon as we stop, breathless and with the star of salvation on our foreheads, we shall see that the same abyss is still there behind and ahead of us, and that it is hard to live on the narrow belt of the present moment, and that we must start running again, and that it makes no difference where in the world we go.

In my fear, my fingers mechanically crumble the fragile convent cakes for Madonna, and she talks to me, surfacing once more out of our story. The dust of the sun has fallen from my head onto her withered hands, as though my sainthood had swiftly passed to her, she talks and asks questions, although this is today quite a different sun that is setting, it is the sunset of an ordinary day at the end of 1965, a day which may still be thought of as Christmas but which for a long time already has not needed to be, and which has found me already very weary and far on in my flight, and left her so far behind in the past that not even this light belongs to her any more, because the images of her memories are lit by a sun that was used up long ago, a light that has moved immeasurably far away and that few living people can have seen:

"Why didn't you become a priest, rather than *invece* one of those bolsheviks, eh? And run away to the other side. Eh, why didn't you?"

On the pathway of my dubious, sleepy meditations, I had almost bumped into Madonna! She too thinks it is only a question of sides, and she too is talking of running away! In this drowsy afternoon, which, according to the traditions she fears instead of understanding, ought to bring goodwill *et in terra pax hominibus,* there occurred for an instant an absurd cosmic rendezvous between the two of us, who had for so long been moving away from each other in opposite directions. I could have said something, I could have said that no one could say I had or had not done something, if it was as far away as it was, and I could have said that what she was asking about was inexpressibly far and from this distance I could not give a coherent answer to her questions from the depths of infinity. I could have said that from this distance things were not what they had been, I could have said that from this perspective what had been done counted for as much as what had not, and that even crimes become obsolete. I could have said anything, everything that the little rhetorician and phrase-monger in me would have been able to improvise in a trice in full consciousness. And, immersed like this in the golden sarcophagus of Christmas drowsiness, I would perhaps have said something, just to free myself from that painful meeting with a corpse in the labyrinth of memory, had I not sensed in the depths of my consciousness that a cosmic circle had just now in fact been closed and that in an instant all our divergent orbits had been wiped out, for we had met once more at the starting point, face to face. So how much was this chain of memories of mine worth in the face of her amnesia, when the roads on which we had spent so much of our life and so many years could be wiped out in a flash, without altering the result? Madonna asked as though she could not have known it before:

"Why didn't you, *bello mio?* And why did they lead you astray?" And then, as though all of that had only just taken place, she began to stroke one of her small hands with the other, instead of my curly yellow hair. "They brought you in the morning to show me how pure and worthy you were, and I said and promised I would make you, if everything was done *in ordine* and properly, make you a priest, and, I may as well tell you, I said I would watch you and see that you carried out God's ordinance in the church and the blessing of the holy water, *la benedizion dell' acqua santa,* I said, and tears came to both my eyes with tenderness and how small you were, meek as a lamb, obeying everything and behaving. And you, *invece . . .!*"

I poured some of the meek little maraschino into a small glass, soundless, glycerine-like, heavy and viscous, and rocked it in the ray of sunlight before placing it in Madonna's hand, just as though she had ordered me to, because that was the best way with her, then she doesn't know whether she asked for it or not, and while that little confusion lasts the thing is done and everything happens simply, without a lot of words, questions or persuading. She drank it nicely, or if she did not actually drink it, at least she sucked and lapped the sweet liquid from our holy neighbor's table and the pancreas is a trivial thing, and, compared to our little Christmas joys, not worthy of attention.

"As for the rest," she said, smacking her lips, "put it away for when my visitors come."

But I had dripped the rest onto my tongue, spectacularly, and she said only that I was a rogue, *mascalzon,* and asked whether it had a taste or not, because her tongue was burnt, which meant that I would have again to roll gauze into a tube and soak the dried-up source of all evil and sin with cold chamomile.

My general weakness made me feel light and sway weightlessly, not now, here, where I have begun to moisten Madonna's tongue, weary with memories, but that bright winter morning, when I was getting ready to go to Madonna and looking vacantly through the misty glazing of my eye at my Aunt, who was standing at the top of the steps to say goodbye, smiling tearfully at me from there as I left and giving Uncle final instructions for bringing me straight home as soon as that carnival and buffoonery were over. She said carnival and buffoonery, and then quickly bent down and began hurriedly wiping the outstretched leaves of the aspidistra with a rag.

The bells had started celebrating well before the beginning of Mass, and when we emerged, approved and praised, from the house of Madonna Markantoni, the Signora Presidentessa, Uncle took me straight to the antechamber of the sacristy, while the church was still empty and cold, full of marble. The sexton Francesco was laying out in the inner area of the sacristy ceremonial gold chasubles, copes and stoles on the high clothes shelf and then he hurried over to me, unlocked the cupboard and began to show Uncle the long silk garments and ribbons they were going to adorn me with, as though he wanted above all to blind him with brilliance and dazzle. He puffed and clicked his tongue continuously:

"Where have you been, in heaven's name, where have you been? It's time, it's time!"

He quickly pulled the heavy, slippery white shirt that reached to the ground over my head. Uncle turned suddenly away as though I had become a woman, and he was going to take his place in the choir and leave me to Francesco, but at that moment he changed his mind and came back, gave my cheeks a lick and pricked my nose with his moustache, saying:

"Well, then, don't disgrace us, don't be afraid of anything, you hear?" Here he gave a little cough and shed a tear, so that his whole forehead was wrinkled and his eyebrows jumped about. "Just you do as Francesco tells you and God has ordained, and listen to the way all the rest goes. Try to remember everything!"

"But of course! It's time, it's time. But of course," said Francesco, "we'll do everything and right away, too. Naturally we will."

"That's it, that's right," Uncle coughed again. "That's how it must be."

"Naturally," said the sexton.

"Naturally," repeated Uncle and as he went out of the sacristy he almost put on his hat, but, remembering that he was in fact just entering the church, he quickly waved it in the air and gave the door a terrible bang with his elbow.

Then I was ready, strangely burdened, belted, crowned with a golden crown. The shoulder straps that carried the big white wings made of real feathers were tight. My bare feet were cold on the stone floor of the sacristy. The priest passed by me, carrying a chalice in front of him, then stepped backwards two steps, tidied a few curls of my hair, moved my wings a little apart, all without a word, because he always harassed me as an altar boy as well, and then he made for the door. Francesco hurried the altar boys with whom I was not allowed to talk because of my purity and composure and stood by the door, signaling to me to stay where I was, and instead of an altar boy it was he who pulled the bell-rope to ring the start of the mass. The organ began to rumble, and Francesco came back to me and told me to go on waiting until he came for me, then hurriedly shuffled off to his corner of the choir. I sat down so that my feet would not get too cold, and wondered whether there was a white bird anywhere in the world. Perhaps all the angels before me died from this cold marble, because in heaven they had thought up silk and ribbons, but not shoes. A crown even, but not so much as a stocking?! My wings were fairly greasy and dirty, but you could see they were white. They had presumably not been pulled off real angels, feather by feather. But no self-respecting bird in the world, other than silly, shitty hens, ever had white feathers. Sea-gulls are various colors. Only swans perhaps... if they really existed. It isn't clear how long it was before Francesco suddenly whisked me out of the sacristy as though everything was in flames, dumped me beside the main altar and left me there, bewildered and alone. I went up the steps towards the priest, who had finished or interrupted the mass up there, interrupted it I think, and who now turned round and poured insincere blessings down on me. A murmur ran through the congregation, because they had noticed me. The organ began to blare as though whole flocks of sheep and goats had started bleating, then quickly changed its tone, it seemed as though some of the gleaming silver trumpets had poked through the closed panes of the semi-circular windows under the roof of the central nave, and they were now ringing out and calling towards the open sea and cracking in the sharp winter sun, while the fat pipes hushed them with a dark rumbling from high up all around between the columns which darkened the side aisles. The whole church was swimming in sound, as though three hundred merry-go-rounds had started playing and now our teeth and the stone flags and the glass all went numb, and now everything was humming in unison softly like the distant steamer, the Oceania, and suddenly everything went quiet. When it had all gone quiet like that, the priest touched me with his finger to make me turn round. He did not say anything, he did not care, and if I had not happened to see that I had to turn round, he would even have started bawling at me, that was how he treated me, unfortunately. The organ began to sing softly, and the girls beside the organ pipes high in the depths of the church began first to croak like crows: "Three kings. . . ." then they sniggered "were ri-i-iding . . ." and then you could hear the organ whistle, and the girls began to sing tenderly, like angels: "from those sun-filled shores. . . ." In that general din, Francesco explained some things to me out loud and I began slowly and solemnly, the palms of my hands together and my eyes raised towards the organ, to scrape the bare soles of my feet along the centre of the church, walking towards that little door at the end, where the steep staircase led up to the organ. My wings flapped unintentionally and I only glanced at Uncle out of the corner of my eye, to see whether he was angry or perhaps sympathetic. He behaved as though he did not know me, and piously as though I were a real angel. Everyone was looking at me, but not all as he did, and I was itching all over from the scratchy top garment sewn with gold thread and gold sequins, I did not dare show it, but still the crown on my head leaned to one side, and my wings, as I have said. On my left and right, every single person was watching me, and among those gazes was that of Madonna Markantoni, *Signora la Contessa, la Presidentessa,* Madonna Markantoni, ever since I came down from the altar and particularly when I came down from the choir between the pews. The stone flags were indescribably cold, that is colder and colder, but the black ones were even more freezing than the white. I felt the icy touch of the stone, or rather the marble particularly at the joints under my toes. The nave shook with a waltz tune from the upper choir:

Bring-ing the gifts fore-told:
Frank-incense, myrrh and gold.

When I finally reached the organ, Francesco was waiting for me there, having presumably run down the side aisle. The church had a central nave and two aisles. The singers tittered at me, covering their mouths with their music.

"This is the balustrade," Francesco explained to me, tapping the balcony rail. "The balustrade comes up to your shoulder, climb onto this bench, but don't let your wings carry you over the balustrade, hold onto it with one hand and with the other we'll perform the holy rite when it's time."

Below me was the whole of the congregation, none of whom dared to look this way. Only the priest was standing with a book in his hand between the lower choirs to his left and right, far away at the other end of the church, facing me. Just within my reach was a taut wire with its other end attached to a big black wine tub by the priest's feet. Francesco had borrowed the ancient golden trumpet from the wooden angel on the organ and given it to me, showing me how I had to blow it, but not yet. Then he took a large white clumsy dove made of compressed salt out of a white napkin. He fastened it to the wire with a ring, and held onto it. Then he slowly lowered it down the wire to my other hand, placed my hand under its belly and cautioned me in a whisper to hold it tightly and quietly. The church rang with silence, all you could hear was coughing in the pews and the cries of seagulls outside. The priest waved his censer to and fro over the tub and spoke, invoking the holy spirit over the waters, and then he raised the little silver perforated mace into the air above his head. The censer jingled like a child's rattle and then it flew even higher towards me, towards the organ, as though it were waving to us and Francesco croaked behind me:

"Blow and let go!"

I raised the trumpet to my lips and at the same moment the organ blared so shrilly, that I almost flew after the dove which slipped out of my hand in surprise. And that must have been agreed with the organist. I stretched after it on my stomach, still holding the trumpet to my mouth, then, realizing that the white dove had irretrievably departed, I took hold of the balustrade again. Its somewhat stumpy wings wide open, the dove set sail, scraping along the wire, and slithered the whole length of the church, increasingly fast, lurching over the raised heads of the faithful, because I must have let go of it awkwardly and it was wobbling. For those few moments all you could hear was the trumpeting of the organ, so as to drown the scraping of the Holy Spirit along the wire. It seemed to last a terribly long time, although the dove had flown off better than a proper bird, waddling in the air a bit like a duck and it had already become small and shapeless in the distance, but very white. Then the priest took one step away from the tub, so as not to be sprayed, and the dove splashed and disappeared into the water, and it was only then that it could be seen that there was water in the barrel, it only looked black — black as the barrel itself.

People used to say, "His spirit has departed — he'll give up the ghost," but what about me? The first thing I thought was "I'm still alive!" Otherwise the singers would presumably not be tittering at me! People were moving towards the tub, clinking their vessels and scooping up the holy water, taking care not to let it drip onto the floor, and I was still alive, I took off my angel's garb, took off the crown, untied the wings, and I was still alive, and suddenly hungry, although I never wanted to eat in real life, and perhaps that was a miraculous sign. And I was still alive when I reached home. And I did not lie down and expire, like so many before me in history. Aunt kissed me as though we were meeting for the first time, as did all the others, they may have looked at me a little out of the corner of their eyes to see whether I was about to expire or something like that, but I didn't, and I have not been taken up to heaven at all, all this time since that great event. Everyone else flew off there before me, only Madonna is still trying to get off the ground, without success. Just as I was a little supernatural miracle, she is a great natural miracle and a riddle of medical science.

I am working this paint-brush over her tongue, as a tailor moistens material with a felt tube before pressing it, and in the window above her bed I see the last embers of the west smoldering, and the fig tree is scattering them with ash like incense, and I would like somehow to understand what happened to all those Christmases and where was it I went that I should now be here again? How did the brilliance vanish from this room, from this rich house, where did the sky run away to, and where is my joy at being alive? Madonna is purring with melancholy pleasure; I am pinioned here as though I belonged entirely and forever just to this purring.

And the feast-day passed.

CHAPTER 8

Everyone would end up in jail at least once in his life, if he did not go against his conscience a hundred times. But one would really need to have a head like a round-topped pin, not to know how to subordinate one's conscience to Great Aims, and thus free it from petty pangs and avoid being jailed. For the conscience is adaptable and it troubles us only if we don't know how to tame it, if we don't train it to jump through the flaming hoop of our ideals. But, if we don't stand in front of it not with the cracking whip of our iron will and the uncompromising boot of our certainty and power, but rather in a sinner's horse-hair shirt — it attacks.

Queste parole di colore oscuro were spinning round my head in Madonna Markantoni's winter garden on an empty stomach, as the sun went down on St. Stephen's day. Scrubbing in the sticky earth with my bare hands, trying to root out the shoots of the wild acacia that was poisoning the garden, I had cut the tip of my finger on my less unfortunate right hand and sat down on a stone like little Miss Muffet, sucking the sandy blood and cursing my conscience and the existence of glass. Because, absolved once and for all from all great ideals, it was only my raging conscience that had thrown me into this prison and now I was serving my sentence, and burdening my conscience still further with evil thoughts about Madonna, and the poisonous wild acacia thoughts were just taking root in my head as though I had sucked them out of my finger along with the dirty blood.

At the garden gate, the postman was already standing gilded with the morning, dissolved in the light and radiant as treasure, waving a gilded Christmas card.

"Here it is!" he announced triumphantly, as though he were bringing me freedom: "A card! From our seventh republic!"

I smiled, pressing the drained pinkish cut against an icy stone, and then I wrapped it in a handkerchief and the postman shut the gate behind him as though he had just arrived from abroad and was going to settle here for good. He even looked over the garden and the house, and as he strolled about doing so, he recited his well-learned lesson:

"It's not a lady of Spain; not a graceful Grecian; but socialist emigration, Deutsche Bundespost, a specialist from Tübingen, the respected manager of the Maddler pharmacy. Well, I'm not impressed by the name Maddler and I do not respect it, it's other kinds of names that impress me. So, a happy Christmas to you, too!"

And I, poor wretch, have done nothing but smile at him since he materialized. I am surprised he's delivering the post so early, but I'm not surprised he's already reeking like a tavern. I lead him, still smiling, into the kitchen, but I feel that my smirk is a grimace left over from sucking blood on an empty stomach and I offer him a drink, and I would wash out my bloody mouth with brandy myself if the bottle were not almost empty.

"I don't like direct greetings," the postman raised his glass, "I like them to be implied indirectly. Your health!"

And so I go on grinning, because it is all quite understandable and normal, and why not. He's that sort of postman. Whatever comes his way he reads, and he always talks like that in comic antinomies, controversies and epic antitheses. He is the only man in the world who still speaks essentially like the traditional ballads: "I've no time for stupidity and barbarism," he says, "I've time only for good sense and honesty." I have no idea what that is supposed to mean, I have ideas about quite different matters. He is *tipus affirmativus,* and he cannot stop at a negative, without denying it. In his own words, that is not all that makes him a unique person, he is unique in other ways as well. He has hit on me to chant to in percentages about how much our industry, our tourism, our skilled and unskilled work force depends on the Germans, and he is twisting his glass around in front of my nose:

"I'm sorry, but I don't believe we're actually a German colony; I believe on the contrary that they can say halt! whenever they feel like it. And we're kaput! It does not follow that this will happen. Something else follows. I mean, what's certain is this brandy for example. Since you have offered me such good brandy, then let's see if there's another letter for you. There needn't be one if there isn't. But if there is, then there must be, come hell or high water. There, here it is . . . I said there had to be one! From the little lady in Zagreb. Madame has written to you. One would not have said it was only the paper that was thick; one would say it was thick for some other reason. . . ."

That is the sort of postman he is, I say, and it is all quite understandable and normal and why not, but nevertheless I did not hit him with anything. I tore open the blue office envelope and I even said: well, thank you, thank you. I opened the letter carefully so as not to smudge the violet mucus of Cara's ballpoint pen and not to hurt my finger, but both things happened, the cut even started bleeding again. I did manage to squint, in passing and upwards, in his direction, so that he would not peer at my letter, at that "dearest husband," but he was waiting, quite uninterested, with his hands lying on the iron frame of his huge oxhide bag, waiting coolly for me to read it to him, because why should he make the effort himself. But when things didn't work out as he expected, he began to enquire, a little disappointedly:

"What's she say, what's she write, how are things up there, what's she say?"

But I was as silent as a rock, only a mine fuse was sizzling secretly in me.

"What do you expect," he went on talking to himself, "we know what it's like. I'm only asking whether there's something different, something new. What does the lady say, your lady, there must be something ... oh my, what a lot she's written! And all that, mark you, for the same stamp ... just one price!"

"Come on," I just managed to stop myself sending him packing, "come on," I said, "another little drink!" and I filled up his glass and went on reading, while he made himself at home, inspecting our little kitchen.

"How's the weather, just tell me that! How is it up there?"

"Oh," I said, "it's all right. She doesn't say anything about the weather!"

He babbled something about how it was impossible to imagine such a fat letter without any mention of the weather and how it was possible to imagine even a short letter about nothing but the weather. How improbable that was and how anything was more probable than that. And the weather report had not been left out because the letter was too long in any case, but because ... and again something quite contrary to anything that might have seemed coherent to me. I simply walked out of the room into the passage, step by step, apparently engrossed in my breviary, abandoning the postman and his crossword meditations.

Cara had early on met a friend from school by the Octagon, and a lot of trivialities about the twenty-fifth anniversary of the year they matriculated, pullovers and the price of Christmas trees in the market, and so, okay, I folded it up and put it back in the envelope, I would read it later, because Madonna was whistling for something in there. She was whistling and whistling, but the postman was in my way and I had to push past his bag in the doorway, but he stopped me and called, come back to the kitchen for a minute, he said, I haven't got much time, I've got time, but the town's big. I finally dispatched him from Madonna's door, almost beside myself: But I haven't got any time at all! If you don't want any more to drink, goodbye, so long, your health, farewell! Devil take you!

With superior and optimistic calm, he said:

"Let me count out your pension."

And now, dear God in Heaven, this blunderbuss! That New year charity had reached even us, here, and he, the great ox, had been rambling on for half an hour about the weather, about the snow, about how it wasn't any kind of New Year holiday for them up there if there wasn't any snow, it was just any other ordinary day. And how we, for instance, think that winter is like winter a hundred, five hundred, ten thousand years ago, from December until goodness knows which month, that winter always comes at the same time. Which is inaccurate! And who guarantees it? The seasons are shifting, once we used to wear white trousers for Easter, the Earth is turning . . . And so he spits on his fingers, turning over my little dirty, disabled serviceman's banknotes. He says:

"Hey, my friend, can anyone live on a pension like this?"

"Yes," I say, "invalidly."

"Ah, I understand," he says wavering and uncertain, because he has to understand at all costs. "I understand. You can't buy white trousers for Easter ... that's just an example."

"You don't understand," I laugh, what else can I do. "Not many can."

"Well, you mean: modestly. Modestly. Like an invalid. Like a pensioner."

"No. Invalidly. That's got nothing to do with modesty, but with lameness."

He got muddled in his counting, and started again, picking up from the table the little pile of forged mournfully smiling May Day girls from the Konavle district and impeccably steaming iron workers, those few golden Dubrovniks with a Cyrillic signature of guarantee and an illegible governor, and began spitting briskly and counting sternly, as though all war damages from Cain's days until the most recent fratricidal ones were being paid out this morning on this comic little Island of ours. He finished and puffed into my face: thirty-one! As though he had been turning over millstones instead of banknotes, and as though stone currency had reached us for Christmas from Easter Island, and then he put the pathetic little weightless mound of crumpled paper into my hand, so that I could not say I had not received it. I had noticed in good time, while he was counting, one thousand dinar note burned through with a cigarette stub, I pulled it out of the little bundle, he gave a whistle, Madonna whistled from her room too, and the postman looked around him in amazement, but nevertheless, in its place I now got new shining steam and smoke from our elite iron foundry framed in virgin fishnet lace and cobwebs, the main proof of its genuineness. I turned the little piece of paper over delicately with two fingers of my left hand, because from the back protective goggles were staring at me above the face of none other than the famed smelter David Štrpac. Actually, you never do know which is the front and which the back. And our astute smelter had not only protective goggles, but protective gloves as well and possibly even a protective crowbar, heavy and made of iron, and behind him hung a hook for hanging something on. In fact it all looks more and more like trash to me, as our forebears used to say, for money is trash. They taught me to kiss bread if I dropped it, but to wash my hands if I handled money. To kiss the bread and throw it away, but to take the money and then wash my hands thoroughly, with the money in my pocket. Hey! Our forebears! I don't know why, but it seemed to me that morning that a part of my former life had alighted on my palm with this smelly little heap, like a panting, bristling and rain-soaked dove in the dying fever of sudden psittacosis, to remind me that this was not simply one more monthly rinsing out of my financial hollows, but to teach me that these menstrual cycles were restoring to me, piece by piece, and at a loss, the life I had given for a song, drop by drop of congealed, insipid, polluted blood. And I felt like treating it as though it were bread: kissing it and chucking it away. Kissing my own blood. Because to wash my hands now that the money was here, when the money was here instead of my life, when the shameful transaction had been accepted, would have been too late and pointless. It would have been falsification, not to say the other thing, which is actually an offence under all kinds of acts! My life has been confiscated, collectivized and nationalized and these are now bonds, which would be no use to me, even if they did bind the payer.

Perhaps I should have answered the postman that economizing did not mean sprouting potatoes, reject vegetables, imperfect goods. That it was not a question of modesty, but denial and deprivation, a cheap life, a sprouting life, a wilting life, a faulty life. Invalidity! Lameness, lameness! Let the postman shout it from the housetops, let him spread that around. But he has gone, evidently offended, poor thing, and now he will leave my letters, if there are any, in the aspidistra pot demonstratively and without a greeting. Instead of him Madonna is whistling like a pressure cooker, traveling blissfully along the rails of a brighter landscape and a lighter horizon, which were once dirty, it is true, but which have been redeemed by our steam, our spiders' webs, our stupidity, our crimes and our lies. But ... you really would have to have a head like a round-topped pin, not to see that all evil comes from a conscience absolved of great aims. Or, if it comes to that, from a piece of morning glass. From the great quantity of glass that is already threatening the world. Because everything rots in the ground and on the earth, even conscience can, if you neglect it, but glass piles up and endures and lasts, glinting evilly from every corner. If only conscience could be hidden, even for a short time! Hidden glass gnaws until you bleed and lies in wait to bite you unexpectedly. A shattered conscience is quiet. But splinters give the glass back its deadly sharpness. Here, a vision of the world crammed with glass is opening up before my eyes. Everything people produce through their labors decays and disappears, or — if it is durable like bronze — then sooner or later they destroy it themselves. It is only out of the cauldrons in which chalky sand is boiled that enduring matter comes in an unalterable aggregate state and clutters the world. And now already a man cannot uproot acacia shoots in his garden with his bare fingers, he has more and more need of protective gloves and hooks and crowbars and other aids. A splinter of glass is already glinting maliciously from every little mound of earth and one day the earth will no longer be clammy, but transparent, brittle and infertile with powdered glass and there will be nothing but crashing and banging in the depths of it. And one little stunted acacia shoot will be worth more than the most crystal gilded Murano vase.

We had said: thirty-one thousand. In this golden age such gloomy little pictures were becoming increasingly necessary. That's another way I am disabled. One month of my youth is now worth only three hundred and ten new dinars, but with or without those crossed-out zeros my life is lame and there is no counting the number of zeros that could restore it to me whole again. Does Mr. Maddler know that he too has been deceived? He says: why don't you come too, leave Madonna. Leave that carcass. He says: spit on that disgusting little pension. Here you'll come back to life, you won't be forcibly disabled. Leave everything, he says. You haven't even got anything that you couldn't leave, he says. Because Mr. Maddler doesn't know how utterly deceived he is! Ah, my old school muddler, do you still muddle up parallels and parabolas? I can't leave this stinking old carcass, my dear friend! I stopped being sentimental about her long ago. At least I would like to think I did. I can't leave her for my own sake, not hers. She has been flapping about on her death-bed for years, no one can help her, and I don't even try. But this revulsion suits me, I need it. To redeem myself in my own eyes, to atone for my youth. And now I live with a corpse, I'm decaying with it, using up my remains, and that's how I know I still exist. And that she will disappear. You churn out money. That's even stupider, if there could be anything stupider, or at least equally morbid. We are both disabled, not even your chemicals can help here, or your powders, not gold nor hard currency, nor invitations; only you don't want to see that, either you have been deceived, or you may even think that it was you who did the deceiving. That you deceived your life, your fate, your Madonna. You didn't, my muddler, you didn't. You've forgotten what our form-master once said of you: he walks through water, without making a splash!

"I'm whistling," said Madonna crossly, "because my nose is blocked!"

"And I thought you were entering a tunnel!"

She looks at me, deliberately opening her little windows wide, so that I could see she was not afraid of those tunnels of mine. And then she said:

"Open that window for me, go on! It's stuffy."

"Not now," I said, "I can't now. We must wash your back."

"Unblock my nose first! *Finalmente,* my back, my back, but first my nose."

And I set about this interesting task more so as to liberate the quiet Island afternoon from the whistle of the jet plane, than for Samaritan reasons. The shrill whistle had slithered assertively into all the rooms in the house, but it was freed only in the open air, and it penetrated even more loudly from outside; it seemed that a crazed meteor was spinning high in the sky above the towers, hissing its burning steam and whirling its spiky steel under the clouds in its lightning flight, or that the sun had begun to spin and scatter itself like a centrifugal fairground firework. If I were now to run out into the garden, and assure myself that none of what was going on outside was reaching us, the nerves of my brain would still go on being rent by that same ear-splitting, maddening shriek, which has settled in it, and when I came back I would no longer distinguish Madonna's jets from the humming that is inside me, I would have to bash my head to knock myself out. While no one has ever fainted from picking a nose. Even if it was a nose through the openings of which someone else's baleful soul was impatiently peering, reaching for the heavens.

The way in which these exotic acts are performed is not particularly edifying, certainly, the whistling stops, or at least is diminished, evaporating in the distance like the hissing of a snake, and it seems to be far away, although it is right here. And it seems less threatening than the distant plane. But I have an auxiliary imagination, which makes my life easier: for me a cheerful sea-breeze is whistling barely audibly round the nylon line; the taut little fishing-rod trembles, and I push my finger into the pike's mouth and take out the hook; scales of sunlight dance over the ruffled sea; and the little worm is still on the bloody hook; the worm is even squirming! So that's what was squeaking!

"Che lo vedo!" demands Madonna, *"Mostra!"*

Go to hell, I think to myself and my stomach heaves a bit from that fishing in the unsteady maestral of my brittle imagination, and Madonna greedily widens her two suction wind-catchers, ventilating her rickety machinery, and sets sail into new waters, while I am left like an idiot, with the little worm on the end of my finger, forcing my jaded imagination and no longer seeing either the pike in the bottom of the boat, or the sunlight scales, but swallowing my bitter saliva and praying to God, whom I had disdained until yesterday almost as much as Hermione, to repeal my vassalage to Madonna *secundum magnam misericordiam suam!* Because the second item on the agenda to which we are now turning is the washing of the back.

When I die, let them put a red five-pointed star crucified on a black cross on my grave. Signs of my martyrdom and vassalage.

My hands had been joined in prayer, my hands had been weapons, they had been a machine for applauding — now they are slaves. And so I have experienced everything. Only now.

And now I also know that I am a fool, and that is why I am in chains, and that is why I am in quarantine. Because stupidity is not a defect — it is an illness. An incurable illness if it is innate. Only someone who has been infected with it can be cured. A defect is not infectious and it cannot be cured, only corrected. That is why stupidity should not be forgiven, even in oneself. We were taught to take off one shoe if we were walking with someone lame. Lameness is a defect, and the intelligent do not close their eyes even when they see it, they make plastic, artificial limbs. But to be considerate to a fool is worse than taking off one shoe. It is like embracing a leper for the sake of solidarity, or worse, for stupidity is more perilous than many terrible diseases — it is dangerous for the healthy as well. We put lepers in isolation and quarantine, and no leper ever opened a cosmetic salon. Stupidity is pandemic, and not even academies of science are spared it. On the contrary, it is most conspicuous where it is most harmful. That is why a fool should be locked in chains until he realizes he must not bite. Only once we have put him in quarantine should we let him be granted care and human rights and all comforts. Let a fool have two bathrooms and a swimming-pool and greater comfort than the sharp-witted. Because humanity must somehow pay back those who have saved it from infection, who have allowed it to live normally, to progress normally, as far as it is able and knows how. A man is sometimes more considerate to a dog than he is to himself, and would certainly be so to an unfortunate human being. But all the dogs in the entire world have never brought into human habitation as much evil, bitterness, misery and unhappiness as one solitary comfortable fool, who thinks that common sense is an illness, and who will never treat a sensible man like a sick dog, but as a biological opponent who must be clapped in irons. A hardened fool is more dangerous than three incorrigible criminals. Humanity is not divided according to race, or literacy, or height, or class, or blood, or sex, but it is brutally divided forever. And on each side there is an equal distribution of representatives of all races, cannibals and missionaries, children and the dying, slaves and plutocrats, the anonymous and all the genealogies, males and females. People cannot be divided permanently according to what they know and have, but according to what they could know and achieve if their spirits were liberated. And in the long-term, a felicitously combined fetus and a gifted infant are worth more to this world than a whole host of grey-haired asses with pointless knowledge amassed in the impenetrable labyrinth of their brains. And a cannibal who is distinguished from the others round the pot of human flesh by his gourmet choosiness is potentially worth more than the know-all who swallows all the great truths of the human spirit with equal relish. And the slave who hates work without knowing why is worth more than all the lords and masters of the world who are enslaved to their work, thinking they are making others happy with their mission. St. Mary Magdalene who was able to distinguish professionally between men is worth more than our holy father the moralist who was unable to end reproduction so he enslaved it with the holy sacrament. One good foul-mouth is worth more to this world than all the doctors of theology who pray for peace and rain, because a regular stool is worth more than the most fervent prayer for health. Only those who look at the world in the short term can prefer a civilized fool to a savage with whose chromosomes nature has juggled felicitously. Anyone who knows that the world is older and that it will endure, values the woodcutter who says: "If only I knew personally what thunder was!" more than the university professor who announces that there are no more secrets for him in the world of electricity. And an ugly nurse who would slap Madonna's sore back and briskly lie her back on her pillows is worth more than me, a fool who has created a ritual out of the pointless washing of a mummy. I know everything now, how to wash and powder the sore back of a crumpled old woman I do not care for, I know how to do it tenderly, more humanely than any sister of mercy. Only now, when my hands have become slaves, only now do I also know that I am a fool. That is just why I am what I now know myself to be. Others do not have to pray, others do not have to shoot, others do not have to applaud or be enslaved to know the little it is worth knowing about all of this. I had to push my hands under her rickety shoulder-blades, to learn so little. Rags of lifeless fabric flap, slimy and bloodless, over my fingers. What am I doing here? This creature is rotting alive! Who is it am I tending? Who am I talking to? Who is putting me through this? She is a corpse!

The next day I sent Hermione scurrying for the doctor. I can see, I say, that those are not bed-sores. She is decaying! It is clear. What we can see on the bed is a relief, a medallion, a papier-maché mask, a mould, a pharaoh's gold cover. Behind this en-face apparition, there is nobody. She does not exist behind it. It is a shield in human form, a suit of armor, a cast out of which Madonna has long since withdrawn, and without realizing, I have been on duty here, and now summoned the doctor. I lift her up and pull up her night-shirt and show him behind . . . there . . .

Hermione gasped in fright and ran out of the room.

"Of course, of course. You always exaggerate a little, always. But this time . . . of course," says the Doctor. "When did you last wash her?"

"My wife washed her," I said, "with alcohol and spirit, didn't she, and then powder. How many days ago? Only, um ... how many ...?"

"Why, every everyday *la ghe fazeva bagni povera Cara.* Everysingleday. *La ghe fazeva, si!"* shouts Hermione from outside.

"Yes, it needs to be done every day," repeats the Doctor. "Every day."

I hadn't known that ... I think, I had not quite ... known that somehow. Or had I lost ... had it slipped my mind? Perhaps it is only now that I know everything ... that if I wash her every day, she will be completely hollow and balsamized.

The Doctor takes me into the passage, holds me confidentially by the arm and says to Hermione:

"Signorina!"

She understands, she knows at once that she has to make herself scarce. How quick she is, in God's name! One Hermione is worth a hundred thousand, perhaps more, of the likes of me. I do not understand a single, solitary thing!

"Is this a door, here?" asks the Doctor, in passing, just in passing.

I don't understand anything again.

"Does it lead upstairs?" He asks and smiles. "Is it a door to upstairs? To the next floor?"

"A door? Yes, yes," I say quickly, "it was a door to upstairs. But you can't, I don't know, it's all rotten. Why do you ask?"

"Why, no reason. Just, you know, while ... we're alone."

I take out a thousand dinar note with its protective glasses and protective gloves, and a crowbar if necessary, for self-defense:

"Please," I say, seeing that we were alone, "here's a trifle for your trouble."

"What?" the Doctor gives a start after looking it over, but he does not let go of my intimate muscle. "Out of the question!

Put it away, absolutely not! Thank you very much, absolutely not!"

My pensioner's allowance twists, embarrassed, between my fingers. The doctor squeezes my upper arm and my hand crumples the note as though in response to the squeeze, and I cannot understand these two intimacies: do I care about that embarrassed note, or the doctor about my untrusting arm? Does anyone here care about anything? That is, if we have not met here, we two, as a beggar and a pederast! What has this arm of mine now become, after all it had once been? Clamped in an unwanted grip, as though in handcuffs. It has not been that yet. That is all it has not experienced, being forcibly chained.

"I wanted to speak to you alone," the Doctor begins. "Did you hear how shocked even Signorina Hermione was? And she belongs here, she is perhaps a friend or relation? You must take a hundredfold extra care of Madonna now that you are alone! You know that everyone has noticed ... you don't know? Why, your wife's departure, haven't they? Okay, and you really didn't know that her back had to be massaged?"

At last the hand on my arm let go in surprise. But I could still feel the iron clasp like an Egyptian bracelet above my elbow. The Doctor sniggered sarcastically: "I'm a rogue myself, perhaps a bigger one than you!"

"That's got nothing to do with it!" I shouted, staring at him astounded.

"Nothing, of course," shouted the Doctor as well, and with his other hand, he began tapping on the door. "And you say ... this door ... No, no, I was only, you know, as a friend ..."

"That's got nothing to do with it!" I shouted again. I couldn't think of anything else.

"My dear!" he rolled his eyes as if he really were gay, "why are you shouting at me!"

My rib cage subsided as I breathed out all the tension and flared:

"Just as a friend!" and I hissed into my beard, "I'm speaking to you as a friend as well."

"Mmmm," he concluded calmly, "well I never."

We were standing there in the cold tiled passage, and I was secretly wondering how I could slit his throat.

Why yes, exactly. Of course!

"Nature is perfect and wise," began the Doctor, after a perfect and wise silence, "and we have to leave her to finish her work alone."

"Nature is stupid! If it were perfect and wise you wouldn't have to prune or clip ... or fit dentures!" I hadn't even noticed that he had a whole porcelain set in his mouth like Hermione's. Oh well, what the hell!

He began to laugh like a lunatic:

"You mean: you have to help nature a little!"

"Doctor," I said, almost calm again now. "These suspicions of yours are offensive. But I don't have to stand here and take them...."

He went on laughing, as though I had only then got to the punch line, and was barely able to say through his laughter:

"It can be ... even stupider ... it can be ... even more stubborn! So that no help is any use!"

"Well, let nature get on with its business as it wishes, what do I care! It wasn't any cleverer at the beginning either. But I'm sacrificing myself here for the sake of this stupid 'business.' For ten years now, my wife and I. And I don't like people making allusions and jokes ... I simply won't have it...."

"Come now, what jokes, what's got into you? I was talking

quite seriously … hahaha … But still, let's leave that now, it's your problem, and no one else should be concerned, isn't that right … no one. Should they. You're quite clever enough yourself. But tell me, I wanted to ask you about that door. There's an attic upstairs?"

"Yes," I replied, with loathing.

"Or rather, I didn't mean to say attic. There's a whole floor above this one, isn't there?"

"Yes."

"A whole floor, and it's all shut up like this. And you're not interested? Not at all? Im … possible! I think you're … gracious! It's incredible! But listen, perhaps we could try the door. It must be possible, it was probably you who took the handle off, of course. You won't believe this, but if you had the handle I would be extraordinarily … I don't know myself, but something in me has always, these old island attics! What can you do, we children of the plains!…"

"Children…."

"You can't imagine … I'm quite childish about this. Do you believe me? Really, my dear … it's quite infantile! An attic!!! Dark. Cobwebs. Ghosts … ah? But of course you know, you're a dreamer!"

And in the end we two infantile dreamers more or less broke down the former door, and set off up the rotten wooden stairs in the dark. Our island doctor had made such a song and dance about that forgotten door that I had to give in, for Madonna's sake, because she still had to be treated — in fact examined! — although it was precisely for her sake that I should not have entertained the idea for a moment. He had insisted so strenuously that I was afraid he would sooner or later produce a search warrant from his pocket. In the dark trumpet of the staircase I turned to that happy man behind me, taking advantage of my temporary initiative as guide and revealer of secrets, and said almost insolently and maliciously:

"Imagine, what if we now come across the noxious remains of the old society!"

"I hope so," he moaned as he climbed, "oh, how I hope so!" Then he tapped me from behind, but I did not turn round confidentially and he explained in a hoarse whisper that nowadays everything was just a replica, just plywood, fake and plastic, and finally he gave me to understand significantly that it was old copper-ware that he found extraordinarily interesting.

"Original pieces!"

"Aha," I said mockingly. "And what about a two-way radio? Not one of them?"

"What do you mean? Don't say you suspect me!?"

"For my personal security," I said. I had acquired that bad habit, unfortunately, in my perpetual innocence.

"Ah yes, yes, yes, is that really how I seem to you?"

"Oh no!" I cried, apologizing. "As far as appearances go, it's impossible to acquire any kind of experience. Because it can happen that it is precisely those who don't appear anything in particular who get hold of some suspicious old dog's bone, and then start drawing professional conclusions about who has forgotten to massage whose back. I couldn't swear, Doctor, that we won't tread on a corpse up there!" We were standing at the top of the stairs, panting cautiously so as not to raise clouds of dust, and he was looking at me, breathless from his climb, not knowing how to take that.

"Or if we don't," I went on, "in the future someone might step on one of our corpses!"

"Mine or yours? In God's name, that sounds almost like a threat!"

"It needn't," I said, "there are so many nice things up here, that it could be me who's for it!"

"Hey! Let's drop it, shall we," said the Doctor in a conciliatory tone, "it's not right that you should be so caustic, you know. If I was at all suspicious about you and the old woman . . . it was, well, because I didn't know how to bring up the subject of the copperware I'm interested in, and you interpreted that maliciously to mean God knows what, perhaps a bribe. And now you're accusing me of all kinds of things: bribery, espionage, denunciation. . . . Well, then, let me say as you did: your suspicions are offensive!"

"There you are," I said, opening the double doors with their primitive inlay. "This was the house chapel. Only be careful, there are holes in the floor, tread on the beams!"

"Dear God, dear God!" He picked his way into the room. "There could well be reasons for murder here! You're quite right!"

In the dark room that little wooden altar was still waiting for my first mass. Madonna had promised she would arrange it with his Holiness that I could be ordained priest here, because this altar was consecrated, and her uncles had said mass at it. The door of the small room could be opened and the passage then served as a nave for ten to twelve people. This was where the sacred sacraments of marriage were performed in the Markantoni family and requiem masses said for the souls of the household's dead. Time had covered over this homely sanctuary, and it was waiting in vain for its last preacher. Someone had long ago hooked the heavy baroque hanging light that hung from the now bared ceiling to a side wall, so that it would not crash down from on high one night and disturb the peace of this dead house. There was no oil or candle in it, only a little ball of sticky dregs in the bottom of the blue glass central fitting that you could not see through for dust. On the end wall above the altar was a cross of dark wood without the body of Christ, and over it was thrown a polished sheet like a shawl carved out of lighter wood. In the corners of the room, on either side of the altar, stood a huge bronze candlestick like those fake wooden candlesticks from the main church, which were carried in procession round the canopy, and which were painted gold, chipped at the tips of their acanthus leaves, full of wood-worm, lop-sided, missing their third lion's paw. But these ones were made of dark bronze, covered with downy dust. The altar was bare, a modest little tabernacle was standing on a once starched cloth edged with tattered lace, like an empty cash-box. And that was all. On the side walls there were tapestries with winged animals, and in the centre of this sepulchral simplicity, my Doctor, in a fever of greed, stepped carelessly, the old floor creaked and the cyclopic candlesticks trembled in their pointless corner solitude, extinguished and cold.

I invited him to cast his snobbish eye into the end room, where I imagined there could be some copper-ware, and he peered hastily to left and right through the room, sighing as though before the tomb of Tutankhamen, forgetting he would ever have to leave this ugly, uncomfortable place, and go down into the future we had built for ourselves, so that things should be better. For us and for our children. I shall not say it was revenge and sadism that made me call him to go down. I simply felt like going, so I hurried him as well. Downstairs was like downstairs, but up here my insides soon started heaving, although I barely knew what there was in this lumber-room. And the only thing that could have kept me up here for a few more seconds was the awareness that all this was the past, damned, harmless and forgotten, and the awareness that up here there was none of that future, that filthy present that was downstairs. But each of those realizations was worth only one fragile and worthless second, and immediately after that I was sick to death of everything!

"Let's go, Doctor!" I said, several times more determinedly, in that irritating way in which we are driven out of pubs. Time gentlemen, please, we're closing. "Let's go, Doctor!"

He could not comprehend that the expedition could end so abruptly, through my whim, brutally and inconclusively.

"I've got things to do," I explained to the Doctor. "You've got things to do."

"Hell I have!" he snapped, exasperated, as he followed me down the stairs. "What do I have to do? No one is calling me."

"Duty calls you."

"Duty, of course! Signora Madonna is snoring.... Signorina!"

"Your home visits are calling you."

"Like Hell. There's no one to visit. If I don't want to go, no one calls."

"Your conscience, Doctor, what about that?"

"What conscience, stuff my conscience, I don't have a conscience!"

When resistance had become useless, when we were already fully launched on our return, and when it was quite clear that there was no question of staying, he began to take a bit of an interest in my insignificant person, and, coughing nervously behind me, he rode me down the stairs. Resigning himself to this return, he began almost to hurry, and, brushing the back of my neck, he hissed into my ear:

"Conscience! Duty! You know what that is? You're just forcing me to hurl myself after high balls for no reason! To make me look stupid. Conscience! That's indefensible cynicism! And I jump like an idiot. What are you talking about conscience to me for! As if I can't see you're deliberately shooting too high!"

I began coughing too, and cautiously asking the Doctor, had it really appeared to him that I had no moral right to ask him about his conscience. And I tried to convince him, clumsily as usual, that I was sure he too was adorned with all the most sacred qualities of his profession, why I was witness to his profound, mortal revulsion, for instance, at the very notion of euthanasia!

"You know what," he said, when we had reached the passage. He rummaged in the pocket of his overcoat. "We could both do with a little menthol sweet." Then he opened a small cardboard box with a few little green rubbery fezes lying among sugar crystals, offered me one and took one himself, saying that our throats were rough from that dust up there. We were standing in the very same spot where we had been guessing each other's thoughts fifteen minutes earlier. But this time he did not squeeze the muscle in my arm protectively, he stuck the tip of his index finger into his little box of Eucalyptus sweets and licked off the sugar, and it was I who grabbed him by the arm, politely and nicely, pulled him slightly to one side, so as to be able to close the door we had just come through. And when I had more or less succeeded in pushing the door against the wall and hooking it temporarily with a nail that was sticking out beside it, the Doctor, stepping slowly, returned to his former place in front of it, as into a spotlight, and, as though the hand of the Almighty Himself had ordained that particular mise-en-scene, he said, sticking his finger into the cardboard bottom of the box, by now quite damp: "You know what, it would be more accurate to say that I almost die laughing when laymen start talking to me about euthanasia and such things. I die of laughter, yes, and not from any profound revulsion. And I still have not yet, Lord be praised, actually died, even of laughter. And I have to confess that's already a lower shoot! If a man throws himself with care he can catch it without mishap, and even if he doesn't save it, he won't be ridiculous; the shoot is direct, you have at least to try.... I'll think about it." He put away his little box like a jiggling compass, and before he left that magic magnetic circle in front of the deconsecrated door, he coughed unnecessarily, pushed his sweet between his teeth with his tongue, and said, flapping his swollen eyelids like an old negro: "Don't nail this door up right away, I haven't looked at anything yet." I stared at him, taken aback, but he was already in the garden and without turning round, imitating me and my intonation quite audibly, he said to himself in great feigned surprise: "That's got nothing to do with it! Ha-ha-ha!" and just waved his forefinger above his head, like Moses, threatening me here behind him, because he could not see the extent of my confusion and astonishment.

CHAPTER 9

The year is nearing its end, Reverend Mother, and these last two or three days must be spent in fulfilling all our remaining obligations and duties to our neighbors and friends, our masters and oppressors.

"But above all, of course, to our Lord! It's a very nice custom, my dear neighbor, and it's good if it is observed."

"When he's settled his accounts like that, a person can set off more lightly on the new hopeless circle along the ecliptic."

"We must not be fainthearted, now, dear neighbor!"

"On the contrary! Hopeless exploits demand the greatest strength! You sometimes need so much strength then, you know, Holy Mother! Someone I know, who was on bad terms with humanity, had a hemorrhage and was ostensibly saved by a transfusion. Ostensibly saved. He was on bad terms with them and they gave him back the life with which he was likewise. What could be stupider! As soon as he was better, that man went round to give back the blood he had received. He didn't want to be indebted to their act of charity."

"Poor man."

"Oh no, Reverend Mother, not at all! He doesn't need anything from anyone! Imagine! That's not a poor man. A man who always has enough to give back everything other people try to offer him or impose on him?! Who knows how much alien blood they pumped into him and he gave it all back as though it were a trifle!"

"And God's charity? That too?"

"I don't know about that. Perhaps he had no quarrel with God. He didn't receive blood from Him."

"We all receive bountifully from Him!"

"Whatever he has so far sent to me has arrived by special delivery via St. Andrew's. That's why I've come now to say warm thanks to you at the end of the year, and to extend you my best wishes. . . ."

"I would gladly talk with you, my dear neighbor, but you turn everything into a joke, God bless you. But never mind. Jokes are also admissible."

"No, keep away from me, Reverend Mother, I turn everything upside down, you're quite right!"

"God bless you!"

"And you too, Reverend Mother. And thank you again and once more. Oh, I forgot to bring your plate. I could slip back. And the maraschino bottle . . . you really are craftswomen at that, it really is some maraschino!"

"Don't trouble. Our little girl will fetch it. And, please, greet Signorina Markantoni. I haven't even asked . . . ah, poor woman. We shall pray, tell her. . . ."

There, that was enough for me. That promise. Not the promise that they would pray for Madonna, as the affirmative postman would say. But that they would send the girl. And when I heard that, my mission was accomplished. And, what was it — just a step back to the house, but I felt I had returned from goodness knows what kind of adventure. And again, not because I had left Madonna, what was it — just a step! It was as though I had gone to the end of the garden. Nearer than to

Hermione for water. But because I had had the nerve to go to St. Andrew with whom I converse in any case so often in my thoughts. Because I had the nerve to speak with his official. Because that sort of thing does not come easily to me and I don't know how to do it. And particularly because I had hypocritically allowed myself that New Year ruse so as to induce the naïve nuns to send me the girl again. Now I was sitting nervously on my couch, mechanically leafing though a slippery English magazine left over from the summer. I must even have been red in the face like the little virgin. A man of my age, God bless him, as the Reverend Mother would have said, he must have been most bountifully endowed by the Lord, and it was all weighing him down, oppressing him. It was all depressing him so much that, the libertine, he wanted to cheat God through His own consulate, and draw His representatives and brides-to-be into participating in his sin. It was not surprising! Look, even in this magazine, here in a sketch by an English caricaturist, not to say a Protestant caricaturist, look: a metal robot is kneeling and praying before a large, ordinary, primitive hammer! No, it was not surprising! The Creator is more primitive than his works and for a long time the good Lord had been an ordinary, naïve, old-fashioned *postillon d'amour*. Anyway, I had not had the slightest intention of scuttling home for the plate and bottle, that goes without saying. I had clowned about until I got what I wanted. And why they did not understand, God alone knows! She had not actually said she would send the girl, although I had expected her to say that: "We'll send the girl." But she had said: "The girl will fetch it." And that presumably did not mean "some time." It meant, in all probability, that they would send her specially. And what could I do? There really was no exceptional perfidiousness in that archaic decameronian cunning! But if God was a hammer — then a robot could not be expected to perform miracles either. It was in fact a miracle that I had not actually become a robot yet, but that nevertheless, thank the Lord, there still appeared, silently, in my hero's dreams, depending on the seasons, at one moment blonde Northern Lucias, and the next funny little virgins. And we had already begun to move some way towards real action, in which we had immediately involved the Church and even a section of its clergy, some of its honorable personnel, in the deception. In other words, the affair was no longer innocent, and it was no longer merely a vision, but a physical act. The sooty little beauty would fall onto my bosom ... and without any of those French imperatives.

Leafing through the magazine on the bed, nervous and excited on my return from my holy neighbor's parlatorium, I felt that now all my time had been broken up, that from now on I would do nothing but wait, quivering, and if that little kid did not appear soon, I would wander round here like a sleep-walker, letting myself go to pieces and serving Madonna like a real robot, which a hammer blow had stupefied, instead of waking it into life, like Buonarotti's Moses. I forced myself to notice things around me and name them. I spoke in a half-whisper, so that Madonna would not hear me, everything that came into my field of vision and to my lips: box, small box, cardboard box, board-hard cocks, in the corner of the cupboard, corner cupboard, a period cupboard with wavy edges, big knife, small knife, two lovely black knives, oh what a surprise! I went from object to object, looking for those surprising black eyes, flexing my eye muscles and straining my inflexible forty-five year-old eye-balls and lenses as though I were drunk. In the cupboard there was also a little jar of holy water from Lourdes. What was water? Living proof of the imperfection of the human eye. What was a little jar, what was a full bucket of water? It was a bucket grown suddenly heavy in which a little circle swung, which would amaze any sensible Martian more than ... you know what, or even some of the scientific miracles of our age. Bernadette was amazed by the Mother of God, but by the holy water trickling in a trickle at her skirts — in the three colors on the jar in the middle of the cupboard, not at all ... Herm ... HERMIONE!

I almost fell over! Hermione was here!

By the heavenly virgin! She was standing like Katya Dolgorukaya by the grave of her ruined happiness. Like a totem, like a Turkish tombstone, crooked, in the doorway of Madonna's room! Facing this way. She was looking at me and fluttering her black blinkers like the Finisterre lighthouse! The nincompoop! I watched her with the imperfection of the human eye; my lenses were completely stuck. I could have named every living thing half-asleep, but what name could I give to this thing in front of me, this *turbeh*, this standing tombstone, as my stomach turned, and the blood drained from my brain, and my brow was sprinkled with icy powder snow! I could say: ASS! What are you doing here, how did you creep in without my hearing you! Muezzin, minaret, steeple, phallus, pillar, stele, wretch, how can you hide, you, you serpent in the wood pile!

I know now exactly what the last moment before a heart attack would be like: my left arm would hurt along that longitudinal line where the skin is bluish, transparent and thin, from the armpit to the ring finger; I would have seven kilograms of agitated pericardium between the lobes of my lungs, an axe in every joint, and Hermione's spiky head stuck in my gullet. At that moment I would remember in a flash all the fifteen thousand stools I had passed on our home planet and then immediately dispatch the immortal part of myself by an ultra-short path into the orbit of the sun. What a spectacle!

In a paroxysm of fury I grabbed the big knife from the table and swiftly forced Hermione to sit down wherever she could. From the other end of the knife a wax skull with broken jaws looked greenly at me. In the upper jaw hissed the pinkish gums of a plastic plate with a row of fiendish little porcelain milk-teeth. The lower jaw was filled from one end to the other with natural teeth, with the taurodonts of a Neanderthal man, with a row of molars in fact, with no canines, no eye-teeth, no sharp teeth at all! Just wide molars, with square black bovine crowns. A surrealistic spectacle shrouded in stench, for my victim was gasping in pre-death terror. She whispered out of her dry throat:

"I commend myself to the moth erofgod!"

The English magazine slipped off my bed of its own accord, and we both jumped, we almost moved closer together than the length of the knife. But Hermione flattened herself in self-defense against the back of the chair, and that saved her. The bells sounded in St. Andrew's. She crossed herself, avoiding the blade of the knife with her hand, and sighed:

"The voice of righ righteousness!"

I stared into her eyes like a hypnotist, and the knife trembled with its tip tensed towards her chin, as though it were searching for it, as though it were stretching out to reach it, to feel a support at its other end as well, to calm itself. And finally — to peel from itself the transparent piece of thin red onion skin that was ruining its executioner's appearance. It was probably because of that stupid bit of skin that the knife was trembling in my hand. That was why I suddenly pulled it back, as though I were going to stab my victim with a swing, and I scraped it over my right thigh to wipe off the peel, and then shoved the blade swiftly back towards Herminone's chin again, to deliver a decisive blow. Hermione jerked and made herself even longer, but the little flag had only partly detached itself from its glue and was now fluttering benevolently on the very tip of the blade without a vestige of cruelty and no style. Hermione wanted to say something else before her end, but I stroked her trembling open lower jaw with the knife and the little transparent leaf finally freed itself. As it fell, it touched the hands raised to her breast, and it was only then, at that light touch, that she gave a stifled cry, waving her hands and letting her rigid head drop suddenly, but I moved the knife away in time so as not to disfigure her, since she was so suicidally reckless.

"Eh?" enquired Madonna from her room, hearing the cry. "They must have taken her innocent children, *assassini!*"

"What're you bleating for?" I hissed murderously through clenched teeth.

"Ithought blood was drip ping onto my hand," Hermione whispered, knowing she would infuriate me still further if she alarmed Madonna.

"Which day was Herod's massacre?" asked Madonna.

"Massacre?" I asked Hermione for an answer with my eyes. "Herod's?"

"King Herod," said Hermione in a wavering voice, "did his blood dymassacre of the innocent children today, if today is the twenty-eighth."

"Today, Madonna," I called in a business-like voice. "The innocent children were the 28th. Today."

"What're you going to do to me?" Hermione wailed tearfully.

"I'm going to cut your throat!"

"Whawhawha ...!?"

"You've no idea how disgusted I am!"

"What have I done, *Dio santo!* I was afraid, er, of frightening you, so I, er, hid. Because you didn't no notice me when you camehome. That's all. What have I done? I was afraid of, er ..."

"Never mind that! For that you would have got two or three of the innocent children, and that would be all. It's not that. You're dying because of treason!"

"At least Herod didn't plunder the belongings and estates of the poor mothers," Madonna meditated aloud, as though we out here were only waiting for her historical judgment. Today was a day of philosophical inspiration. "But Karageorge with his partisans and commissars extorts everything your mother and father and your mother's mother and your father's mother and all your forebears in the old days ... forever. Amen...."

"Me!" Hermione was astounded. "Trea ..., me, me, treason me!"

"Condemned for treason. To death."

"You're not a court martial. Nor the state. Nor the security police, for God's sake!"

"Yes, I am. I've got a knife!"

"Kill me, killme whatdoIcare! But you'll be responsible for the innocent! Herod! King Herod!"

"You are untouched, but you are not innocent! A traitor isn't innocent. I have a license to cut your throat!"

"In the olden days," shouted Madonna, "you could have as many children as you liked, and your position was acquired through the labor of your father and his forebears! And you bear children, and you lose them, so you bear more, and more, and more ..."

"I am untouched, thankthe thank the Lord! That's all I have!" sobbed Hermione.

"I know. If you were deflowered, you'd be nothing."

I was moved. I only need my victim to start crying and I would immediately throw the knife onto the table. I sat down opposite the sobbing Hermione on my couch. Seeing that, she immediately brightened up through her tears:

"You're not going to kill me? I'd rather you cut my throat immediately, you know, rather than de defiled me! *Paroladonor!* Rather than that. . . ."

"Oh," I squealed, "you portrayed me to the Doctor as a murderer. To whom will you accuse me of rape?"

"*Ma insomma,* that's not right either," came Madonna's voice. "They went into limbo, the innocent little children, for they weren't baptized. And him? He went into limbo too, their murderer, because he wasn't baptized either, King Herod! No, he wasn't!"

"Come now, you monster, whatare yousaying!"

"I'm saying that on the basis of your statement the Doctor is calling me Madonna's murderer, and now he's got me between his teeth! If one of these days the old woman . . ."

"She won't," Hermione hastened to assure me. "She won't, you'll see! I'll wash her every day, iron her . . . oh, God forgive me . . . ma massage her!"

It's incredible how little she needed to grasp what I was talking about! How perfectly she knew what it was all about and why I blamed her! In other words there was a lot that was perfectly conscious in her reaction in front of the Doctor yesterday! It had been some kind of revenge after all, an outpouring of hate, an accusation and not astonishment, and not spontaneous horror. And she was even aware of the consequences. Or perhaps she had became so only later, when the Doctor winked at her to leave us alone. Who could tell. She is probably also unconsciously taking her revenge on all those who are to blame for her virginity. In that guilt I am irredeemable, I'm only wondering how I can screw the little virgin, although that is a greater crime. What can you do!

She assured me fervently that the sores would not bring anything untoward, that no harm would come of them. She offered to wash and rub Madonna's back. She bit her tongue and cursed the malicious doctor, and I suffered that soliloquy mercifully, like Suleiman the Magnificent, and let my astonished scoundrel go with a smile and without a sound. I had been secretly wanting a minor quarrel, so that she would spare me her presence while I was expecting my more joyous encounter, so that she would not get under my feet if Andrew's little innocent dropped in.

I went in to Madonna and began independently to prepare for massaging her back. Hermione, abandoned so abruptly, was left sitting motionless in the kitchen, then she slowly got up and walked away. I heard her close the glass door, scrape her feet over the cement porch, go down the steps into the garden, and slowly, slowly make her way across it. And when I thought she had gone, I heard the gate, just one single bang, as though it were the door of the fridge, and not our rickety and shaky, loud, squeaky, heavy great gate. Just one quiet clean bang. That meant she had not closed it properly, but just let it swing lightly behind her, after she had slipped through the narrow gap, as though she had slid out between the pages of a herbarium. It would be possible for a man to be left suddenly alone in this house forever, as on the bottom of the sea. It could happen that no one would ever open that gate at the end of the garden again. Cara would never return. No one would call. Not even the postman. No letters from anywhere. The electricity board would forget the little trickle of current that was used here each month. Questionnaires and forms would be lost in card indexes. My pension would never reach me again. It's all so insignificantly small, what we ask for or owe from here, money, friendship received and returned, it is all so little, so trivial and unimportant, that gradually that little, that insignificant little bit could simply stop, the gate would be left ajar like that, like two pages of a herbarium and no one would even peer in as they went by, everyone would simply forget that there was a three-dimensional garden here. I would probably be left, as in that terrible film, deprived of the ability to cross the threshold. And with time Madonna would perhaps get up, grow younger, and no longer mention a world other than this one. We would tend the garden and live on weeds, bulbs and grass, and in my boredom I would lie with her, for sure, even if she does have a hollow back, even if she is quite overgrown with hymen, and we would sit in the garden like two gnomes, until one day, perhaps three hundred years later, old Tunina would call in and drink brandy with us out of the urn, his eyes full of tears. And then, only after the brandy, only in the delirium of an unhealthy inflamed imagination, would I again be able to grasp the simple truth, that Madonna was actually still lying here, that she was decaying and stinking, as she lay on my left arm, while I rinsed with alcohol the little rags of crumpled tissue under which the suppurating pus of gangrene was fermenting, and that no one had altogether left here, and that time had not stood still, but something had slowed it down, some hyper-clear memory which would not allow moments that were over to sink into the past, but preserved them as they were, and the present was simply extended, the past no longer formed, everything was piling up in the present, terribly clear, actual and permanent. That was presumably what eternity was like, the one we were threatened with and that was supposed to reward us. The permanence of an instant, which becomes horror, whether it is hell or heaven. A reality so terrible that it can only be grasped by an unhealthily raving imagination in delirium.

"And why are you prettifying me today?" asked Madonna in surprise, shivering.

"I'm not. A person has to look his age, and not like an Etruscan!"

"And I'm old, he-he-he! At least a hundred!"

"More, more. Two hundred. Three hundred. A hundred hundred."

"You think so? Is a hundred so little? *In che secolo son nata, cos' ti par?*"

"In the nineteenth century, like all deserving Croats from Pavle Stoos to Karl Marx. . . ."

"E adesso, qual'e? II ventesimo! Orca! Quanti secoli!"

"Madonna," I said, with tears of terror in my eyes, a furrow in my brow and a damper on my vocal chords, "they've all left us. *Tutti!* They've left us alone, you and me! Those from the nineteenth and those from the twentieth century. All of them!"

"Oh, my God, they've been killed!" said Madonna with conviction. "That Karlomarko must have been killed as well, and so many others, *non è vero?*"

"Yes, just about," I said, weeping with all my heart. "Including Krlomrko. But the others weren't. They ran away! We've had it, Madonna. You and I."

"Perhaps a comet appeared to them! Let them go in peace, don't cry, my dear! What do you care!"

"Perhaps there's no one left on the whole Island! Perhaps we're alone for miles around! I've looked at the sky: there aren't any birds. There's not a single ant on the window-sill! It's amazing!"

She looked at me now almost with interest, as though I had announced that there was a south wind blowing up. She thought for a bit and then asked, just to be sure:

"Then the sheep won't all be there, either, for the robbers?"

"Macché!" I exclaimed, "what sheep! There isn't even a small cockerel, but at least we ate that!"

"Bravo!" announced Madonna, "I'm glad of that! And the ants will come again in March, April, perhaps before, *ti vederà!*"

So we fell into long conversations, my Madonna and I, like innocent children, and they weren't senseless as anyone secretly listening might have thought. Nor were my tears, my fear, or my panic senseless. Even though it seems at first glance that it was all a game. It would be senseless to think that words are senseless, that tears and fear are, that everything that wove itself into our interminable conversations was senseless. I would not want to say clearly just what it was, because people would immediately say: a game. But it was not a game. Nor a miracle play. It was the impulse that drives a tipsy man to say witty things. The impulse that appears both in a fever and in the sudden sweet pain of gout, an impulse that is still controlled by full consciousness and that drives us to make the anxious watchers round our deathbed laugh. And which brings profound relaxation and relief, and has no pretensions to last, but spends a long time seeking for a sudden little glimmer. I abandon myself to this roulette of Madonna's associations, and sometimes spend many hours on the very edge of a black circle spinning, inexpressibly light, and then scattering entirely, as it flies out of its center. One day the centrifuge will replace the hospital bed and the strait jacket, and the surgical scalpel, and, as they sit on the roundabout, philosophers will invent what will certainly be a wiser organization of life than they have dreamed up so far. By then I shall have been pronounced a hundred times the one who was not quite all there. Everyone knows how it goes! But the robbers and oppressors will retain their reputation.

That befuddling spinning enabled me to stifle something of my edginess as I waited for the little virgin. But she did not come all that day, and half the next day had gone when she suddenly appeared in the doorway. I had not heard her coming through the garden. The glass door of the verandah was open and I simply saw her awkward black figure standing there. I went rapidly up to her and said somewhat too loudly, right by the crown of her head:

"Oh, what a good thing you've come, I forgot to give the nuns back their things!"

"They sent me for them," said the girl softly from her great proximity, quite conscious of the distance from which she was speaking to me.

I caught hold of her by the left arm, just as the Doctor had held me two days earlier, when he wanted to subjugate me spiritually, and led her to my couch, sat her down, threw the English magazine into her lap:

"There, while I just look for them!" I scratched my ear. "What was it? A plate and a little bottle, eh? Now, let's see...." I knew everything was already washed and properly dried, the plate and the little bottle. I cast around the improvised kitchen this way and that for a bit, and then, seeing that she had not even opened the magazine, I stopped beside her again, touching her knees with my knee and began to turn the pages of the magazine in her lap. "Have a look, here," then I sat down beside her, put an arm round her shoulders and started turning the pages for her. "You see," I said, "this is the leader of the opposition. The leader of the Labour Party. The shadow Prime Minister. Do you want to work for me? I'm their spy! You probably don't even know what opposition is!"

She moved her head slowly as though she were going to

deny it, and then said softly, looking at the leader of the Labour Party:

"Only if there aren't any indecent pictures!"

"Are you afraid of the nuns?"

She did not reply, just sank her teeth into her lower lip, so that one could not tell whether she was afraid of the pictures, or the nuns. She blushed even more deeply and began to turn the pages hurriedly.

I laughed at her, right beside her ear, but she went on chewing her lower lip, turning the pages, until she came to a page with a big plate of decorated sandwiches in strident colors on it. There she stopped, placed her hands on the shiny pages and said shyly:

"I'm not afraid, sir. It's a sacred precept."

"Oh, yes, yes," I said, laying my other hand on her folded hands. "That's what we call ideological principles. Sochlisprinsples. Do you know what Sochlisprinsples are?"

"No," she said smiling and looking me in the eye for the first time, briefly and timidly. Perhaps she thought I was imitating a songbird.

"That's to shorten it," I said, "it lasts too long *and* it's said too often, and it doesn't even need to be understood, so people mumble, gulp, dribble it any old how, as though they were actually ashamed of the word. I wanted to say, when those sochlisprinsples are involved, that, my sweet, is also out of fear of the righteous! But, no, no, not of the nuns! Of righteous people."

"We are not permitted to have anything to do with politics," she said, looking at a stridently red sandwich and following the little yellow plastic spiral of mayonnaise on top of it.

"Nor are we. And how do you know that's politics?"

"I know. It's strictly forbidden."

"Strictly?" I asked, smiling and stroking her little spindle-shaped gleaming fingers.

She nodded and slowly withdrew her hands, then she looked me in the eyes for a second time, briefly, but suspiciously.

"It's a shame, you say, to sully one's soul with such muck! If you sin, then let the sin be sugar sweet!"

"A sin is a sin," the girl recited her lesson, and moved a little way back to the wall, as though she were going to stretch out on the couch. But it was only a retreat from my hands, my breath and my eyes. A retreat, but I did not want to believe it was actually escape, real, final; on the contrary, I wanted to take it as an unconscious invitation to hunt and reach, a call to leap. But in front of me was a ball of black linen, she had moved away, and I had to remove my hands from hers and my arm from her shoulders. In that linen sack there were no knees, nor any kind of little breasts, nor anything definite that I had recently seen when I was tipsy. At one end, two huge shoes poked out of the sack and from the opposite opening, edged with two white linen crescents, there stretched a little curved neck, supporting a small child's head, out of which looked a whole woman, endowed unexpectedly frankly with all the trappings of femininity.

I said suddenly:

"Why, you're a whole woman!"

She bowed her head, but raised her eyes and looked at me from under her eyebrows, inquisitive and flattered.

"I thought you were just a little kid," I began remorsefully to confess my great mistake, turning hypocritically serious at her unexpected maturity. "I was wondering why you were moving your hands away, why you were pulling back. When, there, you have a woman's eyes!"

Then she lowered her eyes as well, and sat looking white under her plaits, with her two wax ears, as though in concentrated prayer, and I began to drop into those ears the alluring poison of flattery and fondling and desire.

She slipped slowly off the bed.

"Is this our plate, sir?"

"Why yes, yes, that's it!" I jumped towards the table, to try to hide the bottle at least, since the plate had revealed itself prematurely, but the bottle was standing there, it fell over as I reached for it, knocking against the edge of the plate … it was all too obvious that everything was ready, right to hand. "Here it is, and the bottle! Your bottle. Why do you identify yourself so much with them, eh?" I asked stupidly and clumsily, as usual acting unconcern and curiosity. She got up and stood beside me. I took the cold, soft lobe of her ear between my fingers, moved closer and said into the microphone: "Before you take holy orders, you ought to be a woman a bit!"

She was burning red like a banner of the Virgin of Carmel. She took the little plate and bottle and went through the passage, with some sort of knees after all knocking against her black habit. I opened the glass door for her. She went out onto the terrace and stopped without looking round. She just moved her head a little to one side, half to me, half to her — their — plate and bottle:

"Goodbye, sssir!" she barely got out in a soundless breath, and, holding her habit aside, stepped hastily down the steps then went along the garden path, crushing the old gravel with those comic boots.

"Ah!" I said mockingly after her. "Ah, ah, ah! Sacred precepts!"

The garden was formless and shadowless in the grey of the afternoon; the child seemed so stiff and awkward in the sooty habit of her wounded virginal immunity as she fiddled about with the gate, that I almost wondered how I could have wanted to unpack her and dig around in that gloomy little sack of immature and ricketty bones as in a bag of peanuts, how could I have such bad taste as to add this principled pale winter paraffin-wax apparition to the museum of the wax lucias of my imagination!

And for a long time now I had not been sure that everyone who left this house and this garden did not do so for the last time and depart forever. Cara, and Tunina, and the postman, and Hermione, and now the little virgin with the plate and the bottle, my last little crooked candle in this twilight of joy and the flesh, blown out by my impatient and hasty overtures in my solitude. And while I could still hear through the half-open gate the sound of her heavy boots on the paving in front of St. Andrew's, while I could still make out at the corner the black fluttering of her short cape, I whistled loudly after her like a herdsman, so that my ears rang, and tears sprang through my lashes, I whistled piercingly and sharply, mockingly as one whistles at stadiums and in the cinema and as one ought to whistle in congress halls and in assemblies, and in squares and law-courts, if it would do any good. I was ashamed of myself. I thought I did not know how to do something I had never done. Given that I had not done it. But there, this little girl had shown me that I did know how. A perfectly good whistler had been discovered, completely unexploited. So it was not because there had not been any reason before! It was presumably only my good upbringing! And how many people were there with talents like that, and they were not even ashamed! I shoved my fingers into my mouth again, but I did not whistle a second time. I only let the current of air blow through them lightly, to see if it really worked. And it would have done. It would....

In the afternoon gray the garden was formless and shadowless. I was alone. With heavy, painful balls, rejected by these virgins as by those rowdies up there, I stood on the raised terrace like *Ecce Homo!* With my fingers between my teeth and a full bladder, which I was just about to empty, right there, from the terrace.

CHAPTER 10

Everyone seems to go, never to return, but the Doctor comes back inexorably. He is drawn back by his copper toys and the silver sacred vessels he discovered yesterday evening in the body of the little altar. He had come for the copper plates and dishes, and been enslaved by the silver chalices, ciboria, monstrances, censers, and other *vasa sacra* rather than the profane vessels. And now, on St. Sylvester's Day itself, he was crouching in front of the little altar, and Madonna was calling me to her in her room and pointing with both her index finger and her unpredictable little finger at the ceiling, because she could not do it any other way, and softly, softly whispering into that divining rod:

"I've been hearing it for several days now!"

I nodded.

"And do you know what it is? Whose footsteps are they?"

"Yes I do," I said, "it's a rat, *pantagana*."

She went quiet and her horns hesitated a bit, they almost lay down flat on her chest. But then she quickly shifted them slightly towards me, just as much as was needed, and stretched them out crookedly, as far as she could:

"You see! You see! You think I'm a non-believer! You see this?"

"Yes, I do, I do. *Ma mi sembra incredibile.* The Holy Virgin is weeping ... and the new Pope has proclaimed horns a sacrilege!"

"We didn't have a mass said for my Aunt Icita this year!"

"Nor last year."

"Nor last year! How can that be?"

"Quite possibly, because last year she was just my aunt, and I didn't think of it. Nor the year before."

"Ma va via, va to prego! How can it be that I didn't pop round to the priest at least, as you neglected to...? I'm surprised, really surprised...."

"You've been ill for ten years, Madonna!"

"Oh, why yes, *povera mi!* But so have so many others too, so what!" She looked at the ceiling again. "Do you hear? There it is again!"

"Pantagana."

"Oh dear, there's wax in the chapel! Go up, it could be a thief!"

"You can't get up there! You've forgotten. The door's been blocked for ages."

"Ben. Then a thief can't get up there either. It must be poor Icita. Leave her in peace."

But I went quietly up the stairs to Aunt Icita, nevertheless. The Doctor was carrying a copper pail out of the room into the chapel, stepping from beam to beam and trying to replace the broken handle. He did not notice me when I sat down at the top of the stairs, then after a while he became aware of me, but he was not startled, he turned calmly round and smiled.

"You've got strong nerves, Doctor," I said.

"Because I'm spending so long rummaging through these pots?"

"You must need them? You've gone back to the profane?"

"Nerves, or pots?"

"Yes," I said, following his every movement with my eyes. "It must be that you need them."

He straightened up, out of breath, his hair tousled, stretching his back, holding his arms slightly raised a little way from his body, as though I had thrust a rifle into his chest, he looked at the things around him on the floor, and asked with apparent unconcern:

"Need, you say? Yes, both nerves and pots, you're right. But you meant nerves. These pots make a man happy, as for being needed, well there again ... what did you say?"

"I said, you're not asking the price!"

"The price," the Doctor gave a little cough, "yes. Well, I leave that to you."

"Me? Why? You want me to ask?"

"To name it, for God's sake! Choose it. Don't let's invent misunderstandings now! At least you're master up here in the attic!"

"I should ask Madonna. It's a matter of ethics. But I am doubtful. She doesn't want people even to know about these old things."

"Jesus Christ! Jesus Christ! You've started shooting into the air again!" He began to mince and strut about like a nervous goalkeeper, and that was fatal. All at once he trod clumsily between two beams, there was a crack like walnuts being crushed. He had gone through the ceiling!

I had to hurry down the stairs, because the ceiling had collapsed right into Madonna's room. Halfway down the stairs I stopped, called the Doctor and when we reached the passage I poured him a bowl of water and told him to wash and tidy himself. Madonna was already clamoring like a torpedo boat, and I hurriedly leaped out into the garden and called back to her from there. Then the Doctor and I loudly acted out the scene of our meeting, clanging the glass door, and we both came into Madonna's room in loud conversation, encouraging each other. The Doctor amused himself with New Year greetings, and I stopped, spectacularly astonished by the little lumps of ceiling plaster that had scattered through the room. I raised my eyes to the heavens which had opened and through which the angels were poking two miserable little twigs. First I raised and lowered my eyes several times, and then I looked at Madonna, to see whether she could explain it in any way. The Doctor felt her pulse, and then looked at me in silence.

"What's all this?" I asked, astounded.

"Oh!" it was only now that the Doctor saw what was engaging Madonna's and my attention.

Madonna at first behaved as though she were in collusion with the supernatural organizers, but she did not hold out long, and suddenly began to cry out of fear and some mystical apprehension. She read in our serious faces that those footsteps of before could also have had a deeper meaning than Aunt Icita's ordinary protest march, and the opening of the ugly wound in the white vault of her one and only ten-year long sky took on an apocalyptic significance. She wept, her eyes fixed somewhere indefinite, and managed to say in her despair:

"They've come for me! They've come! *I xe vegnudi!*"

I picked the plaster up off the floor so that we would not tread on it, and the Doctor soothed her:

"Come, Signora Madonna, there's no question of that, none at all, Signora Madonna! We are the only people here, I, your doctor, and your man here, who looks after you and cares for you, that is, just the two of us, isn't that so, and that's all! And your condition is, I may say, very good! Ex-ce-llent!

Let's just have a look at that back! You know that back was a little … from lying.… There, let's have a look. Well, that's getting better. Just be calm now, it's all getting better … it will all, er, all be all right.…"

"It has just collapsed with age, nothing else!" I said from the floor crumbling the lumps of plaster between my fingers. "There, look, it's dust!"

Covering Madonna up and carrying out a thousand unnecessary and ostensible little acts around her, the Doctor cooed to her, assuring her and himself joyfully as though in naive surprise:

"There, you see, it's age, nothing else! Look, it's dust!" as though it were gold dust.

When she had calmed down a little, she broke into his superfluous cooing: "Doctor, when will I do it?"

"Not this year," replied the Doctor seriously, thinking he could avoid direct prognoses that way.

"Well, which year, Doctor?"

He turned to me, tangling his words quite privately, as though a toothpick between his teeth was getting in his way:

"When do we expect the happy event?"

"At Epiphany," I said, from the floor straight to Madonna.

"Well, that's only a few days, Signora! It'll come quickly. Just a few days … and there."

"Which day?" asked Madonna more loudly.

"Epiphany, the Three Kings!" I replied even more loudly, straightening up, with my hands full of plaster. "The Three Kings, or … whatever you like."

"I want to now!" she snapped.

"Heaven forbid!" I said, "the Doctor wouldn't allow that!"

I went out of the room with the plaster. The Doctor tapped Madonna's arm, cooing tenderly to her, "only six more days, why, that's nothing!" and followed me. I threw the plaster out into the garden and then slowly pressed my back against the door that led upstairs. It went back into its frame, and the Doctor stood in front of me rubbing his chin.

"Have you any menthol?" I asked sarcastically. But it could have seemed that "menthol" was a code word!

"If you want to talk seriously, then it would be more important for us to come to an agreement about the way you are treating Signorina Madonna, some sort of time scale, and so on, that her sufferings should be somehow perhaps curtailed and to see, if it's possible, what we would gain by that, and all those circumstances ... and what it is our duty to do for the unfortunate creature. If you feel like making jokes, by all means, go ahead!"

"Haven't you already been doing for her what your duty demanded?"

"What a question! It depends on what perspective you start from, you know that yourself. Yes. Of course. If you want the suffering to go on, of course. But there are, however, different concepts, treatments, therapies." Then out of the blue he began acting stupidly, like Tartuffe in a village theatre: "I told you a few days ago that it seemed pretty pointless to talk to laymen about the problem of euthanasia or such things. They are difficult dilemmas, at the very least, risky decisions, and the mere attempt to put pressure on a doctor's conscience can be disastrous. There isn't much to consider here, I know what sanctions I have ... every correction of nature...."

"Pressure!... I ... pressure?"

"No, no, of course not, don't start, we're just talking ... it's my duty to say these things...." he apologized, emerging from his new role straight away.

"And what is medicine, isn't it correction?"

"In a way, certainly. So is pruning ... That was a good point you made."

"Well, then?"

"Go on, I'm listening," the Doctor inhaled with new hope, almost fawning.

"What does the law say?"

"I'm asking you, please, don't play the fool, okay?"

"And what would you be prepared to do for the unfortunate creature?"

The Doctor looked for a time at the black and white tiles on the floor of our passage, rubbed his chin with each hand alternately, and then suddenly declared almost violently:

"Nothing for her! But for those copper and silver playthings of mine up there, I would do as much as my conscience allows. Have we understood each other? We have no witnesses, so I do not need to mince my words in any case! You leave my conscience to me! Tell me, is there a chance we can help each other out, or not? I have very little money, I could buy only two or three trifles out of that whole heap ... up there. Even if you manage to sell it all to someone, the old woman will eat up all the income. Signorina Madonna has a strong heart, bear that in mind! Please. I'm only saying. We could both be left empty-handed, if we start intellectualizing. A few days ago you ... set me thinking. And I promised that I would think it over, although, of course, I'm not used to business deals either, having scruples myself. And now, all right, put your cards on the table as well, in God's name! We can always meet or we can part in a friendly manner. Can't we?"

Dreadful, my brothers; both dreadful and fascinating. Appalling.

"Yes," I said, "a strong heart, you say, eh?"

"Exceptionally stable activity of the whole cardiovascular

system . . . given her age!"

"You are proposing violence against that exceptional stability?"

"Of course not! I'm proposing nothing. I'm only asking you what you propose?"

"I see," I said nonchalantly, "all right. I'll think about it. I'll think."

"All right, you think as well!" shouted the doctor and flew out of the house as though shot from a catapult.

When he was already in the courtyard he turned to say something more, but I called to him from the passage:

"And I may possibly consult my comrades on the committee. They're peasants. They have a healthy outlook."

He looked at me without blinking for a second or two, and then set off shaking his head and probably thinking to himself: "And I let myself get involved with him! And I let myself get involved with him!"

Aha! The wind has changed, I thought to myself. Yes. It felt southerly. The pits were stinking. The pressure was low and the air was sticky. There we were. Well. So it was New Year's Eve. Who knows what the coming year would bring. Cara would come back, for instance. Presumably she would. And all the others would in time as well. She would be back on Thursday, in six days' time; just before the happy event. That was certain. She wouldn't leave me in the lurch. Then, that other year would begin tomorrow. Wonderful! Admirable. All new, all different. Starting from the beginning. And that was tomorrow. Today, and even before now, none of those active people up in town was doing anything, and the whole of the main street was filled with lanterns, the square filled with fir trees, and people were patting themselves on the back: Our Town. They were carrying demijohns, buying paper hats, noses with moustaches, waiting at the hairdresser's. The market was carting in whole forests. There were performances of "Cinderella" or "Twelfth Night" . . . or what you will. Europe!

I could have set off as I was, from the terrace, without looking round, and gone straight to play cards. Bolted the garden gate from inside and then somehow thrown myself over the wall, because there was no key. I could have stayed two hours, three hours, four hours. And nothing would have happened. I just wouldn't have been able to tell anyone who was standing in for me. If I had said "the Doctor," the Doctor would have said "First I've heard of it." If I had said "Hermione," she would have found an alibi. Everyone would have said I was neglecting the old woman and that I meant her harm. Which would have been accurate, up to a point. There was even a real criminal trying to emerge in me. I was becoming cynical, to protect myself from scruples.

But I had to turn my back on the way out, turn towards that mausoleum, go back once more to Contessa Madonna, take up the cotton wool and alcohol again, and become a Maid of Mercy at this murky watershed.

When, why, there was Hermione at the gate! She was arriving with the whole heavy burden of my recent insults and crimes. I waited for her, standing on the terrace, my arms crossed on my chest like an executioner. She came towards me across the garden, looking straight ahead, scowling, and when she reached the steps, it looked as though she were gong to kneel down right here, under the guillotine, she was buckling so wearily under the weight of my moral belting, which she had not yet begun to get over. Nevertheless, she stepped out with her long bony legs and, on the contrary, she seemed to be going to take all four steps in one stride. She climbed up to me, long-legged and ominous as Tiresias, besieging me like the greatest scoundrel. She had prepared a speech with examples:

"I just thought I'd tell you: knives kniveskniives don't imp ... don't impress me! When he found in an annual the story about the cr the cruel prince (perhaps you know it, the story, you know all kinds of rubbish as well!), my brother when he found the story about the prince waving his saber and cutting the heads off the lovely irises (no, no, heaven forbid not the head of the priest's servant Iris, if that's what you're thinking! but those blue-lilac-purple flowers, they say there are ye yellowones too, I've never seen any, maybe in the graveyard, maybe there are some there) he went up and down, through the house, the dolt, he threatened all of us with his knife for so many years, waved his knife, a great long slicing knife for prosciutto, shouting: 'I'm that terrible giant! I'm the dan dangerous Fee-Fi-Fo-Fum!' My mad brother, a giant! The fool! (But now he has passed on, so the devil take him!) 'I'm that terrible....' the fool, to his father and mother and me and my sisters and brother. 'Fee-Fi-Fo-Fum', *moniga di fijo!* That's why I wanted to say knives don't imp don timpress me! I'm used to them and I'm not afraid! But here," she suddenly beat her fist against her breast, "you can't dig out what has taken root here inside even with a knife, you *capisci?* I'm just telling you ... like ... like ..."

"Like a brother."

She was aware of the irony, but she allowed me to put that spoke in her exposé, and I stood before her, humbly begging forgiveness, still standing there on the high terrace above my garden empire, in the southerly air, almost moved.

"There are jokes and jokes, but I don't recognize jokes with knives! I promised Cara, so I've come. It's New Year's Eve, so go into town for a while, have a drink. Do what you like, for as long as you like. As you like. Old and New are the same old story to me! A holiday's just another day."

Other interested parties would have seized this favorable arrangement with the said discounts and evident profit with both hands, and I too had almost sent at once for the swiftest pair of horses to be harnessed but nevertheless I merely lowered my visual instruments to the ground, took Hermione by the arm, and, leading her into my gloomy residence, began explaining that there was a reason why I could not accept all that.

"What reason?" she asked, not believing in those reasons of mine, and immediately grabbing hold of the stove.

"I haven't done the old lady's back today."

"Well, do it," she said without thinking, "do it and go go goout!"

I could see it would have been hard for her to do it herself.

"No, no, my dear, I'm not going anywhere!"

"For what reason?"

"If you want to sit here, do; if you want to help a bit with the cooking, fine. But I'll stay at my irksome post day and night, and that's that! Feast days and festivals and days-off are not for the suspect and the slandered!"

"What do you mean slandered?" she scowled, as though I had said Fee-Fo-Fi-Fum.

But I had stolen away to my task, lifted my resigned, waxen Madonna, propped her up and sunk into the alcoholic fumes and little clouds of powder, controlling my sneezing and my desire to sweep Madonna and Hermione and all my damned obligations up and cram them into this little bottle of spirits, roll them under the bed and flutter off on weightless wings into the outside world. Madonna had turned into a waxwork today after her spiritual upheaval, she was gazing at the worm-eaten twig dangling from the ceiling, and behaving like a mannequin which maintains the same movement, the same expression, however you stand it and whichever way you turn it. A taut thread of silence quivered for a long time between that stove out there and this bed here. And when I had already covered up my doll's behind, when I had placed her in her neithersitting-nor-lying position and gone to the washbasin to rinse my hands, Hermione said, suspecting no ill:

"Isp I spoke with the Doctor a littlewhi whi leago. I've fixed everything. Everything's fixed. A fine gentleman, the Doctor."

"What!" I shouted and leapt to the door, "what have you 'fixed' this time?"

"What's the matter," she asked in surprise. "I said it wasn't true you'd neglected the old woman knowingly. That I was only surprised because I thought you'd been massaging her every day and I didn't know you didn't know, or I would've told you, and I was very frightened when I saw her back. And I said you were honorable, and that he, as an educated man, shouldn't be malicious! He-he admitted that I was I wasright! Admitted it. Fancy that! He had to."

"Aha," I said, sitting down upright like a pregnant woman, "did he promise you that he would mend his ways? As an educated man."

"Why do you mock me, for God's sake! I was already afraid I'daga agagain done something wrong, the way you jumped to the door!"

"You haven't, my dear. You haven't. You've only aga again deserved a knife at your throat!"

She threw the tin oven tray with a terrible crash onto the top of the stove, probably because she had incidentally burned herself, but mostly because I had made fun of her stammer, and she threw it down ostensibly demonstratively with such a thunderous din, that Madonna cried out from her heavenly waiting-room, frightened and elated at the same time:

"A Zeppelin!"

But then I saw Hermione really and truly cry. Probably no one had ever seen that before, and she did not herself know how practiced women did it. It looked like anger in her confusion at actually shedding tears. In an instant her thin, bedraggled hair had stuck to her temples and nose, and she had opened her eyes wide, as though she had at all costs to find her burning tear in the darkness of the oven, before it evaporated. Everything round her eyelids went black, even those little yellowish knots of xanthoma around the root of her nose, and the whites of her eyes were crisscrossed with bloody lightning. A vein stood out in the middle of her forehead, little lumps swelled up on her nose, the porcelain plate with its little milk teeth jiggled and clattered, but there was no sound of any kind or sob from her mouth. Poor Hermione simply stared horrified in panic-stricken shame into the dark belly of the stove as though a priceless ball of quicksilver was still rolling away from her into the darkness. And it seemed that if she did not find what she was looking for, this woman would plunge headlong into the burning cavern so that her head would turn to coal.

And so I got up without saying anything, went into the passage, threw my cape over my shoulders and set off to lose myself in the early Sylvester's Day evening, in the early evening of the young year, another one, the eleventh already in this servitude.

And, since all roads to freedom lead across Freedom Square, I set off towards the piazetta, accompanied by angelic singing from behind the closed doors of St. Andrew's, not quite knowing what to do with my freedom. I stopped at the belvedere on the square, as usual, placed my palms on the wall like a preacher, and, facing the red west at the end of the Kvarner Channel, studded with little islands, I breathed in deeply as though I were going to blare protractedly to the oceans in a historic voice with a triple echo: "In the name of the Central Committee, in the name of the workers of all the world . . . " or as though I too were going to proclaim yet another prophecy of total salvation on a scientific basis. But I didn't. I let the sun sink into the vat of lead oxide, and merely tapped my fingers in a superior way on the cement balustrade. And I felt an urge to drum my fingers like this over the destruction of the world, calmly, breathing in the leftover molecules of oxygen and iodine, with none of the pathos of "The Last Adam." To tap the tips of my fingers soundlessly, to squirt saliva through my incisors, spitting out roguishly the acrid froth of exile and loneliness, and to grin like this from the terrace of the world, at all the promise-makers and boot-lickers and all the happiness-spreaders and world-saviors. To grin like a nice pink corpse turned to wax by a vision of paradise. And I wanted to be the last person in fact only so that I could see Madonna being borne rigid aloft by rearing angels, and myself left, thank God, alone, even if only for a short time, just so that I could scratch "a question-mark in the ice" and even if only within the four walls of her mausoleum.

I watched the sun roll like a piglet in the hot milky dough of the golden clay, scratch itself on the tops of the pine trees in the west, prick itself on the needles and cones. And when the wood grew darker, the sea was deserted, and the west turned grey, when the performance out there had come to an end, I was still drumming my fingers on my high balcony, as though in the upper gallery, not knowing what to do with my freedom. I could have run round the whole town before darkness covered half the sky, and before the boat from Rijeka carrying the day before yesterday's newspaper sounded its horn. I could have flown round to Tariba's and settled there until closing time, or hung about in the cafe watching the card-players led by Don Vikica. That was all I could have done. Or set off step by step on a patrol. Only, once the boat had come and gone, I would have had somehow to move, because then the town looked like a church after vespers, the Potemkin lights along the shore went out, and the late Krok, the municipal policeman, would be able to bump into me by the City Arcade, frown at me with a watchful eye, and undertake swift steps in the sense of freeing public spaces of worthless elements.

When I appeared at their door, they thought at first that perhaps Cara had come back a bit early. But then my one-and-onlies-here thought immediately afterwards that Madonna had suddenly abandoned me, and that I was wandering through the world, lost and alone. It was not like that, obviously, and my one-and-only-here quickly cleared the table and we fell on the cards like robbers dividing the spoils. Madame did not think much of that and she said in a petulant tone:

"Lino, dear, maybe our friend has come to hear some news."

Yes, his name was Lino, truly, and there was nothing to be done about it. She was called Olga, and I had once said of them, as a joke, that they were Olga and Lina and that Olga was a good, noble, woman, but Lina was heaven forbid! And so they had begun to take a bit of an interest for a short time in the seaside Zola, Mr Jenije Sisolski, and some secondary questions connected with all that. Otherwise they just let rooms to their regular Austrians, and during the winter they lived quietly and happily in the empty house. *For they were childless.*

"He's not interested in anything," answered Lino in passing, as he spat out trumps. He winked at me. Then asked calmly: "how are the three Ms?"

"Sorry?" I thought I had misheard.

"Mademoiselle Madonna Markantoni. How is she?"

"I thought you were asking about my cards."

"That doesn't concern me, that doesn't concern me at all ... not at all ... your cards don't. That's your business ... those cards. It's nothing to do with me ... We'll just put this jack ... there you are!"

I did not manage to ask how it was that Mademoiselle had suddenly become common property, more common than these cards, but even if I had managed, I probably would not have asked, because those were all words without fixed meaning, the magic words of concentrated card-playing, automatic talk which players use to confuse their opponent and disguise their intentions until the last minute, an idyllic curtain of sound which covers only the muffled thud of galloping blood-thirsty passions aroused by the game. Even by a game! By a bottleneck! Because every contest is a moment of crime, every competition a workshop of hatred. And a noble battle is the same as a noble war: blood diluted with holy water.

"It's not possible!" Olga threw in, in a soft alto from the next room, where she had gone "just to put it on." Then she asked more loudly: "Is it possible, for goodness' sake? Not interested in anything? Nothing at all?"

"There is," I said, out of politeness, "there is one thing that interests me. How is it that Don Vikica has been able to stay his whole life in his house, without having to go off to be a chaplain, or parish priest somewhere.... I've always envied him!"

"Don Vikica? That interests you?" she asked, confused, not knowing quite what to do with such a question, like all people without a sense of humor, who take every word equally seriously.

I was already losing heavily in our card game, so Lino was able to allow himself to interrupt a little to wonder:

"You know, that question isn't, how shall I put it . . ."

"But are you honestly interested in Don Vikica — you?"

"To an extent, to an extent."

"And why not!" Lino went on, taking up the pointless theme himself. "The question isn't, how shall I say, uninteresting. Although he said it, just like that. Don Vikica is the thing that interests him least of all. But the question isn't, hmm, yes . . ."

I slurped my black coffee and did not even count my tricks. It was obvious that Lino could not seize any more of them than he already had. He was even a little unhappy about the extent of my defeat. He felt that servitude had dulled me and that a person ought to spend the few hours of freedom granted him in a happier way. So he meditated with a lump in his throat:

"Ah, what can you do, that's how it always is! In every game some win, others lose!"

"I know," I said, "but people outside the game look on both equally as gamblers!" I did not raise my finger instructively like all good teachers as I spoke, because it was immediately clear that Lino had taken this allusive lesson altogether too literally and, dealing the cards quickly, he ran off again to Don Vikica:

"Because, after all, it's a fact that the man is a bit coarse, he plays cards, smokes a chibouk and hangs around the cafe all day long. It's not an uninteresting question. Imagine, how come they're so broad-minded?"

"Someone somewhere must be broad-minded, damn it! Someone must be, *porco ladro!*"

"Perhaps he was eccentric," suggested Olga, who was following our game indifferently, "so they left him to live as he wanted. As they didn't know what to do with him."

"Oh, then it wouldn't be broad-minded!" I said, still losing.

That would be, rather, a feeling for eccentricity. But that is something all bishops, black and red and white, are short of. Although, one has to admit, in my case they had shown at least a feeling for preventative measures.

The second round of cards was lost for me as well. We went on playing but I didn't have anything worth caring about, and I no longer hid the fact, but said, acting sportsmanship:

"That idea is the gospel truth!"

"Did someone really say that, then?" Lino mumbled meaninglessly, rummaging among his cards and cigarettes.

"We can't know everything that someone there might have ... I said that *idea*. Thinkers think about everything, so presumably they think about gambling as well!"

"Thinkers!" sighed Olga, enthralled. "Oh, those classics!" she tried again, with a real scholarly shudder through all her luxurious erogenous zones.

"Sooorrry?" asked Lino, ostensibly disturbed, as though he were chewing over several stronger expressions at the same time. His wife evidently embarrassed him with such an exaggerated sense of the current political moment.

In fact Olga had so many healthy instincts! But her coffee was particularly fragrant and good.

CHAPTER II

Olga's coffee was so good that I wasn't even aware it was gone midnight, despite being chronically short of sleep. It was only when we heard the town band strike up at the top of the street with a potpourri of the most cheerful ditties of all ages that we shook hands over the card-playing battlefield, clinked our glasses of fast-acting brandy and I flew off into the new year with a twinge of guilt in my slave's soul. That was why I was sitting this morning by Madonna's pillow, deliberately unapproachable and motionless, but in my thoughts and intentions on the brink of a heinous crime, and I gazed at her with the empty stare of a Greek statue, and she could not see me properly, but was trying to work out what had cast a shadow over her white New Year sheets.

The night before, a few minutes after midnight, Hermione had met me with long elastic bows and steady snoring in this same high-backed chair. I briefly wished her a Happy New Year and told her it was from the heart, and that she must forget the business with the knife forever, and she replied that the New Year was neither a Church nor a State holiday, but an atmospheric one, or something like that, astronomical, a holiday of star-gazers, and so one could acknowledge it, and this time alright, whatthe what the hell, devil take what little hap happiness she had. And she said: the old woman waited and asked so many times, and she had justthisminute dropped off, I told her what she's always told, that you had hadgone to thec ouncil, *insomma,* and that everything else was alright, was alright, and I gave her clean sheets, why not, for the New Year.

Madonna almost did not dare look straight at me any more, but only out of the corner of her eye, and out of that problematic, restricted and misty optical corner she endeavored to guess what sort of shadow it was that was not letting the strong morning sun from the east window reach her bed. Between me and her there really had formed a thick shadow like a green jelly, some kind of density was quivering in the transparent light of the morning, a cube of sea in an invisible aquarium. It seemed that if she opened her mouth she would be drowned by this heavy glutinous water and I would no longer need to think about my crime. But she lay as though she had just been taken down from that empty cross up there in the chapel and was looking through me to somewhere out in the garden. Out there two birds were indulging in a saucy springtime dialogue, and in the town a clock struck and high on the hill beyond the harbor a donkey was braying so monotonously that a real local ear would never have heard it.

After an interminably long silence, when I had lost all sense of time through immobility, I bent slowly and deeply down to Madonna, plunging into the aquarium and making my way right up to the thin current of her breath. She went on looking through me, but now it seemed it was because I was too close and her horny lenses could not adapt to such proximity. I pulled a face like a satyr and said, enunciating every word:

"It's done! It's decided! It's all done!"

She went on looking through my navel and then just started fluttering her small fingers uneasily, wheezing barely more distinctly, but all in all she still looked as though she had been taken down from the cross. I went on quietly, almost whispering so that everything around us would not start to rejoice before we did ourselves at our felicitous skill. I prompted her to understand:

"In your favor! They've given everything back!"

And, finally, it seemed that all the color had drained out of her skin, she became as transparent as a tarantula. But perhaps that was only because, as I moved, so much light had poured in from behind my back that it had reflected off the white sheets, drenching her face and hands. Against the bedclothes her complexion looked like washed linen yellowed by strong sun. If that was her true color, then so help me it meant that the final darkness from an insufficiency of blood flow to the brain was imminent, in which case what she had said the day before to Hermione had probably been her last words. Drowning her slowly in that morass of her silent final agony, I had not believed the thing could be serious; I had played with the "the joy would kill her" method, not believing in the crime, not believing in the method, in emotional shocks, or in her ability to perceive. Not believing, in the last analysis, that she cared that much about belated justice. Believing perhaps still only in torture. And in torturing myself. And knowing that time had to be killed, that this day had to be killed, and that this day was the beginning of another year which would have to be killed and spent to no purpose. In this New Year morning, I had filled her, like a hypnotist, with some stereotypical slogans and maotsetungtype thoughts about how everything was ours again how justice had prevailed and how our slogans had prevailed Those same slogans that had once been shouted by the working class in the struggle against Madonna and her kind, against taxes, exploitation, plunder, extortion, bribery, tyranny and all possible dirty tricks and now it was only the crazy Chinese who were still using them today in a strictly scientific manner to dull people's minds, and they no longer meant anything to my generation. The whole New Year morning she just lay, pale, in silence, glancing at me vacantly from time to time, placing her two little twisted hands on the lacy border of the sheet and burping occasionally into her nappies like a nursing baby who had swallowed too much air.

When I realized she had sunk into nirvana and nothing I was capable of dreaming up could affect her, nothing of anything around us that I could see or hear, I got up and went and did a thousand everyday little domestic tasks around the house, and, returning now and then to her room, I tossed out some passing remark about the estate. She lay with a thin profile like a child's toy metal motor-cyclist, whose two cheeks were two almost flat pieces of tin joined by little catches. Only she was not made-up with rouge, like a motor-cyclist, because she had not been flayed by the wind of speed, but illuminated by an unearthly phosphorescence, celestial rays, as though someone had accidentally left the gates of heaven ajar, and as on earth only the faces of communicants are lit when the gold dish, with spectral rays falling onto it through the stained glass of church windows, is placed under their chin. An unliving peace radiated from her, a mummified calm and she was an embalmed saint. *Madonna della motocicletta*. My words no longer found any response at all, and as I did chores around the house I wondered whether, my God, this year was going to be the last. I struck myself as quite comical: I had aimed a pistol at her, but she had not put her hands up; I had brandished a knife, and she was meditating without so much as blinking, I had blasted her from my cannon and she was posing as Madonna. And although I wanted to believe she had heard and registered everything, and was only gathering her tributaries to her like a vast main drain, and then she would suddenly overflow — I must have looked pretty foolish, inventing suggestions about sales, making the most irritating remarks apparently involuntarily and uninterestedly, devising definitive plans about the estate, about paying the peasants, about giving things away ... with no direct reaction from her, who in all other circumstances was more fulminating than was required for one little definitive stroke or heart attack!

Lunch passed in the same way, all too little like a festive meal. Her tongue was becoming increasingly stiff, and I had to feed her increasingly often, to push a little spoonful of food towards her gullet, pick it out of the spaces between her gums and her lips, put it back into her mouth when the stiffened tongue pushed it out. As dessert I served up the slogan: let's use the copper-ware and sacred vessels to improve our meager fare! For the first time that day, when she had eaten and drunk her fill, she looked at me entirely soberly and consciously. I glanced smiling up at those twigs pointing out of the ceiling and then whispered to Madonna:

"There are interested parties!

"What are you talking about?" she asked finally, as though I had announced a visit from Markantoni himself.

I explained in perverse detail what I was talking about, and added that some inconsequential bits and pieces had already gone from the attic, some for that soft juicy steak the other day, some for cocoa, for egg custard and some other things, if she remembered everything she liked. It was clear I had finally killed her. She lowered her eyelids and her mouth dropped a bit open. But then I suddenly realized that she had not believed any of what I had said that morning! She had heard and not reacted! I had underestimated her, thinking I could always blather any old nonsense in front of her. But she had simply not believed it, and it would have been no wonder, if she had calmly replied to my prattling: "Oh, my little Pulcinella! I'm not in the mood for that...!" She had said nothing, however, in case she might find some sort of foundation for my words. She had not, and had remained steadfastly silent. But now, the business of the dishes was at last convincing, not least because of the hole in the ceiling. And with that suddenly everything that had preceded it, the whole morning, had become credible and possible. Now she only said, not believing it herself, what she had been thinking all morning:

"What will they give back? Who will they give it to? You don't know that, eh, do you, *poveretto?* You know how to take, and you know how to plunder. *Niente altro,*" then she demonstratively jerked a piece of gauze over her lower lip to wipe it and asked: "What broke the ceiling?"

I was going to say "a rat," but her renewed authority dissuaded me. The last remnant of her landowner's severity had reared up in her, and fear sounded an alarm in me. I could no longer say that she was simply evil and simply cruel. She was also her murderer's judge.

"It's as I said!" I answered hastily and rushed out of the room. It was a lie, like everything up to then, but it was no longer a morbid game, it was not a method. It was a feeble insistence that the sickening game be pushed to the end. And it was even self-defense and fear that the lie might be discovered.

There was no sound from the other room. I plunged my hands into that most nauseating and most stinking tepid quagmire called greasy washing-up water; the fatty cream sloshed about in the copper basin, filling my nostrils with a thin steam that soils, that gets into the pores and under the hair and that had been making my hands stink for days already. There must have been some kind of portent in the sky. It seemed to me that the bells had not rung all day. I trembled over the iron pot in case it should break, as though it were made of fragile clay. The room had begun to rasp and sway as in a fever, and a pointer in me quivered as in a manometer, as though some level to which I had been filled was oscillating steadily under the pressure of the swollen floor beneath me. I left the dishes, dried my hands, rubbing the skin between my fingers hard and painfully with a rough cloth and fell onto my bed. Perhaps I was short of sleep, and perhaps I had a malicious little lump growing on the surface of my brain and it was pressing on my optical centers or perhaps it was a bit of migraine from sexual deprivation. If it was not early menopausal vertigo. And was it possible that Madonna was so conscious? Had that single-celled being out there always reasoned so clearly and had I just been deceiving myself, carried away by my apparent superiority, mobility, energy, so I had not acknowledged her reason, but had mocked her like a mindless infant, like a silly little animal. Would she remain in future so alert, critical, conscious of everything, of herself, of what I wanted to do with her, conscious of everything going on in me? Perhaps that was why nothing I did worked. Perhaps that was why I was so ridiculous. Because she was waging a battle, beneath a mask of amnesia, irresponsibility and absence. She was studying me and resisting. She was resisting silently and as though accidentally and the more skilful her mimicry, the more innocent she seemed and the more in need of my help and comfort. It would be terrible for a man who had thought he was living alone suddenly to discover that a being who was his equal in every way had been living beside him all the time, watching him, and he had not noticed it in its hiding-place; following him, and he had not been aware of it. It was true that I had felt even before now that a little relationship was coming into being between the corpse and myself. I had admitted it as one admits that ants have a soul and that is why one should not tread on them, and that a tree suffers under the blade of an axe. But not for so much as a second had I had any idea she was so alert. In such a lucid moment she could have understood everything else that happened, she could have perceived all those relationships at once, and it would have been enough. Just one moment of total consciousness was a terrible fact. Who could know when such a moment might occur, how long it might last, what it might leave behind? Would it be followed by total eclipse, or would some bitter memory be left, or at least some subconscious controls, which would go on regulating all its reflexes? Who could tell what this was beside us, when it was not a dead body, a tree, an object? And it was not a person, or an animal. Who could tell what it was watching us and hearing us, when we did not understand an animal, or a person either? We meet and part without agreement, without real contact, not bringing one proper conversation to an end, not waiting for a single word to be heard to the end. None of the people who had paraded through this house in all these hundreds of years had left in it any trace greater or less than Tunina, or the postman, Hermione or the girl. And what about Cara! She had not been here, why a mere twelve days now, and she had already vanished from the house. There were still a dress or two of hers, some shoes, but she was not here, just as Tunina was not (we had eaten the cockerel), and as I no longer was already, because I was a stranger here, because I did not know even how to collect and cherish memories but threw them out. Madonna would not be here either, if the walls were properly whitewashed, the curtains in the windows changed, a fridge and a child's pram brought in. The human community tries constantly to organize itself, but it does not succeed, because it starts from the premise that people get on with one another, understand and know one another, and that they want to gather and flock together. But it is not like that. In every evening newspaper there is always at least one sentimental commentator whining, with the psychology of a kindergarten nanny, gathering around him in his imagination his faithful and good-natured fellow citizens, and coming to agreements with them about green spaces and industrial waste, chiding them and praising them, applauding them and instructing them like a trainer, the editor addresses them as "dear" and approaches them with familiarity, drumming their rights into their heads, secretly fearing the more intelligent individuals. While I can actually see how many individuals turn their backs on everyone who addresses them as a herd, everyone who calls to them through placards, proclamations, loudspeakers. We turn our backs and do not listen with even half an ear to all those flatterers, boot-lickers, demagogues, tribunes and swindlers of the people, simply because no one with any sense would include himself in any of those flocks called citizens, public opinion, electors, readers and so on, but would exclude himself even from the nation, believing he belonged to it voluntarily, not that he was preordained to be a component part of it.

Oh, if I moved my hands near my face they stank. They reeked like a kitchen rag. And I wondered, could I now, in my absurd situation and this unique relationship with my supposed victim, whom I had to groom and to whom sooner or later I would have to explain that I had invented the whole of today's Chinese story for no good reason, could I now, as I was, here, alone in this most idiotic ten-year long position that a chance Samaritan had ever found himself in, could I be anything of all that the newspapers wanted, all that the politicians and civil servants, the priests, the textbooks, the anthropologists, the demographers, the sociologists, the philosophers, the historians or vice-chairmen wanted, when I could not make even an apparent alliance with this one single being, with whom I fed from the same hearth and with whom I was rubbing shoulders under the same roof? I wondered: was I afraid of the fact that I had suddenly discovered a rational human being beside me, and that our relations about which I had only had a vague sense before, would now become two-sided and deeper, and that my secret desire for the destruction of a parasite would become a real crime against a human being? That the biological-medical phenomenon would become a moral issue?

I had not done any of the afternoon chores yet, and already my hands were stinking. The greasy water was getting cold and would by now certainly have become opaque from its thick skin, yellow grease would have hardened on the dishes and cutlery, and I was lying alone in the world, alone in this organized world like a corpse, there was no one to help me, and all that I had from the organization of the world was this couch that pinched me, that pointed its wild springs at my kidneys and on which I was decaying into the earth, weighed down with the stones of half-baked thoughts, obscure ideas and capricious associations.

"There's nothing!" cried Madonna, "it's a lie! Get out of my house, you criminal and imposter!"

She shouted that she wanted a lawyer to defend her, to cancel the will she had never even made, she would not let anyone touch her inheritance or the sacred house of her forbears. She asked that sentries be sent through the town to bring back in chains all those who had plundered her silver from the chapel, that I should be birched along with all the municipal officials who mock the sufferings and tragedy of a noblewoman, the heiress of the great Marcus Antonius. She compared her sufferings to his sufferings in the Roman fortress, and her humiliation to his posthumous humiliation on the Campo dei Fiori, although she could not be compared with him in any way, for she had not inherited his mind, and all the rest was dust!

All right, I said to myself, getting up, I bid you adieu. Honestto-God, I'm leaving! I shall set fire to myself and as I burn I shall leap into the Tiber or scatter my ashes into the wind, like on a threshing floor! I've had enough! I'm leaving this house, and farewell, my ancient love, piss in your clean sheets from now until the Three Kings as much as you like! Then I went to the door of her room and enquired, waiter-style:

"What was it you wanted, please?"

"Get out of my house, I said! Criminal and ..."

"All right. You're driving me out, are you?"

"Get out! Phooey!" Madonna spat onto her chin and wriggled and heaved as though she were going, God forbid, to give birth to herself, to burst through this shell, leap out of her belly and drive me to the ends of the earth.

I stood for a short time in the doorway of the room, looking provocatively at her straining, until she calmed down and turned her head away from me, and, facing the window like that, she started sputtering furiously:

"Dispossess.... dispossess ..." for Madonna pronounces these legal expressions more clearly and surely than many ordinary everyday words.

"*Va bene,*" I said, "I'm packing, don't call me or try to find me."

With nothing but an apple in my hand, I walked though the garden, through the Campo dei fiori laid waste by winter — banished by the Holy Office! The white rose had lost all its petals now, only the frosted pestles and pistils blackened like thorns were sticking up into the air. My footsteps were loud on the silent afternoon gravel. I crunched the sand as though an army of rodents were gnawing crabs' legs. I made the garden gate grind its teeth like a cemetery gate, howl like a mourner and whine like a wounded bitch. I pulled it behind me so that it made a crash to mark the moment when the unimaginable distances had engulfed me, so to speak.

Then I ran to Tariba's and downed two herb brandies, as yellow as gold coins. Tariba's was the only place in the world that was open early in the afternoon of New Year's Day. I thought how sensible it would be to remain on bad terms with Madonna, because then she would welcome Cara more easily on her return. I sat down at a table in the empty bar and began to munch my apple. Tariba was dozing on his feet, leaning on the metal counter with both hands and his belly: In the name of the Central ... My apple crunched in the silence so loudly that it startled him from his slumber, and sucking up the saliva that had begun to trickle out of his mouth, he proclaimed how deadly it was, by Christ, for an educated man to live here, like this so tediously. It was not entirely clear who it was who was so educated, but one would have said he probably meant himself. Seeing that I was just taking smaller and faster bites as I came to the end of my apple and not encouraging him, he switched on the radio that stood among the jars on the shelf, and started shifting soda siphons about. Almost stealthily the muffled voice of a commentator on international affairs stole out of the distance of the perforated ether, but it quickly grew and filled the space.

"It's never been mended," said Tariba proudly.

Scorning all the rules of the announcer's trade and the finest nuances of Croatian accentuation, the speaker on this sluggish afternoon belted out his report at such speed that he might have been swatting flies, and it was almost interesting to wait to see whether he would run out of breath somewhere in the middle of a word, and whether Tariba would not need to have it mended after all. He did not choke, however, but clucked on and on about the Congo, as though he were going to hatch it. We are a people so obsessed with world affairs that we cannot get the unfortunate Congo out of our heads even on the afternoon of New Year's Day, after we have loosened our belts. "The conspiracy recently discovered in Leopoldville is attributed to Moise Chombe and his sympathizers," said the reporter, knowing neither Tariba nor I could imagine surviving without the latest news from the heart of Africa. Then he added at breakneck speed: "It is interesting that Chombe has not even denied the accusation of his involvement in the attempted coup!" Congratulations, then! Since he took part, it would at least be in order for him to deny it! Why had that Chombe not made use of lies, for God's sake, when even we consider it so normal, when we expect it of him and take deceit so naturally as a fashion and diplomatic custom!

"Who is the dishonest one here?" I asked Tariba, handing him the remains of my apple.

"Heaven forbid!" he defended himself, "it's been paid for!"

"Who is the dishonest one?" I asked, pointing to the husky radio waves.

"Aha," said Tariba, perplexed.

"No one and everyone!" I cried, like Cicero. "That's the fashion! It's not that jabbering wanker's fault, he's just a foreign stooge. Now they all lie unconsciously, they lie sincerely and honestly, because the last trace of truth has seeped out of their blood imperceptibly over the years."

He switched off the radio with a sudden movement, and, nodding his head, began to agree.

"Oh, yes, they are robbers, these workshops, they are!"

He was probably afraid that I was now going to chew up that expensive box which attracted and amused his customers and drowned out their curses and quarrels.

A second New Year peregrinus blew in from outside and landed with his right side against the bar facing me, he took off his French cap and his greeting wafted from him:

"Comrade Professor, allow me: Franjo Daska, known as Deciliter."

I nodded vaguely, because I was just heading for the door when this fellow's invasion startled me.

"Deciliter of what?" I asked automatically.

"I have a proposal," said Deciliter quickly, "four decis of white. It's New Year!"

I fished some coins out of my pocket and put them in front of Tariba.

"You've got enough for two decis," said Tariba to Deciliter, pouring the wine.

"I respect the will of the two-thirds majority," he assented, "but don't say my standard of living has risen as a result. I've done nothing but drink fractions today! Happy New and Holythree! Happy holidays! Just let me tell the professor something. Professor, come back!"

I didn't go back, but I did stop by the door, because I do not know how to drag myself away from that corpse up there, let alone from a pie-eyed passer-by, and he came over to me with his glass in his hand, caught hold of me by the broken button on my chest, feeling it and examining it as though he were just about to take a little bite of it, and began in a half-whisper, so that Tariba should not hear, with almost paternal warmth, to wheeze confidentially right by my ear, as though at confessional:

"For this glass I shall repay your charity with a short lesson, my dear Professor. I don't say I'II teach you. You are the first teacher I've seen since I left Oxford in nineteenthirteen. I have a deciliter of first-class brain, and it serves me well. What do you think I tell everyone? I tell them: no problem! I'm a man who always says: no problem! 'We'll punish you!' they say. Go ahead, please do! 'You mustn't do this, you mustn't do that, you can't have one thing, you'll have to make do with another!' they say. That's right, I say, that's how it will be and that's how it must be, I say! I only say: no problem! And that puts everyone off all infamous deeds against poor Daska." He grimaced as he philosophized and tilted his glass in short, sharp jerks. "I disarm them! 'we'll kill you!' they say. Why not! I ask in surprise, there's nothing simpler, dear sirs, comrades, what are you waiting for, go on, kill me! Hahaha, that's what 'no problem' means!" And then, catching me right at the door, he whispered conspiratorially, showing me his tightly clenched fist: — "My confidence discourages them! Please go ahead, go ahead, gentlemen!" he ended, shouting after me, and in that narrow road, he rumbled as though from a barrel, as he turned back into the bar: "God blast you, every piece of advice is worth something! And philosophical advice at least four decis!"

I rode up the steep street towards the little square like a rider on the waves, I streaked across the square and, as I emerged from the corner I caught sight of the little temptation of St. Andrew going into Madonna's garden. I leapt after her before she had banged the gate shut and pounced on her just as she set off across the garden towards the house. She looked over her shoulder, then turned right round in her sack and even went a little further along the path backwards. I bolted the garden gate behind me and, obsessed with my evil intentions, started to walk towards the girl. She had stopped, holding her left fist in her right hand on her belly, as though it were an Indian sign. She stood like Disney's little fortress, barricading herself with invincibility and moats. When I caught up with her, she turned towards the terrace and walked on, with bowed head. I put my arm round her waist and walked beside her. She wriggled out of my hold and moved ahead. I led her into the old, former kitchen, some distance from Madonna's room. As we went down the passage, I heard Madonna sighing:

"He isn't here, *davvero!*"

"Why did you come?"

She bowed her head, because there was a little warm space between my chest and her nose. I pressed my palms against her temples and forced her head up, and for a moment she had Japanese eyes; the crown of her plait unwound as though it were alive, and as though it really were alive it escaped somehow to the left and right over my hands.

"Why did you come?" I shoved my face right into the little Geisha's eyes.

Now she only lowered her gaze, for she could not move her head, and her eyes became even narrower and at the corners the lids moved away from the eye-ball and it seemed as though she were crying, hating me.

"Why did you come?" I asked, almost cruelly by now, but her scrawny body struggled in the wide black sack under the pressure of my belly and, leaning against the wall, it rubbed against the pincers of my thighs. My hands slid down her head to the back of her neck, and as I asked her again and again why she had come, she raised both her shoulders, her head bowed, as though she were trying to pull it in, to protect herself from the tickling touch of my hands, and I couldn't tell whether those hunched shoulders were an answer to my question or just a defense against the tickling.

She put her hands on my chest as though she were going to push me violently away, but she did not push me, I felt just a light pressure, and it was a symbolic gesture of self-defense, not a real attempt: but I moved a little away, made an ugly knot of her hair at the nape of her neck and then moved right away from her, sat down on the old straw couch where the pile of clean laundry she had brought on Christmas Eve still lay. I moved the clothes so that the pile collapsed, and gestured to her to sit down beside me. At first she stood where she was, looping a crown of hair round her head, and then shyly, turning her back to me, moved past my legs and sat down on the couch, as far away as possible from me. She piled up the washing and placed it between us, so that I could now lean my elbows on it and ask:

"Why did you come, paraffin Lucia?"

Now without any other reason she shrugged her shoulders and looked at me like a fawn. So that was the answer to my question. But she also managed to gasp:

"Wwwhyyy?"

"Oho! I was beginning to think they had slit your vocal chords! What do you mean 'why'?"

"Why are you asking?"

"And you're not asking why Lucia and why paraffin? What's your name?"

"Lucia."

"Get away with you!"

"Mmm," she affirmed.

"What a curious world we live in!" I said travelogue-style. "And you're really called ... really, Lucia?"

"They'd change my name if I took the veil. Perhaps to Anassstazia."

"What's all this 'they would', 'if'?"

She smiled a little slyly in her innocence:

"Oh, you never know … perhaps I'm not sssufficiently worthy."

"And it's really Lucia!" I said.

"Yes," said the girl, "Lucia, Lucia."

"You'll never be a nun!"

"Whynot?"

"Why is it you've come to me?"

She shrugged her shoulders and bowed her head again. But now as though she were going to cry properly.

"You little silly." I said, "couldn't you have said you came to wish me a Happy New Year!"

"One mustn't tell … lies. No I didn't …"

"You didn't … you mustn't, my dear, you mustn't!"

The girl was watching me like a Lamb of God. I pushed away the pile of clothes blocking my way, some things fell behind the couch, onto the floor, and she leaned across to pick them up as quickly as she could, but I pressed her down with my hand onto that hard and prickly straw stubble; it seemed that I had covered her completely with my hand like a baby animal. She was lying on her side when I pressed her down with my hand, and all I had to do was straighten my elbow to turn her onto her back, and from down there she looked at me as one presumably looks at an avalanche thundering towards one, which cannot be avoided, no matter what one does. My hand slid from her shoulders when I turned her over, into the middle of her chest, between two indisputable little breasts, which did after all therefore exist, and which could both be touched with the edge of my palm, without my moving my hand. My hand covered her from her throat almost to her belly and it was enough for me to spread my fingers, to press beneath my thumb and little finger both the small, firm, trembling spheres, whose excited tips could not be felt through the coarse material of her vestment, but which slipped animatedly away from the pressure of my fingers, as though they were filled with liquid rubber. I lowered my elbow onto the barely perceptible bony little mound, and so I had the whole of her under my arm, from her Adam's apple to her mound of Venus, comically small and flat. I leaned over her like that and watched as the panic in the face of the avalanche vanished from her eyes, but little shudders of fear at the future weight of my body multiplied. I told her I knew quite well why she had not wished me a Happy New Year, I knew perfectly well.

"Why, then?" she asked in alarm, smiling politely in her fear, to soften my brutality, which I'm sure did not exist.

"Because I might just have said, and the same to you, child! And thanked you. And nothing else. And because you think I'm such a crazy old fool who wouldn't even give you a New Year kiss, don't you?" She gazed up somewhere towards my forehead, surprised and still frightened, and just smiled shyly with her honey-colored irises. "That's right," I said finally, after I had thought for a minute. "I wouldn't have kissed you. Of course I wouldn't." She laughed under her breath. My hand hurried to catch at least one breast, for they had both begun to slip away in opposite directions, with her laughter. This one was pointed now, even under the coarse hair shirt of the convent cape. She laughed gutturally and juicily and almost entirely femininely. For that I kissed her firmly on the mouth, which almost made her faint. She was lying on my left arm and I felt in my embrace a whole, real Lucia, paralyzed by the force of the kiss she had drunk in. Only her legs which had been hanging limply from the bed slowly lifted from the ground, first one, then the other, wanting to cross over one another to protect the antechamber of her virginity; but that spontaneous and unconscious move ment of her legs under the heavy skirt did not achieve its aim, although there was nothing in her way, but it turned into pure play, the rhythm and sound of the rubbing, as though her powerless leg could not summon the strength to raise itself to its neighboring knee and cross over it. With the dexterity of a magician, I succeeded in removing from her shoulders both the cape and the habit, pulling her and peeling her upper body out of that horny hemp or broom, bringing her out, tiny, but drowned in a long flaxen shirt, warm, but inaccessible and unassailable, without an opening, without a slit and without buttons. I dived into her panting kiss, fresh, watery, and even cool, I straddled her and with my knee succeeded in pulling off the bed the remains of her wretched emery-cloth habit, I searched with my hand for the lower edge of the shirt, which had no end or edge, and, unable to reach it, I began tugging and pulling at it as though I were gathering up a sail, heaving it away from gusts of wind. First a warm breath rose up under my hand from the nest of her lap, and then I raised her shirt high up so that she fell completely out of it, with only her arms and head still in it. I pulled from her skin the last white tight bandages and quickly transferred the kiss that had been snatched from me by the raised shirt to the base of her ribs, then towards her armpit, and into the spiral round the dark, rough and hard nipple, pointing upwards like the mouthpiece of a narghile, then moving from one to the other and nibbling in the space between my incisors and canines the rubbery, spongy little mulberries, first the left then the right, bouncing elastically from their base, as they bobbed and swelled and trembled under my urgent kisses, which sucked in sometimes the whole roundness of the tip of the little breasts and then rushed tenderly like drops of warm oil down to her navel, hopping round it over the quivering skin towards the greyish freckles of her lower belly, where my hand, already a bit wrinkled, gently parted her boyish thighs seeking the moist lips never as yet swollen by a strange touch. My unhappy Lucia was almost suffocating under the skirt of her own shirt, her breaths became longer and she was burning with heat-stroke when I uncovered her, but she swiftly and hurriedly pulled at least the edge of her shirt over her face again, so as not to see how virgins were sundered and how her nakedness was reflected white in the broad daylight and in my eyes. She lay before me naked, lumpy and white as the host, whole and all the more complete like this, without a head, with her arms spread out in panic emerging from the crumpled linen.

My eyes which for days had seen only decay, waxy yellow and ragged little curtains of skin on a female corpse, now filled with tiny red stars at the radiance of this child's nakedness, and I raised myself, rapidly freeing my most vital instrument from its slit, and the swollen, violent corpus leapt out, waving briefly in the open space, hurrying its tense conical little head towards that small gate of heavy velvet which stood, only partially hidden, high above the very edge of the sharp straw couch, waiting for the resonant and painful door-knocker of defloration. But, rushing like this to meet the membrane over the unplumbed depths, seeking in a spasm of impatience its little anastasia, the stiffened drill suddenly sagged, drooped, extinguished, to the ground, reaching the entrance with only the arch of its ridge instead of the tip, and stopping there completely unpenetrating, resigned and blunt. It was not anastasia that embraced it, it was overcome by a sudden anaesthesia, and all that could follow from that defeat of the body was a ringing in the ears, a shudder, a twitch, a nervous, painful and uncontrolled flow from the limp semen ducts, shame and disgust, and it is not worthy of mention.

Little Lucia slipped away from beneath the all-destroying avalanche — a mere virgin. I accompanied her half-way along the passage and there drank a whole ladle-full of water, and, when I wanted to follow her, she had already run across the garden and managed to unbolt the gate. So I was left standing by the bucket in which there was scarcely any water left, not enough for supper, so I took just the porcelain jug and set off to Hermione. My balls smarted as I walked from the sharp straw of that shameful couch in the kitchen, and, although that circumstance would have been adequate justification before the entire male race for my cowardly collapse within reach of what was certainly forever the last hymen in my non-existent little career, that unpleasant pain from the sudden straw knife could not calm me or restore my balance, not even with the help of Franjo Daska's philosophical lessons which I tried to inject under my skin as a sedative. I am sure I could have overcome that underhand stab, insensitive to all other stimuli on my honorable pioneer path of penetration, had it not been for those dreadful damned great shoes of hers! The real reason for my unexpected powerlessness was in fact those repulsive clogs I had caught sight of at the moment when I was most prepared, and which I could see now grinding and crushing and pounding the sandy garden path, and which I would go on seeing obsessively all these last few mangy years that I would continue to think about anastasias and lucination. Rearing up like a white stallion above the edge of the maiden's bower, I had caught sight beneath me of those little legs which were still ritually playing a magic love game, disappearing into the vast black boots as though they were descending into Hell. It seemed to me that those two yellow pipes, burdened like this with leaden diver's boots, were suddenly as thin, dry and weak as the withered legs of someone paralyzed, and my rearing had not ended between the dewy thighs of the filly, but on sharp and inhospitable stubble that had been woven by a blind man's hands. The fortunate hands of the blind, which do not know what sparks and lightning conductors are, but which seek a way through directly and independently, move barriers aside and reach their destination steadfastly. Which complete whatever they begin to knit. And for whom such problems as these do not exist. No problem! I do not imagine the girl will announce to her nuns: don't go near that man, sisters, he's a lecher! I had not even tried to explain to her, as the foreign commentator would say. I had not even tried to deny it. And how could I! I could not prove to her that Chombe was not always to blame for everything! I should have had to say that it was her sweet little moccasins with buttons like St. Gulliver's . . .

Reaching Hermione's well, splaying my legs like someone with a hernia, befuddled, muzzy, trembling with spasmodic shudders, I banged the porcelain pitcher like a pumpkin against the stone, and the well sobbed and howled in its depths but the jug rebounded and stayed whole, hanging from my thumb.

"Hey, come on, my sweet virginal neighbor, fill my jug!"

"Ah, here he is, is he! He's alive, *perbaco!* He hasn't died of thirst!"

"Only mind it doesn't overflow, I beg you! Why shouldn't I be alive! My cup of gall is overflowing, but why shouldn't I be! I wouldn't be able to watch it . . . overflow!"

"And I tho thothought you were none of you alive, not you, nor . . ."

"Wrongly."

"Yes, wrongly, yes! But Idru idrummed onthe gate, and why did I drum on it?"

"Because you're a dummy!"

"Because you had bolted the gate, that's why I was drumming?"

"Bolted...? Who could have bolted...?"

"Uhuh, with the bolt, mmm! Which you never do, nor Cara, nor anyone! Ever!"

"Ah, yes, yes, of course! Why, it's New Year ... for heaven's sake! I wanted to have a bit of a sleep."

"Who with?" asked Hermione scornfully, with an expression of disgust and blinking both eyes nervously. "The little girl fromthe nuns, eh? *Porco!* Under-age as well! *Ma propio mi fa schifo, sa'!* I avoid every opp opportunity and occasion and with good reason, I now see. NowIsee. Because an honest girl can always sniff out *il puzzo, il* stench of a wolf! *Vergognoso, vergogna,* you!"

It was interesting, I did not even try to deny my participation in the act of overthrow, I only began in a muffled voice to gabble and bleat and waffle about anything at all that had nothing to do, not the slightest accidental connection, with Hermione's discovery. That was why, when she had filled my jug, she went a long way away from me, calling from her room:

"Go and sleep, you're talking like a wound-up radio, and I don' tun don' t understand you at all!"

CHAPTER 12

And so the wax in my museum of wax lucies is being threatened by rats. Rats are gnawing at my dreams. The one remaining pure and fragrant thing in this antechamber of hell has begun to tarnish and grow moldy under the soles of worn-out gullivers out of which the rats of doubt leap. There is not much in this world to rival a stylish bikini. Perhaps one could find two or three other things, why deceive ourselves! Or, all right, five or six, maybe. No more. Or, to hell with it, maybe there are a million of them after all! But here, in this lair, in this life of mine, there is just one single unchangeable thing of beauty: my dreams about the golden skin, glittering with grains of sand, of summer girls. Sad, barren, hopeless dreams. I could solemnly swear that they are not merely physical. They are, rather, pure spiritual therapy, the determinant of my shaky stability, a dish into which I spit out my disgust with Madonna and with all those millions of joys that have belonged to others. And now that too has been eroded by doubts, I do not even know what kind of doubts or how exactly, but I feel the teeth of the rodents sinking into my lucies, digging out of them sharp-edged caverns and revealing their hollow structure, their wax bones and wax insides, and just enough stuffing for there not to be room for a soul. I do not mean to say, damn it all, that I am particularly concerned about the soul at this moment, but when a man can no longer have faith in his own stuffing, he must come to mention the soul — as the last consideration. My lucies, I say, have been left without souls, and what I mean is they suddenly acquired huge soles, and my forty year-old — let's say — enthusiasm flagged shamefully; the flame of youthfulness had been snuffed out in its autumn. And the huge black shoes had swollen immensely, in their real image, or perhaps only in their significance, like cockroaches with smooth crackling black backs, as big as beached boats with greasy seaweed on their hulls. And one could not help being afraid they would burst from that tempestuous erection, from that internal blood pressure, and spray everything around them with their stinking, yellow, putrid insides, and that would be an autumn shower that would cool me forever. There, that was where winter excursions led, excursions into a reality that was a substitute for dreams, an idiotic winter leap onto an unpunctured, grey, scrawny Lucia!

And then that mad Doctor came as well and asked:

"What is eternal? Apart from God, apart from Hell, apart from those and other such stupidities? What is eternal, I ask you?"

"Oh, how should I know! A shoe-horn is eternal, for example."

"Ridiculous!" said the Doctor. "No, my dear man! No, no, my dear man!"

"And foolishness," I said humbly, "the afore-mentioned stupidities plus foolishness."

"Yes," he said, suddenly disconcerted, "that's true, but actually it's something else."

I replied that I was not saying it wasn't, I hadn't said that, but I was already a little unnerved myself by his unusual behavior. He had burst in to start with like a gunman into a bar full of cowards, but now he had frozen and was hanging about, forgetting what had brought him. And perhaps no one in the world would learn from his lips what it was that was eternal. He covered his mouth with his hand and began to heave as though he were going to vomit:

"Have you any bicarbonate? Let me have some. Damned heartburn!"

He swallowed two whole spoonfuls of the white powder and a glass of water and started belching fire out of his nose and mouth as though he had dropped out of a Russian fairy-story. The he calmed down and went mad again:

"What are you up to with that Signorina Hermione? Where does she come into it? Why have you involved her in our conversations, I don't understand, why and how?"

Aha, I knew that he, an educated man, would make me atone for Hermione's lecture.

"I didn't, I didn't. She just, of her own accord . . ."

"Bringing her into those conversations of ours, my God, a feeble-minded creature. Yes, feeble-minded. Isn't she, you tell me?"

"I'm not getting involved," I said.

"No, of course!" the Doctor squeaked shrilly, "of course not. You're not getting involved."

I watched him struggling with the last little bubbles of gas that were bobbing up from his stomach into his nostrils and, catching him in a pause between two convulsions, I said almost maliciously:

"I don't consider that our conversations were all that learned or intellectual! So so. Average."

"Yes, yes, yes, yes! You're not getting involved, you don't consider! And she, why is she involved? It's got nothing to do with learning! Nothing. It's something else entirely. You know quite well they were delicate and confidential conversations about methods and means of treatment and so on, requiring discretion, it's foolish even to explain!"

"It's never foolish to explain … but they weren't any kind of secret either!"

"What?" the Doctor gave a start.

"I'm saying: I've got nothing to hide. Not from anyone."

"But tell me, please, I want to know what you had in mind?"

"Nothing. I had no idea she would take any action."

"You probably thought I was going to blackmail you, come now, please! The state I found the old … Signorina in, all right … I said at once: that's your business. And there's no point now, for God's sake…! In other words, now you need a feeble-minded creature to intervene to protect you from my blackmail, is that it! Oh come on, please! That's absurd!"

"Listen, Doctor!"

"I know what you're going to say!"

"What am I going to say?"

"Oh, what do I know! How she, by herself, presumably, took it all on of her own accord, as a witness, and so on. But that's hard to believe. And of course, it's impossible to expect of a feeble-minded … obviously!"

"You're attaching too much importance to our incidental conversation, Doctor. There were no deals of any kind between us, no serious discussions, no special relationship, I don't know what you're talking about. I don't know why I need witnesses, and what's this fear of blackmail you mention. Just how would you…?"

"Well done! In short?"

"In short, you needed those old receptacles…."

"… whose worth you well know!"

"… those old receptacles from the attic; and I, a bit more care — for Madonna."

"What!"

"Real care! Help for me, in fact."

"Real care?! All right. You want me to tend her back…?"

"No, no … but we didn't manage to come to any concrete agreement. You broke through the ceiling … and so on. That's why it's best to annul the whole thing. I'll nail the door up again, and as for care, I'll rely on the first-aid book and my own hands."

Neither of us spoke. It was infernally awkward and uncomfortable. He offered me a cigarette, as though we had concluded our business.

"You know I don't smoke, thank you!"

"I don't know anything, why, how could I know? I know nothing. I don't even know my own name!" Then he drew several times on his cigarette and blew the smoke out, sighing, and then said in a tone of bitter resignation: "Well, all right. We made a bit of a balls-up somewhere. Then we hiccupped in our sleep and woke up. And … so you don't smoke, well! Stupid. Really." And he looked at my yellow fingers, hiccupping properly and waking from his stupid dream into stupid reality.

I had been wide awake for some time. I had woken up as soon as I saw him in the doorway today, looking so sullen. I had understood: if there were any adverse outcome from my imbecile assault on Madonna of the previous day, he would be able to declare himself responsible and claim a reward. Or he could simply testify that Madonna had been suffocated with a pillow and ask me, what did I think, should it be put in the report, or we could somehow come to one another's assistance without other formalities.

The stupidest thing was that the Doctor really had begun to hiccup, poor fellow. It sounded as though he were speaking through his stomach: "Hic … hic …" In the silence that had descended, that "hic" could have been a sign of the correct time or a signal from "Lunik," anything rather than the stupid "hic" that had woken the Doctor from his dreaming and dropped him into an ocean of storms.

I was a little horrified at myself. Such calculated tactics! I was used to waking up always last, always too late, when I had already had a good thrashing, and only then hiccupping so that my stomach turned and bile dripped from my nose. Now the victim was this Doctor. But I knew there was no place for self-accusation. It was time to learn something. At forty plus one ought to know everything there was to be learned. The lessons had been plentiful and wearying and thorough, I had finally now to beat them into my head. I pressed my own deserving right hand, quelled, I confess, my compassion, and said under my breath:

"You should not have been so insistent. You really should have known I wasn't going to get involved in … a crime!"

"Sash!" hissed the Doctor agitatedly. "Don't be absurd, for Christ's sake!" and started sucking fiercely on his cigarette.

"Anyway, I'm always prepared to make you a gift of some of those pots and pans."

"Thank you, no, no," he said hastily, but agreeably. "I don't want anything to be found on me. You think you've got me where you want me as it is! But I don't see how or in what concrete … hic … I confess, unless anyone was eavesdropping…."

"Oh, Doctor!"

"No, no, none of your oooh and Doctor, I'm not dreaming any more but analyzing facts. Today there are tape-recorders and all kinds of machines and everyone all over the place listens in to everything. An old medic is no longer surprised at anything. Except himself sometimes. Sitz!"

"You don't say 'sitz' but 'sic,' if you want to make a joke of it."

"Mock me, by all means. Go ahead. I've deserved it. But I didn't say anything, I hiccupped. I wasn't quoting Balzac."

"So?"

"If you are intending to blackmail me, you me, that is, and not I you, tell me first how, in what way and with what kind of proof?" the Doctor began to raise his voice, in exasperation. "I'm not remotely interested in what you are asking from me in return, because there's very little I could do or give you, I'm a provincial charlatan and I don't have the pay of some political charlatans round here. I don't have my own clinic. I don't have a wife or children. I don't have a savings account. I don't have connections 'up there.' I don't have any dollars. I'm not afraid ... of losing any of that. I don't even have a reputation you could ruin. So, tell me, how, how, what could you accuse me of? A crime! Come now! Are you going to accuse me of wanting to steal silver, perhaps? Are you perhaps going to call in detectives to discover my fingerprints on the chalices? You haven't even offered me a chair yet!"

He never sat down in this house, but now he must have decided to wait until things were cleared up, for he had not come because of Madonna, but because of me. He sat down as though he were settling, innocent and righteous, into the dock, but nothing happened or was cleared up, we only went on outwitting each other over the same idiocies as though we were at a trial which we could not extricate ourselves from because some uninvited defense counsels had got carried away in formulating our innocence, immunity and puerilities. It was strange that the Doctor was sitting; he was like a postman, a chimneysweep, a bill-collector; it was strange that he was sitting down on a "home visit." And he had sat down in the wrong place, he had sat down on my chair, and you could see that he did not know the ways of our house, he was not capable of judging which seat would be the most suitable for a stranger, one who had invited himself into the bargain. He did not understand what he should have been able to work out in an eskimo igloo by intuition. He was clearly quite incapable of understanding the way we organize things here, or the coordinates of the interiors of our houses. But nevertheless, on my chair, he suddenly looked like the host.

"You're a South Slav too, aren't you?" I asked him, unable to bear his absolute lack of any feeling whatever for our space.

He looked at me in surprise, but he did not reply. He thought I was getting up a new running start for an attack from an unpredictable direction in our pointless struggle and debate. So I had to answer, myself:

"Yes, a South Slav, and what of it? That's what you would say. Perhaps I would say: so what, then? Nothing! There. But that nothing is important. Really . . . nothing."

"What exactly are you driving at, if I may ask?" the sleepy peasant from the plains suddenly asked, with the authority of his doctor's diploma.

"You may ask, but don't say I'm 'driving at' anything," I said, "it sounds fratricidal! I only wanted to stress the rich variety that links us. The South Slavs are connected by their variety, because they aren't 'northern bears', for God's sake, they're South Slavs! Northern bears are connected, apart from their fur, by common habits, instincts and everything else of a bear-like nature, monotonously and northernly. While we, apart from our fur, are connected by our differences and disharmony. And I tell you, if we lived in the same meadow as someone who was still more different from us, we would be even bloodier brothers, richest in our contradictions. For we're not brutes, doctor!"

"You're talking utter gibberish, and I've no idea what you mean."

"Answer me one innocent question."

"No. No. I'm not going to answer any of your damn questions, and that's that!"

"I'm asking you as a brother in southern blood."

"And don't start politicizing, I beg you! I'm allergic to it, allergic to southern and blood brothers, because I've been a cosmopolitan and all that, from every point of view, since my student days, I've roamed about and lived all over the place, and got on well everywhere, wherever I found a crust, there was my homeland!"

"But that's exactly what I wanted to ask you!" I exclaimed, encouraged. "Just that. To tell me how you found your way around in this atmosphere, in your new domicile, this coastal, island, and ... what can we do, this Romanized atmosphere? This isn't Cosmopolis, after all, but our cradle!"

"All right. Why? Fine! Of course."

There we are! Ah, I had immediately felt cramped as soon as I sneaked into that mystical historical preserve, protected by the hedge of the constitution, but I managed to restrain myself now that I realized my Doctor did not belong so much to a different nation, as to a different world, a different spiritual system, a different intellectual level, God forgive me, where a person's emotional intelligence is enclosed within the impenetrable, thorny hedge of the universal and the cosmopolitan. And it was far more difficult to squeeze through that hedge than people generally believed, because it enclosed a world that was so big and organized and well-protected, that it would be more correct to say you had to squeeze into that world out of a smaller, besieged one, itself vigilantly supervised from outside.

I laughed in the Doctor's face. I laughed and waved my hand.

"Oh, I know what you mean," he said, "wherever your homeland is, let your crust be there!"

"Why no," I said, "what do I care where anyone eats! But I wouldn't want to feel foolish here in my own house, as though I were in the wrong place. You're sitting in my chair, how can you not see that! That's where I cut my 'crust'!"

"What do you mean 'yours'? Does it matter? It's all yours!"

"No it's not, it's not. But stay there! Stay as long as you're here! All the chairs here are actually ours and we can spread ourselves about as much as we like! The house has been nationalized ... no, sorry! Taken over by the state, internationalized! I just find it comical that you feel so perfectly at home, that you really don't care, that you breathe in a cosmopolitan way even in my chair, under this patriarchal roof in the shadow of St. Mark...."

"It's not Mark, surely, but Andrew."

"Yes, St. Markandrew."

I said I managed to control myself. And I did, and I was all ready to have a joke with the doctor, seeing that we could only call to each other through the hedge, and there was no room for nuances or bantering. But he wasn't in the mood for jokes. He had actually grasped the fact that I was not cynical, but rather inclined to something like mockery and bitterness, and that he was under no threat from either blackmail or any kind of accusation, but he probably could not forget that he had nevertheless lost the copper and silver-ware, and he was preparing to leave this house with a sigh. He set off as always, like a man to whom everyone gives way, he stood in the doorway, his back turned towards the house, patted his pockets and sighed. Then he stepped out into the courtyard, and, with his back to me like that, he said:

"There's no prospect, no. No. There's no prospect whatever."

I followed him to the door, smiling enquiringly. I crossed my arms on my chest and smiled enquiringly again. I thought he was talking about the pots and I cast a still smiling glance at the door behind me in the passage, for no real reason. Catching myself in that indelicate movement, I stopped smiling because it would have been offensive. I stood in the doorway, one step above him, but still lower than him, and so, my arms crossed high on my chest, I looked with a forced frown up through the top of the fig tree, as though to suggest that there were some loud sparrows up there, arguing so strenuously that I could not make out whether the Doctor would have wanted to say something else as he left or not. But at that moment he spoke loudly and unequivocally and as though there were suddenly no sparrows any more. I heard only his voice, suddenly colorless and firm, as though dictating the water level of a river:

"There's no prospect of my curing her." He tapped his pockets helplessly and took a step or two. Surprised at his painful sympathy, almost consoling him, I started to present the thing as hopeless by its very nature, but as he left he turned to me with loathing and spat out through dry lips: "so as to get my revenge!"

I was as sorry as hell that, at the moment when he looked at me like that, I had not been smiling enquiringly and sardonically as before. But there was nothing for it by then. The whole thing only lasted an instant, and he went away through the garden, stretching aero-dynamically, inaccessible to voice or stone. A rapid hic-hic from the universe still echoed in my head. And one of my ears rang. The ear that means good news.

Yes, only three more days without Cara! She would already be talking to everyone up there about her return, and perhaps she was worried about us and would set off earlier. Perhaps she no longer knew what to do with her freedom, and wanted to return as soon as possible, and that was why my right ear was ringing three days early. But, before anything at all changed, I was afraid I would have to settle things with Madonna. I would have to deny the lies and restore our former relations. Stand in front of her and say: Nothing has been decided. Nothing ever will be decided. Nothing can be decided, Madonna. Let's stop dreaming and just die slowly with no illusions, as is fitting. I spent half my life fighting to see that you and your case should never be resolved, as though that were the most important thing in the world. And I'm presumably not now going to spend the last little half struggling to have it resolved! When not even that is important now. Ask Cara! She fought as well. But, you should know, she showed me sympathy when I was on the point of death. Because she is honorable ... and women are adaptable. They marry generals and become generals' wives; kings — and they are queens. A queen's husband isn't a king, at most he shouldn't sing anti-royalist ditties. But she married me, and now she is a pensioner, a nursemaid ... almost an invalid, like me, not only because of me, but instead of me. If I were a king ... oh, I would decide everything in your favor with a wink of my eye, because it's just as meaningless as fighting you. But that really would be your death sentence, because then Cara would be a queen, and not a nurse. Who would keep you alive? Up to now she has done, she and the hope that everything would be resolved. Things were good for you until now. It's good for you that things are as they are with Cara and me, isn't it? You've been living a borrowed life on the rubbish heap of the revolution, and have even been constantly hoping that it would bloom for you. Well, it won't, my dear lady! It blooms with carnations for others, for those who made it. And a decent gravestone would suit you far better than any aspiration to blooming. Just you be content even without carnations!

"And, please, forget that little joke, do! It was a little joke! Just a little joke!" I fawned the next day to Madonna. "Or have you forgotten: Peace to men of good will!"

"Imbecile! I won't put up with the insults of your little jokes or *scherzi,* and it hurts and offends me every time you think I believe you!"

That's what she said, the old devil! Anyone near her would sometimes question his own sanity.

"But after all, it's best this way, what would you do with all that land anyway?"

"I'd shit on it. That's what. You villain — *vigliacco!"*

"I know ... heinous, villainous!"

"That's right, monstrous!"

"Tutto in rima?"

"O in rima, o no in rime, sei vigliacco come prima! He he he, disse Dante a Garibaldi quando scopri l'America ..."

She was touched that I had asked for forgiveness, and all I needed was for her to forget my attempts at assault, my useless lies and pantomime.

It must be that Tunina had meant something different, not so literal. The joy would kill her. But perhaps it did not bring her any joy at all? Perhaps she has just been performing her hypocritical pantomime over the whole affair, because she is of Jesuit extraction? Her part in the historical game, because of her forefathers, as the last offshoot of a lineage who did not want to die out humiliated by herdsmen, who wanted her estate to survive her, that the land should carry her name when no living being did. Perhaps she was only half-consciously carrying her tragic baton to the end, and was in fact delighted that she had not given birth to disinherited sons, and that no one could take anything from them, since they did not exist. Or had the century-old line perhaps long ago decided to come to an end at the threshold of this age, aware that with them something would disappear which is needed by every age and which is indispensable to the world. Perhaps the last generations had felt the joy of vengeful extinction and anticipated the division of the estate far more consciously than the landless Tunina and his kind. Perhaps Tunina is primitive. And perhaps those of his kind who would be devoured by worms and fierce fire if their land were taken from them, and I, and those like me who shed our blood for this land, perhaps we are all fools. The Markantonis deceived us, for they held on to it tightly although it did not mean anything to them. They only needed it so that they would not have to dig. As we need our blood, but we still shed it, as though it were insignificant, for this land that we have to dig in any case. Perhaps it is we who are primitive even compared to the instinctive wit of this Madonna. Perhaps we create our destiny out of our own needs, and they, in their destiny, have nothing in common with us or with our modest needs. Perhaps we do not understand their destiny. We have atrophied in a century-long drought, and what was for them a need is for us happiness, what for them was rain is for us a blessing, what was just earth to them is our destiny. They cannot rejoice in the way Tunina and I imagine, and for them there is no joy that could kill them. We are killed by good and by evil. By happiness and by pain. We are killed by laws and by lawlessness. We are killed by life and struck down by death. We die for freedom and are killed by captivity, we are killed by love and by hate. We are killed by everything. By enslaved labor for the Markantonis, and by liberated labor on our own land. But they kill themselves, as they want. They write a book, ten books, they write what they want, how they want and then they walk calmly away, into the cells of the Inquisition, from where there is no return. They manage to write down, exactly, all that they think, in as many books as they want. And then they suddenly go off in the direction they have decided on, so we have to dig them out of their graves later, to get our revenge. Or, if they have nothing to write, like our Madonna here, then at least they refuse to die, out of spite, even when socialism excommunicates them and their own body betrays them. Neither life nor death is their destiny; they take them or leave them according to their personal perceptions and in tune with the genealogical plan. We do not understand their destiny. What is it, what does it consist of? Perhaps it is that gift of decision. Perhaps their quick wits. It is somewhere beyond us in any case. Their destinies cannot merge as ours do, for we date from yesterday and are therefore consistent, identical, stereotyped, as though mass-produced. Each one of them is an excess, but at their end — even three and a half centuries later — the same accusation is always heard, only read in a different voice: ... *We condemn the memory of Madonna Markantoni to eternal shame; we deprive her of all honors, functions and benefices: we confiscate all her possessions and goods to the benefit of the Holy Office; we cast out her memory ... and give it all into the hands of Monsignor the Roman Governor or his representative here present, to handle and dispose of it according to the laws....* Once in dark Gregorian bass voices in unison, now in brighter coloraturas — all to the benefit of the Holy Office, all into the hands of monsignor the representative. Eternal shame lasts as long as a shoehorn, the law changes its cap, but property is divided, and again provokes worms and fierce fire. And arouses appetites even for a repulsive urn. They leave ash in the wind, or a contorted skeleton, but also a voice which is heard among the wise, while we travel on into history, weighed down by always the same destructive termites' hunger, in the name of which we read over and over again the same monotonous condemnation through the centuries, like grace before food.

CHAPTER 13

For the next two days I abandoned Madonna and went down to the sea at the time when the boat came in. There was no need, because the last thing Cara expected was for me to meet her: she thought I had to be at Madonna's side. And she never traveled with a lot of luggage because she didn't want to show the world that we were just poor folk, who dragged old mattresses, ocean bales, or bundles of pillows round ports. She never let me know when she was coming, and anyone interested could take that as a sign that we loved each other properly, with none of the public slobbering and arm-waving by the gangways of ships that problematic marriages need. There was no need for me to go, because it wasn't even night as it had been when she left, not that anyone chases other women here even on the darkest nights, and the only hunting that does occur on moonless nights is in fact done by lantern light, with harpoons near the shore, or nets on the open sea. It's true that on summer nights all the dark nooks and crannies heave with excited breathing but those are foreigners with their own women, and we locals raise our faces to the stars, sipping a little of the fresher air from up there, although all the air here is equally healthy (but there you are, it's a universal habit), and we stroll off doing our best not to look round. That is the delicacy and courtesy we offer in addition to all our other services. In the tourist season and post-season, and particularly in the pre-season, in the spring. Now, in winter, a woman must be accompanied at night because of cats and similar surprises, although you don't meet so many mice now as in the summer, or those lone frogs, crouching for no reason, motionless as a yogi, on the concrete or paving stones, and leaping up as though prodded precisely at the moment when my wife tries to pass. That was a curious phenomenon, which could not be avoided. Now one had to watch out mostly for cats, particularly the more sluggish ones, those that do not come running up from a distance, those few spoilt kitchen cats which air their kitchen fur by night and lie in the dark like little heaps of rags, not stirring until a passer-by comes within reach, and then they start to stretch and pour themselves out like half-empty bagpipes just by your shoulder, or above your head, or at your feet, so that ... Yes, I was saying, I went down twice needlessly, because Cara did not come early, but I went more in order to leave Madonna, to confirm and reinforce my success of New Year's Day when I popped out to Tariba's, admittedly she had not known, but nor did she sense my absence. I thought that after a decade of slavery the time had come to show Madonna our style of life. To demonstrate it to the Markantonis after our century-long enslavement! Cara was not capable of doing it, and these eighteen days were an excellent opportunity for undertaking the first attempts and preparing a little revolution. Mind you, it would have been a good idea to have had the inspiration earlier, to have started right from the first day, from the night I took Cara to the boat, and then to have refused Hermione's turns on duty and accepted Lino's invitations for cards, and been away for an hour or two from time to time, or even a shorter period several times a day with Madonna's agreement, or at least her knowledge.

Now it is a little late, but the success is obvious. For what could happen to anyone in that time? Nothing. And if by any chance she passed away in our absence, we would still arrive in time, *de facto*. It would be as though she had died in our arms, and that is how it would have appeared. So, why not. After ten years we ought to be able to summon that little strength to free ourselves from the terrorism of the town and our fear of Madonna. Besides, where does it say that Cara and I could not from the outset go for walks in the evening along the summer couples' paths, where the town spies do not penetrate in winter! It might perhaps be a little chilly, but once we got used to overcoming our nervousness of Madonna, then with time we would be able to risk the opprobrium of the town as well, and stroll along the Main Street or sit down to a cappuccino. I'll certainly take that on myself!

On those two days, as I went along the quay to meet the boat, I saw that the time had in fact come for an even more daring undertaking. Escape from the Island. But how could we do that!

I went out early, before the boat sounded its horn, so that Madonna should not associate my going out with the boat and begin to expect Cara or any one of her dear departed to arrive that very day. And when I was already walking along the shore the boat would just be turning in front of the harbor, aiming at the opening in the walls. We would move like that towards each other, as though we had God knows what designs on each other, and as though this whole décor around us had been set up for our meeting. The harbor wall, and the retinue of gulls, and the harbor-master, all blue uniform and insignia, and the large audience scurrying behind me, because people always let the boat's whistle take them by surprise, and the huge moving cage with grey-painted iron bars that rolled on two large Sicilian wheels, used by the Post Office. In this island harbor *mise en scène* with its banal symbols of the free white boat under the spreading wings of the gulls and the one grey prison-like hand-cart, like the ones in which they used to drag ruffians through the town streets for people to spit at them, I understood that it was time, ah yes, to embark! That it was time to set off into my past life, into that town of wrath *(into that day of wrath and doom impending, heaven and earth in ashes ending),* not to wait for Cara on the quay, but, if she came, to leap up to her on the deck beside the gangway and call to her. Stop! We're not setting foot on that soil again! Let them live and die without us! We'll stay on this heaving deck until all of them there on the quay leave us for God knows where, with their shore, with this contorted theatre! We must just hang on until this rocking stage turns round — and they will not be there any more! And we shall be able to turn discreetly towards the changing room, cast off our stupid Samaritan roles, cast off our anonymous, reclusive existence, sit on the windiest deck and wait without fear of ever again seeing that dog's life we have rejected, return from this exile to that town where the people we do not want to meet have forgotten us and where we can drink our fill of water from a tap!

But as Cara was not there on either day, her little hat nowhere to be seen among the travelers, I had to return the same way, following that Post Office cage which the respected Doctor Guillotine, who was concerned for the health of the people, sent down to the quay to collect all my dreams of revolt, and all my fluttering banners, and all my war cries of self-encouragement and heroics. Ever since I grasped that I am the eternal capital of all revolutions, because I am weak and because I cannot help myself on my own, I tread this red bauxite sand as though it were filled with blood, and as though my ankles were steeped in these blood-matted grains, and I shall never be able to get into bed again, for the sticky particles will drag after me in necklaces, and I shall not be able to wash them off, and there will be no rest for me until I grow into this bauxite soil like a vine, and until roots spring from my Oedipus-like swollen feet, that will hold me, that will make me vital and strong and self-sufficient whereupon I shall forget all about revolutions.

On my return on both occasions I made Madonna some flimsy apologies, that it was chilly as hell outside, and that there was nothing much to see round about — just so that she wouldn't think that I had been relishing my freedom. But the third time Cara arrived at last, and I no longer gave a damn about that great corpse up there any more, let her think whatever she liked!

I spotted Cara in the same place I had left her so many days before. She was standing on the deck beside that truly beautiful suitcase, as though she had just stepped off a tram and had paused for a moment at the stop under the chestnut trees. I think that suitcase is the most beautiful and valuable thing we possess. An object of significance. And precisely why we should have a suitcase that is so splendid and refined, God knows! We scarcely use it, and there are so many other things a person does not have, for goodness' sake! Cara is the kind of woman who should have all her possessions in the style of that suitcase, and a hundred and one other little things and articles and three shiploads of treasure besides. There was no one as well turned-out on the whole deck, and there would not have been if the late "Queen Mary" herself had sailed in. Ah, what can you do, I know, it's a waste of breath!

Cara and I did not signal to each other as it is customary, over the heads of all the people, waving, necks outstretched, standing on tiptoe. We just smiled at one another, I did actually move right up to the ship under the deck where she was standing, I did not want to wait by the gangway. I looked at her from down there, well, after all, but she always knew how to behave decorously, she pressed her skirt against the railing with her knees and asked through all the hurly-burly something like "how're things, up there?" and I told her with my head and shoulders that everything was all right on the whole, and I wanted immediately to ask her too how things were up there, for Zagreb is as much up there as Madonna's house, and everything in our lives is always up there, but I must have made an unnecessary movement and Cara simply nodded her head, thinking I was just saying any old thing because of that bloody audience around us, who always expect that people on ships must announce things hastily to people on the quay and vice versa as though the end of the world was at hand. But she did seem a little mysterious to me, and I made repeated question marks with my eyebrows several times in succession, but she answered something along the lines of "No problem, why not, go ahead, carry on killing!" and in a moment she was smiling again, with shadows round her mouth and across her nose, and seeing that I did not know my wife, because you can't ever get to know women at this distance and in public, I resigned myself to waiting for the smell of her skin, which is what I usually judge best by. My golden can was coming down the gangway towards me, its label had fallen off, and I was just waiting, hungry in every way, to see what kind of juices I would extract once the contents had been declared.

"How are things!" I said, kissing her on the cheek and taking the suitcase. "Kids all right, everyone all right?"

She only nodded, mumbling. She smelled of the distances that stretched between the morning rising of the sun and this midday. And I could not pick up any of her personal smells in this conventional contact in front of the boat and harbor crews, and in front of the town's citizens.

We dug ourselves out of the herd by the gangway and joined the little procession that had left the harbor and was trailing along beneath the town walls, lugging a whole shop of articles that could not be found on the Island counters. Cara had a kind of broken, slow-motion step like a long-legged marsh bird, and she talked about everything incompletely, but reasonably contentedly, although everything up there was apparently somehow different; and all the conventionalities were in order — greetings, health, messages and the rest, and finally she said we should hurry not to keep Hermione waiting. I said that Hermione was not there, that Madonna knew I had gone out and I set about presenting her with a brief sketch of our future style of life and partial emancipation, but as soon as I began she quickened her pace slightly frantically, and would not let herself be reasoned with, and it was impossible to broach anything serious with her the rest of the way home. She only reproached me breathlessly as she hurried up the steps towards the little square:

"You shouldn't have done that to me. If you found it so hard, you should have told me and I wouldn't have gone anywhere. What a thing to do, leaving her alone in the house!"

"As if it mattered! She's not going to steal anything!" I shook myself angrily, as I dragged the suitcase at this breakneck speed up the steps and steep little streets. "What are you so afraid of? She's not going to slink away to the cemetery behind our backs!"

She did not reply, however, and did not even look round at me any more, she sailed, almost charmingly, but somehow sideways, as though hiding, along the walls towards the house.

By the time I caught up with her, she had already put on

her house-coat. In her haste, she had at first forgotten her hat, then she took that off as well, although I believe hats should be taken off first. She fluffed her stiff perm up a little and went into Madonna's room, saying in a completely calm and everyday tone:

"How are you this morning? I expect you didn't get much sleep, I know you. I was told you were asking for me. Would you like a little warm tea, mm?"

Madonna was silent. Silent, silent.

Cara had perplexed her with her calm manner, charmed her with that sly "you didn't get much sleep," but it was not clear whether she had also driven away her doubts. Cara busied herself a little around the bedside table, and then went out of the room just as busily as she had gone in. As she came out she covered her mouth with her hands in alarm and began to roll her eyes, wondering what was going to happen. Then she set about cooking, because lunchtime had already passed: I had placed my bets on the new cook today, prepared everything, laid the fire and — gone hungry.

I had already asked her several times how things were up there, it was of inexpressible interest to me, but I simply could not get a proper answer — not even the least little taste, to orient me or to cheer me up. So I came up behind her and threatened to chop off her head if she did not give me the answer to three questions, all three of which went: how are things up there?

At that she suddenly shuddered and without taking her eyes off her work she said first, disconcerted:

"I don't know. It's all somehow different." Then she thought for a moment, looked at me askance and said, apparently more brightly, "different, somehow, really. It's all different," as though she wanted to soften the impact of her first, so serious words.

I was surprised, in what way different? Somehow! What did different mean? Different from what? Different from before? Different from how she had imagined it would be? What did different mean?

"You're different yourself!"

"Why, yes. Me too. Everything. Society, people."

I took up a warlike position, straddling a chair and looking over the back of it, knowing that this always irritated Cara for some unknown reason, and said didactically, sadistically:

"Well, we fought for a different society didn't we, for ... a new man ... For the new, for ... difference!"

This time she didn't react at all, she would not let herself be interrupted in sorting through the rice, but said in the same tone, taking no notice of my attack:

"It's a different kind of world now. Different."

"But that's what we fought for, wasn't it, a different kind of world?"

"A better one, yes," she said suddenly, as though she had got muddled in counting her rice.

"How should I know what's better? How should we know what kind of new world? How should we know why we fought? We thought we knew then, when we had to know something ... to orient ourselves ... to write on the flags ... while we were fighting. We fought, that was our thing. Like these people today, in their own way, why they're certainly.... Hey! But you wouldn't by any chance have got yourself involved in some sweet little adulterous affair, since you're so different, would you, honey, eh?"

"Is it so obvious?"

"You've blossomed," I said. But she was worn out, more tired than she had been before, here with Madonna. "That is, you're different...." I wanted to correct my lie, I wanted to say: "You're serious, stiff, tense." Perhaps I would even have dared say "run-down," but probably sensing that I was lying, sensing that I felt awkward because of that pointless compliment, she went back into Madonna's room, as though I had been droning on in some monotonous afternoon speechifying over Tariba's air-waves about who had engaged in long, animated conversation with whom, which could be listened to or not, parts missed and others caught with the corner of an ear. I was left in the middle of the kitchen, my hands in my pockets, where I had moved to let her past when she walked round me. My glance slid over the slippery English magazine on the shelf. The question flashed through my mind: "And what about me? Does anything show?" and I concluded that perhaps that was why she had become so serious, that little pictures of the leader of the Labour Party and spirals of mayonnaise could not be palmed off on her. I heard Madonna suddenly begin to lisp about something, but I could not decipher a single word, although I had learned to follow her speech better these last few days than in all the preceding years since it became bad. She was lisping in a calm voice, as though Cara had not been away for that long, as though everything was forgotten, but too softly and too indistinctly as though she were speaking Calabrian.

I strolled slowly and idly into the room, dragging my feet, for I was no longer a stranger here now as I had been a short time ago, before Cara's departure, I went in to hear what was going on and to dispel my thoughts about that stupid magazine. Cara had to bend devoutly over Madonna, so that the old woman could examine the quality of her curls with her fingertips. Her hand quivering like a little flag on a bicycle, Madonna brushed her fingers over Cara's artificial curls, like an infant that had not yet learned to grasp. She was annoyed and growled softly as soon as Cara tried to free herself from that uncomfortable position, and said calmly and almost warmly:

"La ga i capelli . . . ti ga le locks . . . far far finer than all three of you, than the first two I mean. Theirs was thin and straight as needles." Then catching sight of me, she let go of Cara's hair and threatened: *"Ela, moscardino!* What will the Holy Church say, what will God say?" But then she turned back to Cara seeking to justify me in her eyes. "But they weren't divorced, in actual fact; she died, the first one first, then the other, of catarrh, not a hint of TB, or anything else nasty. Catarrh, who would have thought! He's a widower . . . did you tell her . . . *così giovane vedovo!* Eh, they'd all want him, I know it! But you're lovely too, aren't you? Tell me the truth! What's your name, eh? And do you speak Croatian?"

"Cara, Cara, it's me . . . " my third wife burst out, she obviously didn't feel like equivocation, but I stopped her hastily, not to have her complicate the story.

"All my wives are called Cara," I said. I say, *"cara mia,* my darling, and there you are!"

"Hehehe . . . " she began to snigger, *"ma quella* your other wife was not . . . *cosa voleva dir . . . ecco, non mi piaseva affato,* she wasn't *cara mia* to me . . . but – a harridan! *Il mio difunto padre diseva per la nevista,* my brother's wife, *diseva:* harridan! *Significa . . . come . . . un* harridan, *non so. Insomma lo stuzzigava.* And my brother! My God, he nearly exploded every time . . . *Che da rider che me fa!* Harridan!" she said almost seriously, to Cara, pointing at me, "the other wife of him was a harridan! Believe me."

Cara and I had long since ceased to be amused by her meanderings through the murky limbo of her spiritual miscarriages, the more so since one could no longer tell how far she was deliberately twisting reality, and what was the fruit of amnesia and disintegrated consciousness. So we turned each to our own occupations, but just then she sighed:

"Haaaah, it doesn't do my stomach any good to laugh! I have a weight in me, *un peso tremendo!*"

Cara and I looked at each other. Epiphany! The camels were coming! The three kings, he-hey! There, the three kings were coming too: bearing fragrant oil, bearing gold and frankincense. So let us therefore be prepared, for the bearing of gifts is approaching for which you traveled these three hundred kilometers this morning, the offering of the kings which has made me so anxious all these days — is about to begin. A new cycle according to which we two must live is beginning. Neither the changes of the Moon, nor the Gregorian week, nor the sun's circling, but Madonna's Day, ovulation, period of mystic ripening, sluggish swinging of our tireless metronome; from evacuation to evacuation — that is our rhythm. Not a single life and not a single movement in Heraclitus' cosmos corresponds to ours! We are a peerless trio! Eighteen days, what is that? It is neither the lunar nor the solar nor the lunisolar, but the evacular calendar, with calends in the sign of the urn, with nones and ides in the sign of picturesque vessels for urination. And poor, poor us, my Cara! Poor you!

"Ahaha!" sighed Madonna more and more frequently, "not when I laugh, nor when I talk to people. Only *quando sto quieta, quel peso* I do not feel so much …"

We ate our last, eighteenth, lunch on the eve of this year's first calends, and Cara had to lie down to sleep off her exhaustion from her journey, nerves and trepidation at the uncertain situation she had found here, about which I had not once informed her; while I took up my watchman's duties, my close-watchman's duties, glad that Madonna had accepted Cara again so easily, even if as a completely new person, glad finally that she had buried us so painlessly and light-heartedly, with just a little catarrh, and that she was not committed to us, but to our help, so we did not therefore need to offer her anything apart from help. But I wondered as I stood in my sentry-box, watching beside this urn over the muffled awakening of those intestines out there, what front this was I had been posted to, what operational headquarters had found this position for me, what army I was a soldier in, a fighter in what revolution. Or, if I had been demobilized, as suited my nature, what kind of a world was this in which there was no better meaning for me, no other content for me and for Cara? What kind of world was this? Whose was it? Who had taken it over? Who had devalued our destinies like this and degraded us to such an extent? Who was it who could do that? And who else in the world carried out these duties of ours, these duties of burying dead bodies? Who gave part of himself to clean up the battlefield for a healthier life? Who had ever buried such a large part of his own life, in order to see an anachronistic corpse to its grave, long since dug out and by now almost caved in. Who was there in the world, apart from us here, sitting waiting over the intestinal orbit of the most worthless, most barren, most useless feces that were ever produced and ejected? The overflowing of a black pit! Maybe some sister of mercy, some mother or daughter, or some paid woman. A father, son, nurse, servant, slave. But I, what was I doing in the world of these unfortunates?

"Ahaha!" sighed Madonna from in there, as though mocking me, *"un peso tremendo!"*

Yes, perhaps I had been too heavy. Yes, indigestible. And Moloch had simply ejected me, with one little anal effort. Me. Cara. Thousands of others. It did not matter who was what or where; the main thing was that we had been discharged, shaken out, emptied out of the bowels of the Almighty, even after eighteen years of constipation and painful straining. And the main thing was that now, without us, everything was different. The ones who had not been ejected — had been digested without trace, disintegrated. And now everything was different for them, as well. Quite different.

And it was probably just as well! It struck me as a little comic, but really it was just as well! The collective had freed itself of the faint-hearted almost as successfully as it had digested and decomposed us. It had neutralized our poisons. And so society was now really a society, a partnership, a brotherhood, and no-one's defeatism could undermine it. A real society! And there it was, universally committed to making its latest far-reaching mistakes. But there was no more faint-heartedness, and that was so important! Admittedly, people did not even make mistakes with real enthusiasm the way they used to. As long as we were making our mistakes with enthusiasm, it was stupid all right, certainly, but somehow more human. Making mistakes like this without enthusiasm must really be infernally dreadful! At least for us, who must first of all believe.

Cara was sleeping too lightly and tensely and she seemed to be registering my gloomy emanations through some extra-sensory perception. We had become too close, the two of us, for her not to connect telepathically with my lugubrious thoughts. Without opening her eyes and without stirring in bed, she said as though dreaming:

"We must go and get that pipe for the drain today. Or we'll be fined."

"Only, please," I said, "we'll tell Madonna we're going and we'll go. Let her get used to the idea that we've got our own legs that can carry us through the wide world. No Hermione, no duty officers!"

She stopped talking when I said that and I thought she had dozed off again. I knew she did not like the idea. And it was not the right moment, what would happen if the worst occurred?

Oh, that was a really mean trick, this business with the drains! We, chance tenants, in a nationalized house, had to put in these "installations essential for the health of the inhabitants" at our own expense and within a set time. For the council had decided to take a further step towards abolishing black pits, instead of the medical and social institutions paying us for doing their job for them: nursing a neglected and helpless old woman, whom they had reduced to penury! This was the way our society, which had profited from her, prospered by taking this further step, or as many as it had to, raking in taxes on top of it all.

"Ahaha!" said Madonna from time to time in her false labor pains.

Yes, yes, ahaha, I said to myself as well. Just keep sighing, black pit! You are lucky they have not set us a time limit on you as well and thrown in a fine for your not having been abolished at the right time. And in fact your life depends on a simple administrative prerequisite, because as far as they are concerned you too might be merely a black pit, of somewhat smaller capacity, only some thirty-six meals, but still, it's quite true! Ahaha, yes!

Cara got up and trudged barefoot over the worn linoleum and over those ancient tapestries with their hunting motifs that had long since ended up on the floor, she was shivering slightly and asked me to stoke up the fire in the stove. She was still wearing her new, representative, ceremonial, or as they say, certainly infinitely saucier underwear; it almost seemed to me from my stale viewpoint that this black, lacy, tight and cobwebby fabric was the dissolute prop of a film-star or trollop. She wrapped her housecoat round her in passing and began to arrange her hair, then said indignantly:

"It's incredible how everything has been prostituted!"

"Maybe it's more attractive that way?" I said mockingly, trying in vain to establish exactly what it was that airy, elegant brassiere under her wrap was covering.

She glanced swiftly at me, probably trying to grasp the ostensibly enigmatic sense of my remark, and then she went on:

"People live literally from buying and selling, in the most shameless sense. Do you believe me? Why are you looking at me like that?"

"Go on, go on, I believe you," I said, turning my eyes away from her. But I thought how comforting it was that, in that underwear, she too, it seemed, made the same associations as I did. Although the underwear was beautiful, although everything was all right, although it was all more beautiful than that everyday stuff. Even so! It was unusual for her to be wearing it, when she knew it was worth as much as a month of my life, and when she knew that a complete outfit and total arrangement of life in the style of that sumptuous underwear and that gorgeous suitcase was worth more than my entire life. It was a real luxury for anyone other than those who had prostituted themselves.

"What I meant was that up there now character, morals, ideas, are no longer sold under the counter, as was the case until recently. While you were up in town there were still some sort of scruples and black marketeering. Now, it's all flung down on the counter like bales of material, fingered, crushed, taken out into the daylight among the passers-by, bargained over. Invoices are even made out with official stamps. In all this filthy buying and selling there's some kind of commercial morality developing; people don't just pilfer, they give out the requisite receipts. It's true that no one says in so many words: one high office — a hundred thousand; or — one dishonest silence — a sinecure; or so many dirty tricks — a villa. That doesn't happen, it's true, but not out of fear or consideration, but because all those things have different names now and the criteria have changed. Instead of statements and records at criminal hearings, ornate contracts and written agreements are made over an official black coffee. If you could only see what it's like!"

"Those are images from dreams!" I laughed at her, because she did not usually go in for exaggeration. "You've been seeing Morpheus in your afternoon sleep, my love! That may be some future world but such a paradise is still a far cry from this lovely friendly little developing country!"

"Honest to God," she swore. "They wear stiff white cuffs, like the ones people used to write lines of verse and sayings on, and then, with those cuffs on their sleeves, they make graceful queer movements from the time of the Charleston like this, but they don't say 'Oh, yes?' and 'Ah, no!' — they warble: forget that conscience, mate, don't give me that shit! If you won't, someone else will. Who's next?"

Just then, as though in response, there appeared in the kitchen doorway our late, faithful harridan in all her totem-like longitude that Madonna hated so much, and, catching Cara in full swing, miming the Charleston in her décolleté, she was almost idiotically embarrassed, losing a little height in that whirlwind of air, and, indifferently balanced, she suddenly began to marvel at Cara's underwear, coughing out her afterworldly catarrh.

Cara smiled good-naturedly, if a little self-consciously, although she knew no one else would have burst in like this without knocking. Reflex action drove her to try to wrap herself in her robe, but she still had to disclose portions, at least partially, to Hermione's eyes because she was greeting every fold, every tuck and every seam with cries and ovations, and clicking her dentures merrily the while as a mark of enthusiasm.

"Ialmostsaid Idid *BIANCARIA!* And how can it be, love us, when it's so-so black, then how can it be when it memeans *bianco,* deargodinheaven, white!"

Seeing that she had managed this scholarly exhibition quite well, she looked around her admiring surroundings with a serene brow and in doing so chanced to look also at me, and, fearing there was never going to be an end to the surprises now, the thought flashed through my mind that in her inspiration she might wink prophetically at Cara and say: that'll be something your husband bought to bribe you to forgive the funny business he gets up to when you're not here! A male floozy, youcapisci! — But she just could not get over her amazement that such things could be fashionable, or that something you never saw on a woman should have to be so finely made; but she admitted that it was practical because it would not get dirty, and have to be washed all the time, so those washing machines of theirs would go to pot. They dream up one thing, another goes to the dogs!

"Well, well, so how is it, howisitupthere?" she asked Cara importantly. Her turn now.

"What can I say?" said Cara distractedly, "they're stealing cars. Hooligans," and she smiled herself, trying to soften her pointless answer which might have offended Hermione by seeming to make fun of her.

But Hermione had made a serious decision to preserve her reputation achieved a short while before with the *biancaria,* and she launched into a sociological discourse, without etymological support:

"It's our luck these cars have come! If it wasn't thosecarshad come those hoohoohoo ... what's their names, would've raised another revolution!"

"Why who, the hooligans?" Cara laughed.

"The hooligans. Hoohoohoo, they're all the same, *perlamadona!* If they'd had all those things in the road in those days, what luck! These hoohoo ... how shall I put it, they persecute individual drivers, just drivers, they don't persecute whole nations and humanity. You wouldn't believe it, but it's true my mad brother saidhedid in my ear he said, heardhim myself, we've nothing to lose, he said, except our chains and irons, and we'll get, he said, whatever we want, *tutto il mondo!* That's what they all think, that's your best proof it's egoism and not commu-com-munism. It's villainy, primitivism and backwardism. They make speculations, authenticate ... discredit ... *che il diavolo li porta* ... they steal, loot and cover up for each other, because what can they lose, nothing — and they get *insomma* ... a year or two in prison and that's all! It's good luck, good luck, I say. So, they're stealing, eh?"

"They're stealing big time, my Hermione. They cheat and steal wherever they can!"

"Well, let them. But, no more politics! Let them steal, for God's sake, it'll come in handy. Maybe they need five to make up six. Like us. They cheat here as well, so why not in Zagreb! If there was only ..." she turned to me, lying self-effacingly low on the couch, "if there was only one of those ... what did you say to the old lady ... a vo vo volcano! But there isn't. It's a shame. To vomit cash, by God, to vomit cash! And not only money, my Cara, my dear, people steal all sorts ... just move and your fingers reach for other people's things, and take what you can!" and then, so that Cara could not see, she flashed me a blackmailer's glance out of the corner of her eye, "They think we don't see all their bruvaras and braviurias ... bravuras, and alltheir bravuras, eh?"

"Come on, come on," I muttered murderously through clenched teeth. "Don't summon Herod, you devil!"

"And then, are there up there any foreigners? Is there the occasional outoutlander? They told me that so many outout-side ... visitors come to Zagreb, even now, in the wwwinter. Is that true? But why not, they don't even have to go bathing up there, there's no sea none of that dirty business, there's no sun even for the locals, and they don't have plastic-beaches ... They just walk about and gaze around them like idiots. And why wouldn't they come and see, blessus, the Viennese theatre, Lordsaveus, the Sava and Drava rivers! I heard that there are a live lion and crocodile there ... Ah, well, it has twentythou-sand inhabitants, and not like us eight hundred poor souls, if that! And then at noon a cannon fires, and everything shakes! Yes, my dear: BOOOM! And even at night there's no peace, there's music playing at midnight, people throw snowballs at each other, roll on the ice ... oohmy, I'd like to see all that, morethananything! I wouldn't worry about anyone stealing anything from me, if I could just see Jelačić Square ..."*

"Republic Square," I trilled maliciously from my corner.

"Repuplic? What do I need that for? I've got that here!"

It was so entertaining that I almost abandoned myself to the delights of this sketch, and so exciting that I had to inform Hermione belatedly and apparently nonchalantly that it was not a question of some little bureaucratic speculations, but of conquering and transforming the world.

"Hoho! No less! Oh come on, come on, you don't need me

---

* Jelačić Square in the centre of Zagreb was renamed "Republic Square" during the Second, Socialist, Yugoslavia. (Translator's note)

to tell you! The world is not, whatsitsname, under underage, to be taken over by de-deception, foo-foolishness and si-silliness!" she said scornfully, for she was evidently now flexing her muscles, looking at me as though I were the leader of all revolutions.

I tried as best I could to throw the blame onto others; like Augustus, I stretched out my hand towards the mountains and cried:

"There are all those Eastern countries! They exist. They are there. What are you ranting on about!" I was challenging her to see how far she could take her treachery, because I could see that the business with little Lucy had really got up her nose.

She answered readily, running away from us as from immature litigants:

"*Rosso di mattina!* The shepherd's ... er ... warning! That's your East for you!"

That was really too much, and if she had not gone away with that proverb of hers, perhaps I would have had the last spicy word, but I said nothing and let her sail off unpunished. And as the early January dusk was already beginning to gather, with no rosy glow and no promises of any kind, I started hurrying Cara to get dressed so that we could finally go to pick up that wretched asbestos pipe. In order to forestall any arrangements Cara might make with Madonna I had warned the newly arisen Hermione that she should not appear in Madonna's room for some time, because Madonna would think she had bewitched herself into the likeness of my late second wife. But ever since she had burst in from the garden — which she had possibly never left — she had been flapping round the kitchen like a bat, and not even after Cara's explanations did she succeed in disentangling that little ball of nonsense, but she agreed not to go into the bedroom, unless Caspar, Melchior and Balthazar suddenly blew in, in which case she would certainly save what she could of the situation. However, Cara assured her that Madonna's time would not come till the next day, and that she could doze calmly here by the fire until we got back.

Then, quite unexpectedly, Cara began her long lament.

When we emerged into the half-dark she suddenly burst into tears, shuddering in the cold air. She stretched her neck, swallowing her own surprise at this violent outburst of uncontrollable convulsions, and she continued to sob softly as she walked beside me as though in future this was going to be her way of breathing which she would not be able even to try to hide from passers-by.

I wanted to turn back, but she went on utterly decidedly, crying quietly. And I wanted her to speak to me but, drenched in tears, she only said:

"It's the whole thing, up there, down here.... And everything that's happening to us. That's all. Leave me alone, it'll pass...."

I did not want either to console her or to question her because the poisonous suspicion had suddenly arisen in me that Cara had met something or someone, that it had been hard for her to come back to me in this graveyard, and that in the panic-stricken moments that beset a woman of forty she had might have involved herself in some licentious folly of which she was ashamed or frightened. I knew she had not come in order to say: "I'm going back there, I came to tell you I'm going back and leaving you." No. I knew she had not come to do that, because then she would not have talked with such disgust of the life she had found up there. But nevertheless, I was afraid she had not told me everything, and I could see that something in her was broken. And had I not watched her with my own eyes from the harbor this morning up to this present moment, it might have occurred to me that someone had briefly exaggerated and shamelessly dramatized my absurd lucination, my infantile poking round the little virgin, although I do not believe that could have upset her so much, however caricatured it had been. She would have said I was a silly, vain ass, and she would have been offended with me, because I had been publicly unfaithful to her, I hadn't been capable of finding a worthy replacement for her ... and that sort of thing. That would have been all, she is a wise woman, she would not have sobbed like this from the bottom of her heart over that.

In order to get this idiotic pipe we had to go right out of town to a building site where a whole lot of them had been dumped, including one for us. Cara never stopped softly shedding tears the whole of this time. We walked in the dusk side by side, without speaking, going across the park to avoid meeting people.

"You know it all!" she almost shouted. "You know because you were up there five years ago, you know because you listen and read and think more about it down here than I do! There's nothing apart from what you know. Nothing out of the ordinary has happened to me, and you've no need to be suspicious! I've just suddenly realized what you've known and been saying for ages: that there's no point in our expecting anything from up there any more, because there's nothing in that new society that could make us happy. So what will be the social consequence of this whole unholy mess!"

"Ah!" I waved my hand in relief, "social consequences are always in the hands of the socially consequential!"

She was scornfully silent for a moment, rejecting my simple liquidation of all problems. But somewhere in the middle of the park she said pathetically through her now tearless sobs:

"Where is all your enthusiasm? Instead of making puns you should be asking yourself what you once were and what you've now become. It's appalling. Why, you don't believe in anything any more."

"Well! Fancy that, as if I were the only one!"

"I'm talking about both of us. We don't believe in anything. We won't believe in anything. We don't want to believe in anything any more!"

"That's true of millions nowadays."

"But you don't want anything!"

"Oh, but I do. We want too much! But the exaltation has passed, like all exaltation. We were conceited, arrogant, self-important, we thought that if we had nothing to lose we deserved everything! But we didn't know that everything in the world that was being destroyed by our bullying and disdain was a loss for the world that was becoming ours. We thought we were opening up a golden era, but, well, I wonder whether anyone would want to take this world over from us the way it is now! We were incapable of understanding that the world does not give in to brute force. We thought it began with us, and that it would be exactly as we had sketched it. But we should have realized that, on the contrary, some things had been tested and resolved definitively and sensibly long before our time and that all we had to do was learn them. We did not need even to agree with them, or adopt them, or understand them. Just get them into our thick heads! That's what the humble and the sober do. We were presumptuous fools, for the most part. But we do still want a tremendous amount today as well. We want darkness to swallow up our stupidity, but it won't, it devours our souls and leaves us our stupidity to stop us crying over what we've lost. So what could I have become? In fact, I did become something, of course, I became a priest, a vestal virgin beside that urn, priest of that shitty shrine! I became what those who brought me up, ordered me about, preached to me, pestered me, wanted me to become. I didn't become a guardian of their spiritual lairs or of their infallible lies, or their black pits, but only of this one little forgotten black pit here . . . which is almost comforting! Why yes! There's not a trace of her illustrious ancestor in this specter here, but nor is there any trace in us of what we ourselves once were, or of what we wanted. We were our own great forefathers; now we are our own degenerate posterity! Now that you've begun to talk about all this as well, now that you've seen that you are not my flunky, it will be easier for me to bear this exile, and I shall possibly even begin to love Madonna in a way. Because she is something that I dare to despise in the name of my past, that I dare to condemn and reject, that I dare to hate. That is why I must love her. As long as she is alive, I shall feel at first hand that we have achieved something, that we have invested our youth in something, that we have destroyed something that threatened to fall on our heads. When she disappears, I shall feel only innumerable things which I oppose and which my entire soul resists. So, what's to be done? So, let Madonna live! Let her endure, for me to busy myself with her! Let that past vegetate on since it's so innocuous and piteous compared to the evils we ourselves created. She really is a monster; although she's partly of our making as well, but she's a real monster even without us, she's a very suitable object to embody much of what was poisoning mankind, that had to be wiped out, she's convenient for our contempt, handy for justifying the exploits of our heroic youth, everything we undertook in faith and sacrifice and work, even our rashness and arrogance and even our unintended crimes!"

"What a gloomy subject!" said Cara with conviction. "Was it worth undertaking anything for that?"

"It's absolutely too late for that sort of question, my love! Belated questions like that lead to pointless reflection, on how for example my destiny, my vocation has been in a way the meaning of Madonna's life, or at least of her old age. And then: should anyone take the only sense of such an empty and barren existence away from it so lightly, even if that so-called sense were pure nonsense, like everything else, like the whole of life! Even if it were only a fixation. Should a person do that? Let alone turn his youth, his life's force, his best energy against that barren life of which he is the only meaning! Do you see? But this is just raving, both naïve and morbid, and belated questions must be wiped from the mind! They are not our main problem. We are still living. Our present life is what is tormenting us, and that is neither meaningless nor naive."

By the end of the park Cara was weeping still more bitterly. We went down onto the building site where people were putting tools away and stacking them by the light of oil lamps. We were given a heavy pipe a thousand meters long and picked it up, and everyone looked doubtfully at Cara, but she could do it. Having no money to pay for transportation we would even have picked up two of these pipes "indispensable for the health of the population" and carried them like this in the dark towards the park without thinking how we were going to get any further. I set off in front, Cara behind me at the end of the pipe, but the men from the site called to us that the paths twisted sharply among the trees in the park and we would have trouble maneuvering in places, which was true, so we turned and made our way along the path beside the sea, just below the park, with dark tree-tops overhead instead of sky, joined together by the long heavy asbestos pipe, and also by the weight of our common knowledge, which was dripping into my stomach, like poison, and flowing out of Cara's eyes in desolate weeping. Below the path the sea lay dead calm and we were able to talk softly along the pipe.

"What do you think," I asked, "will the waste water flow towards me or away from me?" For I had felt under my hand, through a painful neuron, the throbbing of her tears as they trickled quietly along the resonant pipe.

"The waste water will flow at an angle of 3% . . . I don't know," Cara lectured, laughing through her tears, "depending how the pipe is laid. Ah," she remembered, "have you got the wide bit? That means it's going to run from there to here. Is that right?"

"Yes, that's right, only it isn't right that you should be so logical. It's not modern."

I had taken up this senseless conversation to help us forget and Cara no doubt knew it, because she too now found absolutely everything senseless, apart from what we would have liked to forget.

"You think so! No, no, you don't know! They're extremely sharp and clever! In fact, I really like those boys and girls up there, you know! They're perfectly built for a world like this! They're the only thing that's been a terrific success, these youngsters. But there seems to be a hidden paradox there, I see now. They've probably managed to duck out of the way and that's why they're so free. It really would be paradoxical otherwise. I'm not much good at paradoxes, am I, clever-clogs? I've proved that."

"No, no," I said, preoccupied with other thoughts. "It's only now. Only now, that it's all over for me too, and I've always been good at paradoxes. What you've seen is obviously not the fruit of my mad and disordered imagination, my wounded pride, my bad temper, my complexes, or all of the above. . . ."

We chatted on, groping like sleepwalkers along the fine

grooves of normal reason. At our feet below the path the sea comes to an end at the edge of the shallows; all that is left of the great, heavy, dead, open sea lying beneath the firmament is just a coverlet, a thin membrane of still water, immaterial, woven of the subdued celestial radiance of night. All the seas of the world end at this docile line, and it seems to me that the two of us are walking along the edge of the universe. By going round the dark wood that is still hanging over our heads, we have found a strip of no-man's land between the watch-tower of death and the void of the universe, between the Earth and the Ocean, and now we are neither fish nor birds, we are floundering at zero altitude and shedding our past tears like sweat, harnessed to this hollow shaft, lugging this deaf trumpet of our own judgment day.

Out of breath, we slowly transferred the pipe to our other hands.

"Perhaps our children ... who knows, after all...." sighed Cara.

"Yes, perhaps the children."

"Or, more likely, our grandchildren."

"Or great ... great ... great ..."

We were silent again, for a long time, and then from the other end of the drainpipe her voice came uncertainly, despondently:

"It was all easy to bear as long as we could think hopefully about going back...."

For a moment it seemed as though I could feel the warmth of her hand through the pipe. I wanted to stop, throw the pipe down on the ground, hug Cara and weep over her: Never mind, my little one, we must find another source of strength. The same thing that brought us here for instance — flight from everything up there! The wish to delay our return as long as possible. Because — I wanted to say — in a choice between ordinary eternal death and this happy life about which 'the best minds of the century' have (fleetingly) fantasized, we decided daily in favor of the latter. The choice is pitifully limited, but that does not mean it is simple! Living means constantly choosing that harder alternative! But I did not pronounce these words of wisdom, which are always implied but not spoken, I did not even say, as usual, that we would take up Buddhism. I voiced my anxiety of the day:

"I thought you were going to come back sick with longing for the city."

Cara was silent for a while and then she took up precisely what had not been spoken:

"Madonna is still holding her own, there is hope!"

"Those hopes are, luckily, illusory!" I said, in sing-song tone. "We'll find a better meaning!" (But if anyone still has the slightest belief in that meaning at this moment, let him show himself: I'll crawl through this pipe!)

As she has perfect pitch, Cara continued in the same register:

"I know, I know. Once she's off my hands, I've got my penance with you waiting for me."

"Right, either that or new conflicts with this terrible world we've sacrificed so much to create! So we'll survive these few more years from one of Madonna's stools to another, between two lots of shit, that one up there and this one here!"

"We ought to get ourselves photographed, the two of us, with this drainpipe!" she said grimly, resolutely wiping her tears away. "We're too poor for me to fling the pipe onto the ground!"

"If you want to ... come on, let's smash it!"

"It's one thing to want something, quite another to do it."

"Calm down," I begged her, "calm down, that makes no sense whatever!"

"So what does?"

"This, my pet, is salonite that costs money! Asbestos-cement from ancient Salona. If it were produced in Zagreb it would be called zagrebite. And through each of them would flow one and the same fluid of life, and it wouldn't occur to you to snatch anything out of it. You would just let it flow by, as swiftly as possible."

CHAPTER 14

That was my first wedding night with my third wife, the new permanently waved one, the wife who had not only unselfishly taken on my unhappiness but had in the end wept it with her own tears, for my unhappiness had become hers as well, even more hers than mine now, as much hers as it had been mine once. I looked forward to that night, not in the way I would have looked forward to any caressing, but like a boy, even with stage fright at the first affirmation of his maturity. And I told Cara who was washing outside in the dark hall, standing in the tub, that Madonna was quite used to having no one sleeping in the bed in her room any more. My first wife who had slept there had died eighteen days ago, my second wife, luckily, had never got into the habit, and therefore let the third one proceed with caution! It was the last minute to say this because Cara was almost beginning to hesitate about how to trick Madonna and stay beside me.

Outside it was deathly quiet as in a snowy pit, but a cosmic frost was beaming down from the glassy sky, for this clarity had opened up a path from the depths of space. I kept frantically putting more wood on the fire so that the hall should not get cold, and we had had a good fire going all day not only because of our baths, but because of Madonna's condition, to heat up the walls in case we had to air the house at night. I had already washed off the afternoon sweat from carrying that pipe and now, wrapped in a blanket, I was drying my hair in the current of hot air reflected off the iron plates of the kitchen range. I could hear only the sound of that hot whip against my ears and the alarming roar of the fire shackled by the iron and pipes, and from the hall the occasional splashing of water and the slopping of soap in the folds and curves of Cara's smooth skin. These were the only sounds under the sky tonight, as though nothing had happened recently on the old continent, let alone under this crumbling roof, as though we had sailed into some mistaken, deaf, lenten year, in which the sun would never return, and in which we would soon grow old. But out of these sounds of silence there suddenly thundered through to me, from just here, right above my head, what sounded like an explosion, a piercing male voice:

"Well, what's up with you?"

I jumped and sat up. There was no one there, naturally, for Cara had locked the door into the garden, and if anyone had come in they would have had to walk past her naked in the tub. Like a distant hallucination the voice had no echo, the silence rang in my ears and I thought it must have been a trick of the air in my eardrums. But a childish sinking fear had wound round my heart, the terror of isolation and ghastly powerlessness against the evil voices of loneliness, and I did not dare stir from the spot, just like a few days earlier when I had found Hermione here hidden in the doorway. I asked Cara as calmly as I could whether she had said anything, and she replied that she had heard me call something, but she had been rubbing her ears ... or maybe I had put the radio on? Yes, I heard it too, I say, a man's voice, it asked how we were! How come?! Because I hadn't opened my mouth or switched on the radio, it was a strange voice, not remotely like Madonna's, not even her altered one. We could not both be hallucinating! Perhaps there were some acoustic tricks here as well, like the ones in stone cupolas! I went timidly towards the bedroom door. The light from the kitchen reached part of this space, and I saw Madonna's eyes shining as though the lids had been rubbed with phosphorous. Half-sitting, as usual, she was looking this way, towards the door, and just as I was about to ask her if she had called, she croaked in a raucous voice:

"Coraggio! Coraggio!"

Her voice was suddenly so deep that it no longer resembled hers in any way at all.

"How are you?" I asked, shouting in my agitation. "Shall I turn the light on?"

"And how are you?" she asked in a sailor's bass voice instead of replying.

I shuddered a bit in my blanket toga, and said we were well, while she, her eyes gleaming like a cat's, remarked:

"Disinherited!"

I went straight to Cara and told her what has happening to Madonna. She said her eyes were probably shining with fever, as she often gets feverish with her motion, but as for the voice, she had heard that voice as well now, but she did not know what it could be. Perhaps she couldn't cough any more, or her vocal cords had simply seized up as well. And poor unhappy Cara sighed that we were surely not so down on our luck as to lose Madonna suddenly now, when we needed her perhaps more than she did us!

The thin, tense skin stretched over the top of my head stung me, my sparse hair itched at the roots, and I felt shivers rushing through my skull from sheer terror and from that terrible sigh.

What little faith in the future we still retained, like a last bullet for ourselves, could easily have been puffed away on the breath of that sigh!

When Cara later slipped into bed beside me in the dark, virtually the moment the electric light switch in the kitchen had clicked, Madonna rumbled from the bedroom, in her pirate's voice, somewhat louder than before:

"Well, eh? Are you well?"

I began to shake hysterically; I felt I was going to burst into tears of despair or go mad. Was one of the gods above asking us how we were? Who was making fun of us? That simply was not Madonna's voice! She is an occult medium and her cries are the materialization of the evil spirit that is destroying us. I wanted to leap out of bed and pitch into her with a chair, the chamber pot, an axe, to silence her, to bury her in the pillows and choke her!

I had thought that this night was ours, and this bed the only thing that belonged entirely to us, that no one could take from us. And now it seemed that Madonna knew quite clearly what was going on, as though she had crept into our room and intended to embitter our most intimate moments.

Cara stroked my forehead and soothed me for a long time before the knot in my chest dissolved and the pressure in my temples and the top of my head dispersed. When I took her in my arms she said:

"Do you know that your first wife really is dead?"

"The main thing is that this third one is as warm as this," all at once I breathed the whole nightmare and all the poison out of my soul, "and that she should smell of pungent frankincense dissolved in the warm milk of a young ewe! Eh? What do you think?"

"If frankincense is soluble in milk!" laughed Cara gaily, but soundlessly, in my ear, as though the hot breath had sprung up from the glowing plate again.

"Your eyes are like two kohlrabis from crying! Of all the women with whom I have produced two children and to whom I have been married for more than twenty years, this one tonight is the biggest crybaby! I'm going to look for a smilier one!"

Cara laughed in my ear again, gasping and quivering like a kitten, for I had found that spot in the small of her back where everything begins.

We spent most of the night awake, waiting tensely for Madonna's comet, following her rambling and watching out for the sudden riders, who generally arrive at the gallop and in their haste do not know what to do with their gifts, and then you have to leap head over heels to assist them.

We kept watch, I may say, under the open sky of marital bliss, and *a great light shone forth as at noon*. Selected angels from eastern rituals took it in turns to play to us on a dulcimer; but, even deafened as we were by the drums of sex, every real sound from the other room woke us; dazzled as we were, our eyes were pierced by the black outline of the shiny glaze on the clean chamber pot ready by the door. The spasms of our tingling limbs and the throbbing of our blood, the tremor of frenzied skin, and every gasp, every groan was restrained, smothered and interrupted by the fear of the presence of a stranger, of the sudden overflowing of that black pit. That Bethlehem ride to meet the kings was painful drunkenness on the hard straw of strained consciousness; a night watch and the tensing of a cold trigger right over the chasm of carnal sleep and warm pleasure; sinning against the uncharitable sacrament of life-long maidenhood.

But still — I closed my crazed Cara's mouth with my hand,

for a real woman forgets fear and consideration; she forgets everything around her when there is a man inside her. I had to double my own vigilance for her too, blinded, stupified, and without the slightest ray of consciousness. Dead to everything that was not warm throbbing in the depths of her belly.

It was not until towards dawn that we fell asleep, but as lifelessly as one sleeps after violent weeping and absolute coitus, and we would have slept through the collision of the galaxies, let alone Madonna's time had it come early. I recovered my self-confidence that night, not that I had really ever lost it even on that ill-fated straw couch, nor would the question arise for a few years yet. But I shall never be able to regain any other kind of self-confidence, although it's already obvious that this won't last until death and it cannot be enough for life.

We were woken at an uncertain hour by an overcast morning, and we lay felled by the leukaemia of thinned blood, in hypotonic lethargy and cooled by a sexless slackness like drowned bodies on the bottom of a dead sea. Yesterday's immense tenderness had disappeared, and Cara had at first anxiously sniffed the air, then extracted herself clumsily from her hole by the wall, thrown herself over me pressing her whole weight onto my painfully swollen bladder, so that I groaned and got straight out after her onto the cold floor. She went into the bedroom and when she returned, satisfied that Madonna was still asleep, she asked how that great hole in the ceiling of Madonna's room had come there all of a sudden. I replied, yawning on purpose, that it had — fallen. The plaster had come away; I'd been poking about up there with the broom handle, there was a cobweb on the ceiling and there we were, we'd have to fix it with plaster. So we got that out of the way. She made some chamomile tea and took it in to the old lady to wake her up.

Finally, when I had dressed and after the day had begun I still felt it important to tell her:

"A lot I care about that past! You don't live from it, whatever it was like. We should forget it. Everything becomes tolerable when you forget the beginning!"

"If you forget the beginning, what'll be left? This here?"

"Oblivion, my friend! When the people it shook up die out, everything becomes interesting. For others, of course. For those who are left. Or, at worst, uninteresting and tedious. But it doesn't shake them up, and they don't give a damn!"

"Yes," she replied uneasily, at once on the brink of tears again. "In fact it's just as well that's the case. Let it all fade into the past, into oblivion, and not happen again to a single other generation!"

I was afraid Cara was going to start her lamentations all over again, because she was in that kind of state just then, and who knows when she would become inured and forget. I preached her the maxim of the faint-hearted that everything was in harmony *with the most ancient laws of the world*. What little there was that we could still believe in was so generally accepted, nowadays such a universal good that in practice it belonged in good measure to all civilized people and was common to all religions and all ideologies. No one had a particular right to it and no one had to swear by it, or cover himself with flags, or commit himself with pledges, or sacrifice himself to conspiracies, in order to declare himself for what little he believed in. Emblems and parties served quite different purposes nowadays, unfortunately, the least of which was leading people to true faith. And even the person who says he does not believe in anything is man's friend and fellow-fighter, and like thinker. The only people who are not are those who, in the name of their obtuse understanding of the common happiness of us all, trample on what little scrap of belief in man's future human beings have preserved ... I endeavored to show her that disillusion is the result of naïveté and inexperience, and that one must dig oneself as fast as possible out of that shit ... when at that moment Madonna cried out gruffly, no longer in a bass voice, just hoarsely now, from her room:

"Aaah!!!"

Cara rushed into the bedroom, and I followed quickly after her, dragging the pot up to the bed. The chamomile was spilt over the white sheets. Madonna was just trying to turn onto her side and groaning "aah, aah." The covers had slipped off and we could hear a gurgling like young wine in a cellar. Cara and I took her under the armpits and knees and lowered her slowly onto the pot, taking care not to stretch her or contort her, but trying to keep her as she was in her half-sitting position, in which she always lay and into which she had by now grown. Then I fled out of the room closing the thin door behind me, and opened the kitchen window to send that whole intense stench out into the night, and hastily swallowed an enormous mouthful of hot tea from the stove. I steamed my face and eyes in the dense steam pouring out of the pan, because it was terribly cold outside again, and it seemed once more that real winter was only just beginning. I had to put more and more wood on the fire, heat water, and hand Cara prop after prop like a practiced stage manager.

When the ritual was already drawing to a close, while we were laying Madonna in the bed, I drew Cara's attention to the sore patches on her back.

"I've seen them," Cara replied calmly, lifting the shirt, "but they're healing beautifully."

I knew that those sore patches had almost healed, but it was as though I was only now really aware of it. Shiny young pink skin had covered them as though under that wrinkled and furrowed old skin Madonna was really hiding a fresh young body that would one day free itself from its hard shell. The Doctor would be triumphant when he saw that. He would look at me ironically and say with delight: "Well, there you are, it's amazing how wonderfully it's healed. You needn't worry any more!" Because he doesn't know just how much that really does delight me now!

I picked up the pot and carried it victoriously towards the door to raise it up like a holy relic and hurl it against the walls, against all Normans and criminals, but Cara took it from me and carried it out onto the terrace facing the sea. From there she suddenly tapped on the kitchen window, motioning through the corridor towards the garden, her eyes wide open, telling me more with a grimace because of the strong smell from the pot than a voice:

"The priest! The priest! You meet him, let him in!" I read from her lips.

I went out onto the porch, irritated by this visit just when the heavy waves of stench from those greedy bowels were flowing through every corner of the house. Don Vikica was coming towards me in a white surplice with a pocket prayer book in his hand. Behind him scampered two little parrot-acolytes, one waving a silver censer which was barely smoking, and the other carrying an enormous font also of old silver the color of roof tin. Seeing me with my hands in my pockets and my eyes on the ground, the old priest stopped at the top of the steps, greeted me in drawing-room style and said:

"If you would permit me…?"

"Fumigate!" I said, in the voice of a drunkard. Just as people who stammer do not always find the best and most precise word, but the word it will be easiest for them to say, so I squeezed out — like an oath — fumigate, fumigate!

He stepped youthfully into the hall and called:

"Peace to this house!" and then began to mumble privately as though Latin were more natural to him, *"Pax huic domui et omnibus habitantibus in ea!"*

The acolytes piped after him in their chickens' voices:

"And to all those who live in it!"

Don Vikica opened his prayer book, uttering the ritual words loudly and distinctly. He blessed the house and its inhabitants. We were confirmed on the old soil. By the land-register and holy water. Cara bent her head towards me as though she wanted to sniff with closed eyes whether or not we really were inhabitants of this house. Using a silver spoon, the priest had taken the frankincense from the open container in the acolyte's hand and was scattering it, with a jeweler's precise movements, over the glowing coals of the censer. Praying, chanting, and sending curls of blue-grey fragrant smoke through the house, he peered round the door of Madonna's room. The acolytes wrinkled their noses as they followed him, glancing at each other and stifling coughs. Then he gave them back the censer, clinking its little chains, handed them the prayer book to hold, and with both hands began to lift his surplice to uncover the pocket of his trousers. He took a stump of white chalk out of it, stood up on tiptoe and on the inside beam on top of the bedroom door he wrote out in chalk the magic signs: *19 C+M+B 66*. Standing stretched out on his toes like this he slowly farted twice, and his shoes hastily squeaked. Cara clinked some coins into the acolyte's purse. Madonna asked from her room whether he had fumigated everything as it was laid down.

"Yes, yes, he has," I said, while Cara accompanied the trio into the garden.

Then Cara came back, we closed the windows early because the cold air was driving the smoke and stench back into the house, and we found ourselves, confused, beside Madonna's bed, as though there was still something we had forgotten to do. Relieved, flattened, as though recently confined, glowing all over, her face almost rosy, her eyes closed, breathing in the incense, she announced blissfully:

"Like two angels, you are to me, my lovelies!" and she smiled, abandoned like that to her vision of heaven.

Ah well, so, after all, again and still, an angel! For all who baptize the water die like that. Like a little dove of salt, I had merely fluttered through the atmosphere, and here I am on the balustrade of heaven where past and present have met. The late Madonna and the present Cara are standing in the choir of virgins. The future resounds emptily and hopelessly with gilt salonite fanfares. We are in heaven. And this is eternity now.

Glossary of Italian (or Dalmatian Italian dialect) expressions used in the text and other references

a, ecco! E quell altro? · well, of course! What about the other?
aiuto! · help!
altretanto · likewise, in the same way
andato a finir · it came to an end, ended
anima serena / contami la tua pena / E sta lontan di me · 'Gentle soul, / tell me your trouble / and stay far from me!' Popular saying in times of trouble or alarm.
angelo mio! · my angel!
anima · soul
antenato, avo lontano · ancestor, distant forebear
asasinati · commit a crime
assassino · murderer, assassin
bel campione, cara mia, ti lo senti? · a fine example, my dear, do you hear him?
bella roba · a fine thing
bello mio! · my lovely!
ben · good
beneficienza · public good
bersagliere · member of an Italian infantry unit (they wear wide felt hats, with cock's tail feathers)
biankarija, biancaria · underwear
'to choose and be chosen' · a common constitutional

formulation about the right of every adult citizen without a criminal record to vote in elections and himself stand as a candidate

Böcklin, Arnold (1827-1901) · Swiss-German painter of 'The Island of the Dead,' which it is believed was inspired by one of the islands in the Bay of Kotor

bon poeta. Vero poeta · a good poet. A true poet

brutto bugiardone! Ti lo senti! · the great fibber! Do you hear him?

Buonarotti, Michelangelo · there is a legend that, when he had completed 'Moses,' the sculptor tapped the work with his hammer and said 'Speak, Moses!'

C+M+B · initials of the Three Kings or Magi, Caspar, Melchior and Balthazar, as a sign that the ritual of blessing the house has been carried out (in the year 1966)

Campo dei fiori · square in Rome (see Markantun de Dominis)

capisci · you understand

caro mio · my dear

cento anni precisi · a hundred years exactly

che coraggio! · what courage, arrogance!

che da rider che me fa! · how it makes me laugh!

che il diavolo li porta · Devil take them!

che lo vedo! · let me see!

che sorpresa! · what a surprise!

coda · tail

come no! · why of course!

come si ciama quell masculzon de Turco? · What is the name of that Turkish brigand?

contessa · countess

coraggio! · courage!

corpus Domini nostri · (Latin) the body of our Lord

cosa volevo dir … ecco, non mi piaseva affatto · as I wanted to say … there, I didn't like it at all
così giovane vedovo · a widower so young
cuore ingrato · ungrateful heart
dappertutto · everywhere
davvero · really, in truth
deboto · nearly
de facto · in fact
de resto · besides, otherwise
Deo gratias · (Latin) Thanks be to God
Dio mio! · My God!
Dio santo! · Holy God!
dunque · so, therefore
e adesso, qual' è? Il ventesimo. Orca! Quanti secoli! · and now, which is it? The twentieth. Gracious! So many centuries!
ebete · fool
Ecce homo! · Behold, a man! (Pilate's words when he showed Christ with his crown of thorns to the Jews)
ela, moscardino! · hey, you dandy!
elenco · list
el mio · my
el signor Lucić · Mr Lucić (Hanibal Lucić, 1485-1553, poet from Hvar)
el tè · tea
el tuo · your
Entrez! Restez! Tombez! · (French) Come in! Stay! Fall! The beginning of a Croatian school textbook section on French imperative verbs
esatto · exactly
et in terra pax hominibus · (Latin) and on earth peace to men (people)
ex-King Farouk · of Egypt, deposed 1952

farabut · swindler
farrò quello quelloche potrò · I'll do what, what I can
fiera · feast. On the island of Rab an entertainment that includes the entire town of Rab, with dancing, traditional costumes and crafts
figlio mio · my son
finalmente · at last
Finisterre · the most westerly point of Spain on the Atlantic coast (Lat: the end of the world)
Fyodor Mikhailovich · Dostoevsky, a reference to *Crime and Punishment*
galetina · biscuit
Gilda in the sack · reference to Verdi's 'Rigoletto'
Gods, Graves and Scholars · a novel by C. W. Ceram
grazie · thank you
guarda · look
Hanibal–Hasdrubal · Hannibal of Carthage had a brother named Hasdrubal
i ghe da bever, dunque · so, they gave him to drink
il cerchio dei santi · the halo of the saints
il mio difunto padre diseva per la (nevista) · my late father said of his daughter-in-law
in che secolo son nata, cos' ti par? · what century was I born in, what do you think?
indentro · inside
infermiera · nurse
in Latino · in Latin
in ordine · all right
in punto · exactly
insomma · in short
intanto · however
into that day of wrath and doom impending, heaven and earth

in ashes ending · Thomas of Celano, c. 1250, transl. by W. J. Irons of hymn beginning *'Dies irae, dies illa'*
intrigoz · tease
invece · on the contrary
i xe vegnudi · they came
Jeftić, Bogoljub · Prime Minister in the Kingdom of Yugoslavia known for his reactionary and violent policies
je nemohla · (Czech) she could not
kampanare · to ring
kanat · sheep-fold
kandelica · candle
Karageorge · Rebel leader in the first Serbian uprising against Ottoman rule in 1804 and founder of one of the two main Serbian royal dynasties
Katya Dolgoruka · 'She stood like a statue by the grave of her ruined happiness,' caption under a kitsch illustration in a cheap novel about life at the Russian Imperial court
kretino · idiot
Kulin Ban · ruler of Bosnia in the 12th century, the period of his rule was considered a happy time, so there is a saying in Croatian 'Since Kulin Ban and the good times'
la benedizion dell' acqua santa · blessing of the water
ladri · thieves
la ga i capelli · she has hair
la ge fazeva bagni, povera Cara · she washed her, poor Cara
lo go buttà · I threw it away
lo mazza · they'll kill him
La Santa Sede · The Holy See
lo stuzzigava · he teased him
Lucias · the nine most beautiful, most intelligent etc. Swedish girls, chosen each year in a questionnaire in *Stockholm Tidningen* (the prize is a trip round the world, including

the Dalmatian coast)

Lucheni · Italian anarchist, who stabbed the Austrian Empress Elizabeth, wife of Franz Jozef I, in Geneva in 1898

lumin · little flame

Lunik · the name of several Soviet satellites

ma che da rider … · how funny!

ma dell' altra parte insomma · but on the other hand, however

Madonna della motocicletta · Madonna of the Motorcycle, allusion to e.g. Raphael's painting 'Madonna della Sedia'

magari · at least

maledetta · cursed (fem.)

maledizion de 'sti biglietti · what a curse these pieces of paper are!

ma che da rider · what a laugh!

ma mi sembra incredibile · it seems incredible to me

ma propio mi fa schifo, sa' · but actually I'm disgusted, you know

Markantun de Dominis (1560-1624) · born on the island of Rab (where the novel is set), Bishop of Senj and Archbishop of Split, who rebelled against the Pope and emigrated, among other countries, to England, where he was appointed Dean of Windsor and engaged in anti-papal activities; later he returned to Rome in an attempt to make peace and ended his life in prison, dying before his trial. In December 1624 The Grand Inquisition pronounced their verdict that his body should be disinterred and publicly burned on the Campo dei Fiori, together with his portrait and writings, and the ash thrown into the Tiber.

mascalzon · good for nothing

ma va via, va te prego! · so go, go, please

me romperà · he'll break

mi ricordo come se fosse ieri · I remember as though it was yesterday

Miroslav Tyrš (1832-1884) · Czech patriot, founder of the Sokol Gymnastics Society

misera plebs contribuens · (Latin) the wretched people who pay tax, the common folk

moglie · wife

moniga de fijo · son of a monkey, fool

mostra · show (me)

neanche per idea · no way, not a chance

niente altro · nothing else

o, corpo di Bacco! · in God's name!

o in rima, o no in rima, sei vigliacco come prima, disse Dante a Garibaldi quando scoprì l'America · in rhyme or without rhyme, you are a villain as before, as Dante said to Garibaldi when he discovered America (a well-known comic saying)

Olga and Lina · reference to the naturalist novel by the Croatian writer Eugen Kumičić (1850-1904), who published under the pseudonym Jenio Sisolski and who was called (unjustifiably) the 'coastal Zola.' The main characters in the novel are two sisters, Olga and Lina, one wicked and the other noble.

oštija · curse, expression of surprise, confirmation, protest

oui, nous aussi, nous sommes les internationalists · (French) yes, we too are internationalists

pazzienza · patience

pantagana · rat

parola d'onore · word of honor

parolazze sporche · filthy words

parona · padrona, mistress

pax huic domui et omnibus habitantibus in ea · (Latin) peace to this house and all who live in it

per dio · for God's sake

per il Padre Santo · for the Holy Father

per l'amor di Dio · for the love of God

Pius XI · Pope from 1922 to 1939 (long dead at the time the novel is set)

piazzeta · small square

porco · pig

'The Last Adam' · reference to the well-known poem by the Croatian poet Silvije Strahimir Kranjčević (1865-1908) 'The Last Adam' ('Zadnji Adam'); the 'question-mark in the ice' is a quotation from the same poem.

postillon d'amour · (French) messenger of love

povera mi · poor me

poveretto · poor little thing

poverina · poor thing (fem.)

povero diavolo · poor devil

preciso · exactly, clearly

procurator · (Latin) manager

puzzo · stench

quando sto quieta quel peso... · when I am still (I don't feel) this weight....

quel · that

quel poeta · that poet

'queste parole di colore oscuro' · 'these words of colour obscure' (Dante, *Inferno,* III, 10)

questi due · the two of them

rabochyi klas · (Russian) the working class

ritardando · musical term: gradually slowing down

rosso di matina · pink sky in the morning

Santa Barbara, san Simon / Liberene de sto ton, / De sto ton, de sta saetta / Santa Barbara benedetta · Saint Barbara,

Saint Simon / Liberate us from that thunder / From that thunder, from that lightning / Blessed Saint Barbara

santissima · most holy (fem)

scherzo · joke

Secundum magnam misericordiam suam · (Latin) through Your great mercy (second line of the psalm beginning *Miserere mei Deus,* Have mercy on me, Lord

selvatica · vulgar, coarse woman

sempio · fool

sempreverde · evergreen

si · yes

significa ... come ... un ..., non so. Insomma lo stuzzigava · it means ... like ... a ... I don't know. In a word he teased her.

'Siren of the Adriatic Sea' · allusion to the Hungarian poem of that title by the Croatian poet Nikola Zrinski, translated into Croatian by his brother Petar (1620-1671)

sopraddetta · the afore-mentioned

sospir · sigh

Starčević, Ante (1823-1896) · Croatian politician, known as the 'Father of the Homeland'

Suleiman the Magnificent · Turkish Sultan (1494-1566), a character in the Croatian composer Ivan Zajc's opera 'Nikola Šubić Zrinjski'

sursum corda! · heart up! Have courage!

Sanpjero · Saint Peter

sporkulja · dirty thing (fem)

suo · his

testardo · pig-headed

ti lo senti? · do you hear?

ti me capisci? · do you understand me?

ti vederà · you'll see

tu es primus inter castigandos · (Latin) 'You are the first of those who must be punished', from the novel *The Witch of Grič,* by the Croatian writer Marija Jurić Zagorka

turbeh · Turkish grave-stone, mausoleum

tutta la notte · the whole night

tutti · all of them

tutto il mondo · the whole world (allusion to the statement in the *Communist Manifesto* that the proletariat 'has nothing to lose..., but will gain the whole world'

tutto in rima · all in rhyme

un peso tremendo · a great weight

va bene · it's all right

vasa sacra · (Latin) sacred vessel

va te far · be off with you!

veramente · truly, really

vergognoso! · shame on you!

vigliacchi · villains

Vo imya centralnavo komityeta, vo imya trudyashchichsya vsyeh stran · (Russian) In the name of the Central Committee, in the name of the workers of all the world

vsyo ravno · (Russian) it's all the same, it doesn't matter

'Where there is no hope, where fortune is evil' · line from the finale of Verdi's 'Aida'

'*... with the most ancient laws of the world'* · line from Puccini's 'Turandot'